"IF YOU'VE HAD A CHANGE OF HEART, McCORD, SPEAK NOW, OR SUFFER THE CONSEQUENCES…"

Amy slipped the shirt from her shoulders, revealing a nude, lace-edged bra that barely covered her breasts. "But I warn you, if you try to leave here, I'll have to kill you."

Jesse managed a husky laugh, though it nearly choked him. The sight of all the cool, pale flesh had the blood draining from his head and rushing to another part of his anatomy.

"I'd be a fool to risk death. Do with me what you will, Ms. Parrish."

She wrapped her arms around his waist and ran hot wet kisses down Jesse's chest to the flat planes of his stomach.

She felt his muscles quiver before he clamped his hands at her hips, lifting her off her feet. His mouth was almost bruising as he devoured her with a kiss so intense she could do nothing more than hold on as he took her on a wild roller-coaster ride.

As Amy started to pull back, Jesse kissed her again. "Before we're through, I'll make you forget everyone and everything except me. And this. Just this…" he growled.

MONTANA LEGACY

R.C. RYAN

FOREVER

NEW YORK   BOSTON

Cover design by Diane Luger
Book design by Giorgetta Bell McRee

Forever
Hachette Book Group
237 Park Avenue
New York, NY 10017

ISBN 978-1-61664-189-4

Forever is an imprint of Grand Central Publishing. The Forever name and logo is a trademark of Hachette Book Group, Inc.

Printed in the United States of America

To Tommy, Bret, Patrick, Johnny Ryan, and
Ryan Paul—the next generation's band of brothers.

And to my darling Tom,
proud patriarch of the clan.

MONTANA LEGACY

PROLOGUE

———◆———

Montana—1988

Last one to circle Treasure Chest Butte is a dirty, rotten skunk." Ten-year-old Jesse McCord urged his horse into a gallop, leaving his cousins, nine-year-old Wyatt and seven-year-old Zane, in his dust.

The three cousins lived with their parents and grandparents in a sprawling, three-story house on their grandfather's ranch, Lost Nugget, which covered thousands of acres of rangeland in Montana. Because of the vast size of their families' holdings and the distance to the nearest town of Gold Fever, the three were homeschooled and spent much of their spare time exploring the hills and rich grassland that formed the perfect backdrop for the thousands of head of cattle that were raised here.

The three were alike in coloring, with dark, curly hair, now slick with sweat, and their grandfather's laughing blue eyes. In town they were often mistaken for brothers, which pleased them enormously. They were, in fact, closer than brothers. Not just blood-related, but best friends. Since birth, they'd done everything together.

"Hey, wait for me." As always, Zane, the youngest, had to scramble to catch up.

By the time he and Wyatt slid from their mounts, Jesse was kneeling beside a fallen log, fishing something from the dirt.

"What'd you find, Jesse?" Wyatt looped the reins of his horse around a nearby sapling and crept closer to drop down beside his cousin. Zane mimicked his older cousin's actions.

High above them, the peaks of Treasure Chest Mountain glistened gold in the late summer sunlight.

Jesse held up a dull bronze-veined stone the size of his fist. "Looks like a nugget."

"Gold?" The two boys watched with rapt attention as Jesse turned it this way and that, grinning each time it caught and reflected the sun.

"Could be. Or it could be fool's gold." He rubbed it on his sleeve, hoping to clean away some of the dirt. "Coot's got a shelfful of fool's gold."

"Is it heavy enough to be real gold?" Wyatt held out his hand and Jesse dropped the stone into his palm. After testing it, he grinned. "I don't know what real gold ought to feel like."

Jesse shrugged. "Me neither."

"Let me see." Zane closed his hand around the nugget and felt the heat of the sun-warmed earth radiating from it. He looked up. "You think it's part of the lost treasure Grandpa Coot's been searching for his whole life?"

The three cousins exchanged eager glances.

Everyone in the McCord family knew the story of their

ancestor Jasper McCord, and the sack of gold nuggets he and his son Nathaniel had found at Grasshopper Creek in 1862, which was later stolen by another prospector, Grizzly Markham. Though Markham was found dead scant weeks later, the sack of nuggets was never found, and rumor had it that he'd buried the treasure somewhere nearby after slitting Jasper's throat. That was how Treasure Chest Mountain, the town of Gold Fever, and even the McCord ranch, Lost Nugget, came by their names. Now, following the lead of three generations before them, the McCord family continued the search, much to the scorn of folks around these parts, who believed that the gold carried a curse. Hadn't it consumed the lives of every McCord male?

Jesse broke off a low-hanging tree limb and began pushing it into the dirt. When it was firmly planted he took out a handkerchief and tied it to the top.

Wyatt eyed it. "What's that for?"

"We need to mark the spot so Grandpa Coot knows where to dig if this turns out to be real gold." Jesse pocketed the nugget, then, enjoying the drama of the moment, looked around to make certain no one was nearby. He felt a tingling at the base of his skull. What if it turned out to be part of the lost treasure?

This was, he realized, why his grandfather continued the search, despite all odds.

His voice lowered to a whisper. "We have to keep this a secret. We can't tell a soul except Grandpa Coot. We have to swear an oath."

The two younger boys nodded solemnly, looking to Jesse to show them how.

Jesse spit in his hand, and the other two followed suit.

Then the three rubbed hands, mingling their saliva, while Jesse said, "I swear to God I'll tell nobody except Coot about this gold." He looked properly stern. "Now you have to swear it."

"I swear," Wyatt said.

Zane swallowed, feeling the weight of this momentous occasion weighing heavily on his young shoulders before saying, "I swear."

Jesse pulled himself into the saddle and waited for the other two to mount.

As they started toward the distant ranch house he turned in the saddle. "Remember. Since we all swore, if anybody breaks the vow, something really bad will happen to them."

"Like what?" Zane brought his horse even with Jesse's in order to hear every word.

"I don't know." Jesse shrugged, thinking about all the adventure novels he'd read as part of his homework assignments. "Maybe anybody who breaks the vow will be banished from Lost Nugget ranch forever. Or they'll die or something."

The three boys slowed their mounts and looked properly worried. Not about death, which seemed too improbable for their young minds to conceive. But being banished from the ranch was the worst possible punishment they could ever imagine.

Each boy knew he would take his secret to the grave before he'd risk the loss of this place he loved more than anything in the whole world.

CHAPTER ONE

———◆◆◆———

Montana—Present Day

D amned north pasture's a sea of mud." In the doorway of the barn, Jesse McCord shook rain from his dark hair like a great shaggy dog and shoved past wrangler Rafe Spindler, who happened to step out of a stall in front of him, nearly causing a collision.

With a rough shove he growled, "Get the hell out of my way."

Rafe jumped back before huffing out a laugh at Jesse's mud-spattered jeans and boots and faded denim jacket with a torn pocket. "Looks like you've been wallowing in it."

"Up to my knees. And it's still rising." Jesse's usually infectious smile was gone, replaced by a flinty look that most of the wranglers mistook for impatience. Those closest to him recognized that look as one of pain.

Tall, lean, and muscled from his years of ranch chores, Jesse was, like all the McCords, a handsome devil, with a hint of danger about him that men found daunting and women found irresistible. From the bloodshot eyes it was apparent that he'd been up most of the night.

Jesse turned toward the white-haired man bending over a calf in a stall. "Cal, I'm going to need a crew to get on it right away."

"I'll see to it." Cal Randall, lanky foreman of the Lost Nugget ranch for more than forty years, didn't bother to look up as he continued examining the calf. "I'll see who's left in the bunkhouse before I head on up to the main house."

When Jesse strode away, Rafe ambled over to lean his arms on the wooden rail. "I know we're burying the old man today, but that doesn't give Jesse the right to tear my head off. Like it's my fault it's raining on the day we're going to bury Coot. Damn Jesse. He's just like the old man. Ornery as hell. Hated days like this. Only good for ducks and funerals, Coot used to say."

Grumbling among the cowboys was as natural as breathing. Especially for Rafe Spindler, who grew up not far from here and signed on as a ranchhand after the deaths of his parents while still in his teens. Like so many of the unmarried ranch hands, Rafe was a hardworking, hard-drinking cowboy whose only pleasure was a game of cards and an occasional fling with the local women. Though something of a hothead, Rafe could be counted on to do his share of the toughest, dirtiest ranch chores.

Rafe lowered his voice. "Jesse's been working up a head of steam ever since Miss Cora told him his cousins are coming in for Coot's funeral."

Cal straightened. The ranch might consist of hundreds of wranglers spread out over thousands of acres, but gossip had a way of spreading faster than fire through a bale of hay.

Cal nodded toward the calf. "Keep an eye on him, Rafe. Any change, you can reach me up at the house."

Cal's movements were slow and deliberate as he trudged through puddles. His only concession to the downpour was the wide-brimmed hat pulled low on his head. Autumn had brought more rain than usual to this part of Montana.

After a stop at the bunkhouse, Cal crossed the distance to the sprawling house on the hill. His thoughts were focused on Jesse McCord. He understood the young man's anger and misery. As the only grandson to stay in Montana and share the old man's dream, Jesse was feeling the death of his grandfather, eighty-year-old Coot McCord, more keenly than anyone.

Gabriel McCord had earned a reputation early on as a fool and a dreamer. When he'd begun buying up huge tracts of land around his ranch, folks in the area said he was, like his ancestors, just a crazy old coot, and the nickname stuck. Even his sister, Cora, ten years younger, who some said was just as crazy, had eventually taken to calling him Coot. The old man embraced the name and wore it like a badge of honor.

By the time he died, Coot had bought up over two hundred thousand acres of surrounding land, and he had planned on going over every inch of it with a fine-tooth comb searching for his ancestor's lost fortune. Folks figured if that didn't make a man crazy, nothing did.

Cal didn't share the opinion of the others. There'd been nothing crazy about Coot. Driven, maybe. Determined, definitely. But he was the truest friend a man could want. The old man might not have found his treasure, but it wasn't for lack of trying.

As for Cora, she may have been a bit eccentric, wearing her brother's cast-off clothing while she wandered the countryside alone for weeks at a time, creating paintings of the lush landscapes, which sold for ridiculously huge sums of money in the international art world. But that only added to her charm. She was a true artist. She didn't paint for the money. She painted because she was driven. It was as necessary to her as breathing.

That was another thing she'd shared with her brother. That determination ran like steel girders through all the McCords. That's what made them all so ornery.

Cal stepped into the mudroom, cleaning his boots on a scraper before hanging his hat on a peg. He carefully washed his hands at the big basin before walking into the kitchen where Dandy Davis was flipping hotcakes. As always, Dandy wore a crisp white apron tied over clean denims and a spotless plaid shirt with the sleeves rolled to the elbows.

The wranglers had a bet going that Dandy probably owned more than two dozen shirts in the same plaid, and an equal number of pairs of denim pants and shiny black boots.

Dandy had come to the Lost Nugget looking for work as a wrangler. Instead he'd been pressed into service in the kitchen, and agreed to cook until a replacement could be found. Twenty years later he was still cooking.

He kept his kitchen spotless, spending hours each day polishing everything from pots and pans to countertops. Any cowboy who forgot to scrape his boots or wash his hands before entering Dandy's kitchen did so at the risk of life and limb. His demands were tolerated because he was, quite simply, the best cook in all of Montana. His chili, spicy enough to bring tears to the eyes of old-time cowboys, was his most requested meal on the range. But running a close second was his slow-cooked pot roast, tender enough to fall off the bone, served with chunks of potatoes, carrots, and winter squash. When Dandy was baking bread, the crew found excuses to go up to the house, knowing he was always good for a handout of hot, crusty heels of bread slathered with the honey butter he made from his own secret recipe.

Dandy turned from the stove. "Morning, Cal. Just coffee, or do you have time for pancakes?"

"I'll make time." Cal smiled at the woman in the denim shirt and oversized bib-overalls. Gray hair curled softly around a face too pretty to be improved by makeup. Whenever her hair needed cutting, she simply snipped a curl here and there, and fluffed it with her fingers. She had been, for all her seventy years, completely without artifice. "Morning, Cora."

"Cal." She looked up from the newspaper. "They wrote a nice piece about Coot."

He nodded. "I saw it." He waited until Dandy set a steaming cup in front of him. "Rafe tells me the boys are coming in."

"They are." Cora nodded absently and finished the obituary before setting the paper aside. "Isn't that nice?"

"Yeah." He glanced at the empty chair across the table. "How'd Jess take the news?"

She shrugged. "He's angry, Cal. He said his cousins should have been here all along, instead of waiting until it's too late. I've told him it would please his grandfather to have all his grandsons together, but right now, the only thing Jess knows is that he's lost his best friend, and he

doesn't want to share the good-byes with anyone else."
She stared down into her coffee. "I know how he feels.
I hate the idea of saying good-bye. It makes it all so
final. I can't imagine this place without my brother." She
sighed. "But I'm glad Wyatt and Zane are coming in for
the funeral. It'll be the first time we've all been together
since their fathers left years ago."

Cal accepted a plate from Dandy and began pouring
syrup over the mound of lighter-than-air flapjacks.

When the back door slammed he looked over to see
Jesse McCord hanging his hat on a hook before crossing
to the table.

"Morning, Jess."

"Aunt Cora. Sorry I dashed out so early, but I got word
that the rain washed out a culvert under the road leading
to the north pasture."

"I've got some men on it." Cal sipped his coffee.
"Cora tells me that Wyatt and Zane are coming."

"Yeah." Something flickered in the younger man's
eyes before he looked away. "Just coffee, Dandy. I'm not
hungry this morning."

The cook filled a mug and set it in front of him before
returning to the stove.

Cal glanced at Cora. "What time's the service?"

"Noon." She sighed. "Coot told me years ago how he
wanted to go out. He always said he'd feel like a hypo-
crite being buried from a church. It was nice of Reverend
Carson to agree to drive out here and say some words.
It'll add a nice touch, don't you think, Jess?"

He shrugged. "I doubt Coot cares one way or the
other. Just so he's laid to rest on the land he loved."

Cora nodded. "He did love this land, didn't he?" She

closed a hand over her great-nephew's. "It gave him such pleasure to know that you loved it, too, Jess."

He felt his throat closing up and, afraid of embarrassing himself, shoved away from the table. "Think I'll drive up to the pasture and give a hand with that culvert."

"But Jess..." As he stalked out of the room Cora turned to the ranch foreman. "Maybe you should go after him, Cal, and tell him you don't need his help."

Cal gave a slight shake of his head. "He needs to be busy. Work's good for the soul, especially when it's troubled."

"You'll see that he's back in time for..." She fisted her hands in her lap, unable to say the words.

Cal pushed aside his half-eaten breakfast. Funny how quickly an appetite could flee. As he started away from the table he paused to drop a hand on her shoulder and squeeze. "Don't you worry. I'll make sure of it, Cora."

And he would. Even if he had to hog-tie the young hothead and haul his hide home like a sackful of spitting cats.

There was nothing Cal Randall wouldn't do for Cora.

The Harley roared along the open road. Water sprayed up like geysers as the wheels glanced over ruts. As it came up over a hill it slowed, then came to a stop.

Wyatt McCord whipped off his helmet and stood a moment, listening to the incredible silence. Gradually the sounds of the countryside began to seep into his consciousness. The trill of a meadowlark. The distant lowing of cattle. The whisper of the wind through the ponderosa pines.

It was as though the years rolled away. It was all here,

just as he'd pictured it in his mind for the past fifteen years. It was, he realized with startling clarity, the only place he'd ever called home. When his parents had taken their leave of the Lost Nugget, he'd grieved the only way a sixteen-year-old could. By breaking all the rules. Dropping out of school. Getting into as much trouble as he could.

It had taken him years to put his life in order. Long after his parents had given up on him, he'd returned to school to earn his degree. But he'd never been able to put down roots. Instead he searched the world over for a place that would call to him. He'd meditated in Tibet and climbed Mount Everest. He'd traveled to India, just to experience the culture. He'd worked on a luxury yacht in the South Pacific, and had even wrangled sheep in Australia. Through it all, he'd made enough money to live comfortably. Not that he needed much. He'd learned to travel light. Maybe his mother had been right, all those years ago, when she'd teasingly suggested that he'd been dropped on their doorstep by a Gypsy.

He had the look of a Gypsy about him. Thick shaggy hair the color of coal spilling down the collar of his faded leather jacket to brush his shoulders. A dark stubble covering his chin and cheeks, giving testimony to the fact that he'd been on the road for more than a dozen hours. There was a world-weariness about him, especially in the set of his jaw and the challenge in those piercing blue eyes.

He pulled on his helmet and climbed back onto his Harley before roaring off in a mist of rain.

He'd told himself he was coming home to bury his

grandfather, but it occurred to Wyatt McCord that he'd actually come home to bury his childhood regrets.

Cal stepped out of the barn just as the motorcycle roared to a stop. He hurried over, his weathered face lit with a smile. "Welcome home, Wyatt. It's been a while."

"Yeah." Wyatt set his helmet aside and offered a handshake. "How you been, Cal?"

"I've been better. Your grandfather's death hit us all hard."

"Was he sick?"

"Nope." The older man's eyes watered for a moment before he blinked. "He was climbing around some rock cliffs like always, and took a nasty fall. As soon as he called in his location from his cell phone, I phoned Marilee Trainor and then raced out there with some of the wranglers. Before the medevac could fly in, he was gone."

Wyatt stuck his hands in his back pockets and looked out at the towering buttes in the distance. "Sounds like old Coot, doesn't it? I think that's the way he'd have liked to go."

"Yeah." Cal nodded. "Your great-aunt's inside. You go ahead and I'll get your bag."

"No need." Wyatt reached into his saddlebag. "All I've got is this duffel."

He climbed the steps and let himself into the house, pausing at the mudroom to drop his bag before continuing into the kitchen.

"Aunt Cora."

She was instantly out of her chair and into his arms. "Oh, Wyatt." After a fierce hug she held him a little away.

He took that moment to shake Dandy's hand. "Good to see you again, Dandy."

"And you, Wyatt."

Cora was studying him with a look of disbelief. "Oh, look at you. You're the picture of your daddy."

"Except he wore denim instead of leather." He grinned. "You haven't changed a bit, Aunt Cora. In fact, I think those are the same overalls you were wearing the day I left."

She gave a girlish laugh. Wyatt had always been able to charm her. "They're Coot's. I always liked his clothes better than my own. I think I'll like them even better now."

Wyatt sobered. "I know what you mean." He dug into his pocket and held up a battered watch on a chain. "I've been carrying this ever since the crash. The authorities found it in the wreckage and sent it to me. I like having something of Dad's."

Cora cupped it in her hand and studied it before looking at him. "Coot gave that to your daddy when he graduated high school."

Wyatt nodded. "I know. That makes it twice as special to me."

The old woman wrapped an arm around his waist, loving the big, sturdy feel of him, all muscle and sinew. Like his daddy. "Come on. I'll take you up to your rooms."

He leaned down to kiss her cheek. "Don't bother, Aunt Cora. I remember the way."

As he retrieved his duffel and walked away, she stayed where she was, listening to his footsteps as he climbed the stairs.

Dandy set a fresh cup of coffee on the table. "Here, Miss Cora. You look like you could use this."

"Thanks, Dandy." She sank down onto a chair, wondering why she felt this sudden urge to weep. Instead, she leafed through the paper until she found the obituary, thinking Coot's grandsons might want to have a look at it later.

Wyatt paused in the doorway of the suite of rooms he'd once shared with his parents, memories of his childhood sweeping over him. He'd always loved living in this big, sprawling ranch house, knowing an entire family lived just rooms away. His cousins, Jesse and Zane, had been his best friends and constant companions. If his father was busy, there was always an uncle or his grandfather to talk to. When he needed help with schoolwork, his mother, one of his aunts, or his great-aunt Cora was always available to lend a hand. There had been a strong feeling of camaraderie in this house when he was young.

Gradually, as he grew into his teens, he'd begun to sense the unease. His father and mother yearned to break free of the constraints of ranch life to travel around the world. They resented the treasure hunt that had become Coot's obsession. Angry words triggered endless arguments. As a teen living in his own selfish world, Wyatt seemed barely aware of the tension until his father and mother had ordered him to pack his things. When he realized that there were no plans to return to the only life he'd ever known, he became angry, distant, difficult. While his parents attempted to share their love of world travel with their only son, he repaid them by dropping out of school and out of life. It was only years later that he'd managed to pull himself together and make something of his life. But by then, with his parents gone in an instant, killed in a plane crash, his anger had turned inward, directed at himself.

He'd overcome the anger and guilt. And now, just when he'd accepted a life alone, here he was, back where it had all begun.

He carried his duffel across the polished wood floor of the foyer and paused in the big open parlor, with its massive stone fireplace and familiar overstuffed chairs. Over the mantel was a portrait of his mother and father and the boy he'd been at eight. Dark hair cut razor-short, laughing blue eyes, wide grin with its missing front tooth.

He was smiling as he made his way down the hallway to his old bedroom. Just beyond was the master bedroom and bath, but except for a quick glance, he returned to his old room and tossed the duffel on the twin bed, still covered in the red-plaid comforter he'd chosen for his fourteenth birthday.

He'd slept in youth hostels in Europe, tents in the Andes, and fleabag hotels in plenty of towns he'd rather forget. But in his mind's eye, he'd never forgotten this room.

This was the only place he'd ever thought of as home.

The sleek little sports car, in candy apple red, took every dip and curve with the grace of a dancer. At the top of the rise Zane McCord pulled over just to drink in the view.

Green pastures dotted with cattle. Weathered barns and outbuildings. And that grand sweep of the brick-and-stone house atop the hill where it could be seen for miles in all directions. When he was a kid with a wild imagination, he'd thought it looked like a castle. His own private keep, and he the white knight, saving the kingdom from peril.

Now he saw it as it looked through the lens of his camera. It was all here. The wide-open ranges, with no houses or factories or offices to spoil the view. No people. Just acre after acre of cattle, and the men who tended the herds. There was something mysterious and romantic about this land. This ranch.

He'd been so afraid it wouldn't look the way he'd remembered it. After all, he'd been just a kid when he left. But he'd never forgotten this place. The simple beauty of it. The soaring majesty of the mountain ranges. The icy purity of the streams and rivers.

After years in Southern California he'd really feared that his childhood memories had become fragmented and magnified, taking bits and pieces of the things he'd liked best and making them seem even better than they'd been.

Ignoring the rain, he stepped out of the car and leaned on the hood, breathing deeply. Even the air was different here. It hadn't been just a kid's imagination. It *was* cleaner. Sweeter. Purer.

He relaxed for the first time in hours, softening the sharp angles and planes of his face. A hawkish face that would never be mistaken for movie-star material. His jaw was too square. His steely-eyed look intimidating to most men and intriguing to women. He idly touched a hand to the scar along his jaw. As a kid he'd taken a nasty fall from a horse. Because the Lost Nugget was more than a hundred miles from the town's clinic, most injuries were handled by one of the cowboys. Zane's cut had been treated no differently. Half an hour after being stitched up in a bunkhouse, he'd been back on the same horse, racing to catch up with his cousins. A few years ago a well-known plastic surgeon he'd met at a cocktail party in Malibu had wanted to correct the damage. Zane had refused, considering it his own special medal of honor. Every time he caught sight of it in the mirror it brought back memories of earlier, happier times.

He was smiling as he climbed back into the car. On the oldies station Bob Seger was running against the wind. Zane found himself keeping time to the music as he shifted gears and raced off in a spray of rain and gravel.

Cora looked up at the sound of a vehicle approaching. Setting aside her cup, she hurried through the mudroom to watch as a sleek little sports car came to a smooth stop directly behind the motorcycle. Seconds later a man stepped out and paused to look around.

Cora sucked in a breath, then raced out to greet him. "Zane. Oh, Zane."

"Aunt Cora." He gathered her close and breathed her in, feeling a rush of emotion at the half-forgotten scents of lavender and paint that had always been so much a part of this special woman.

She clung to him for a moment before stepping back and tipping up her head to study him. "Look how tall you've grown. Why, you must be well over six feet."

"And a couple of inches." He chuckled. "Who'd've believed it of that skinny little kid?"

"Skinny and absolutely fearless. As I recall, you did some pretty foolhardy things when you were a boy."

"I'd appreciate it if you wouldn't mention them.

Besides, I had to keep up with my cousins." He glanced around. "Where are Jesse and Wyatt?"

"Jesse's gone to look at a washout up the road, and Wyatt is unpacking in his old room." She nodded toward the car. "Why don't you do the same?"

He retrieved an overnight case and followed her inside where he greeted Dandy with handshake. "I hope those perfect pancakes I remember from my childhood aren't just a fantasy, Dandy."

The cook grinned. "If you haven't had breakfast yet, I'll let you find out for yourself."

Zane shook his head. "I had something at a place called the Grizzly Inn they called a biscuit-sausage-egg combo. I think they make them out of cardboard and use them over and over on every tourist who happens by."

The two men shared a laugh.

Cora looped her arm through his. "Think you can find your way to your old rooms, Zane?"

He nodded. "Yeah, Aunt Cora. It may have been years, but I haven't forgotten the way."

As he started toward the stairway she called, "The service for your grandfather will be at noon."

Zane glanced at his watch, relieved that he had an hour to prepare. "In town? Or here at the ranch?"

"Here. Coot always said he wanted to spend eternity right here on his own land."

Zane nodded. "I'm not surprised."

Zane McCord strode into the section of the house where he'd lived as a boy with his father and mother. Like the Lost Nugget, everything here was bigger than life. The formal parlor, with its Italian marble floor and priceless

Persian rug that his mother had insisted upon, still looked out of place in this homey setting, as did the custom silk draperies and furnishings. But Melissa McCord had been as out of place in Montana as her choice of furnishings. From the time he was a kid she'd made no secret of her distaste for ranch life. There had been endless arguments between Melissa and Wade, and when Zane's father had finally agreed to leave the ranch, it had been a last-ditch effort to save his marriage.

As he walked through the rooms until he came to his parents' bedroom, Zane frowned. The sacrifice his father made had been in vain. The marriage had already been irretrievably broken, and his father had died out in California without even the comfort of his family.

Zane backed away from the ornate master suite and followed the hallway to his old room. He'd rather spend his one night at the Lost Nugget in here. It was as he remembered it, right down to the horse posters on the walls. As a kid he'd been in love with the idea of traveling across the wilderness with a herd of wild mustangs. That was why, when producer Steven Michaelson had offered him the job of assistant on his documentary about the government roundup of wild horses, he'd jumped at the chance.

Zane tossed his overnight bag on a chair and headed toward the bathroom. He was glad he had time for a shower and a change of clothes before his grandfather's funeral.

While Dandy prepared a meal for the mourners, Cora walked to the great room, where a fire blazed on the hearth. If she closed her eyes, she could almost believe

Coot was here with her. Though the paintings on the walls, of wide, sweeping vistas and snow-covered mountains had all been done by her, the furniture was big and solid, to accommodate her brother and his sons, who had all been big men. It made her smile to remember.

She clutched her arms about herself. "Oh, Coot. It's hard to believe all our boys are so grown up. We've lost too many years."

How ironic, that it took Coot's death to reunite the family. The same family that had been shattered by Coot's obsession with finding his great-grandfather's fortune. He'd been heartbroken when two of his sons, whose wives had grown weary of the search, had left the ranch, and Montana, for good. He'd despaired of ever seeing his family together again. But here was Wyatt, son of Coot's middle son, Ben, back from whatever godforsaken place he called home these days; and Zane, son of Coot's youngest son, Wade, in from California.

Cora turned to look out the window at the mountain peaks, barely visible in the rain. "I know it isn't much. A day or two. But at least for whatever time they can manage, we're all together. And that's a tribute to you, Coot."

CHAPTER TWO

Come on, Jess." Cal slid behind the wheel of the battered old pickup and waited while Jesse stored a shovel in the back before climbing into the passenger side. "Your aunt'll have my hide if I don't get you up to the house in time for the service."

"Doesn't matter." Jesse wiped his muddy hands on his jeans. "Coot won't like it."

"Now what makes you say that?"

The younger man glanced over. "He never liked fuss, Cal. Neither do I."

"This isn't fuss. It's the only way we have of paying our respects. Coot knew that. It's why he told his sister just what to do in the event of his death." Cal's voice lowered. "This is important to Cora. She's hurting as much as you, Jess."

"I know. I wish I could ease her pain." Jesse turned to stare out the side window as the truck rumbled along the rough road. Next to Coot, Cal Randall was the closest thing Jesse McCord had to a father, since his own had died twenty years ago, leaving him lost and bewildered at the tender age of twelve.

Cal wasn't one to give advice, but when he did, Jesse heeded it, however reluctantly. "I suppose I'll have to wear a suit."

Cal nodded. "Me, too. Though I've no use for them."

Jesse looked over. "Didn't know you owned one."

Cal grinned. "Haven't had much need for it, but now and again it comes in handy."

"Especially if you're trying to impress a lady."

"I'll leave that to you, Jess."

The two shared a smile.

As they rolled to a stop by the back door, Jesse caught sight of the unfamiliar vehicles. "Well, well. Looks like the gang's all here." He stepped down from the pickup and turned from the Harley to the sports car. "Let's see. Which one do you think belongs to our free spirit, and which to Hollywood's golden boy?"

Cal shook his head. "Let it be, Jess. They're family."

"Yeah. I keep forgetting." His tone roughened. "Of course, it's hard to remember when you don't see someone for ten or fifteen years."

"They're here now. Here for their grandfather. That's all that matters."

Jesse nodded. "And by this time tomorrow, they'll be gone."

He stormed up the steps, hoping to escape to his room. Instead, after scraping mud from his boots and washing his hands at the big sink in the mudroom, he stepped into the kitchen and came face-to-face with a roomful.

His great-aunt looked up from the table where his grand-father's lawyer was seated beside the minister. On the other side sat his two cousins.

"Well." If he couldn't manage a smile, at least he didn't groan. "Wyatt. Zane. It's been too long."

"Yeah." Wyatt stepped forward to offer his hand. "The place looks the same as I remember."

"Yeah. Some things never change." But Wyatt had. Even the proper suit and tie couldn't erase the long hair and casual air that gave him the look of an eternal surfer. Maybe, Jesse thought, that's what Wyatt was. Always dashing off to find the next big wave to ride.

When he turned to Zane, Jesse was startled by how much his younger cousin had changed. He'd expected a smoothness to Zane, a polish that could only come from easy living. After all, the suit was custom-made. The shoes Italian. And the watch on his wrist cost more than Jesse's last truck. But there was a toughness in his younger cousin's eyes, a strength in his demeanor that didn't quite fit the image he'd formed in his mind.

"How's Hollywood? I hear you're working with some hotshot director now."

"Steve Michaelson." Zane stuck out his hand. "I assisted on his latest documentary. It'll be on PBS next fall. Good to see you, Jess. I wish it could have been under happier circumstances."

"Yeah, well, too bad you had to wait until Coot was dead to pay a call."

"Jesse." To avoid an all-out war, Cora stepped between them. "I was just about to introduce Vernon to your cous-ins." She looped an arm through each of theirs. "Boys, this is Vernon McVicker, Coot's lawyer. Vernon, these are my great-nephews, Zane and Wyatt McCord."

The man who pushed away from the table had sad, tired eyes in a long and lean face. Sparse gray hair was combed straight back, adding to his hound-dog expression. As he approached he studied them as he might specimens, with more than casual interest. "You'd be Wade's son," he said to Zane. He turned to Wyatt. "And you'd be Ben's."

They both nodded.

Relieved that she'd managed to smother Jesse's temper for the moment, Cora managed a smile. "Jess, why don't you go ahead upstairs and get dressed while we wait. Reverend Carson is here to begin the service, as soon as we're ready."

Jesse was grateful for the chance to escape. The last thing he wanted to do was stand around making small talk. "I'll just be a few minutes."

As he stalked up the stairs he thought about the two cousins who were no more than strangers now. There'd been a time when the three of them had been inseparable. They'd grown up wild and free on their grandfather's ranch, swimming in the creek, riding bareback across the hills, daring one another to try every dangerous, reckless stunt a young boy's mind could imagine.

They'd all lived here in various wings of the house. One big, noisy family. Even after the death of his father, Jesse had felt safe and protected, because he'd been surrounded by so many family members. But gradually the cracks in the family had begun to show signs of stress. Ben had left first, taking Wyatt away. Later it was Wade, heading off to California with his wife and son.

Jesse undressed and stepped into the shower, letting
the hot water beat on the knot of tension at the back of his
neck. After toweling himself dry he slipped into a crisp
white shirt, tucking it into the waistband of dark pants.

As he ran his fingers through his wet hair he paused.
He didn't blame his cousins for leaving. They'd been only
kids when their fathers had had enough of old Coot's
ravings and had pulled up stakes, in search of a better
life. But they'd had plenty of years to come back after
they were old enough to be on their own, if that's what
they'd wanted. The fact that they'd never returned to the
ranch meant one thing to Jesse. They hadn't loved their
grandfather enough to spend even a week with him. Not
a single week in all these long years.

Jesse slid his arms into the suit jacket, hating the way
it felt. Stiff. Phony. That's what this whole fiasco was. A
service. For what? So the minister could say a few fancy
words about a man who'd never set foot in his church?
Coot was gone. Nothing would bring him back.

He took a last glimpse in the mirror, straightening his
tie, then slammed out of the room and down the stairs.
What he really wanted to do was to get into his truck and
drive up to the hills where he and Coot used to spend so
much time together. That would mean more to him than
any stuffy service. At least then he'd be able to properly
grieve.

And he would, he vowed. As soon as the others left,
and he had time to himself, he'd bury his grandfather in
his own way.

They stood together on a windswept hill. The rain had
stopped, leaving the surrounding countryside looking

fresh and green, frosted with the pale pink blossoms of bitterroot and waving tassels of golden bear grass.

Jesse looked around at those assembled. It was the first time he'd ever seen so many ranch hands together at one time. Even their roundup barbecue, traditionally held after the cattle had been brought down from the high pastures in late summer, never included all the wranglers, since some were needed to tend the herds. But today, out of respect for the man who had built this amazing spread and had been its heart and soul, every last man was here. Dandy Davis, wearing a spiffy western suit and string tie. Cal Randall, looking as uncomfortable as Jesse felt in his dark suit and cowboy boots. And Cora, in an ankle-skimming dress of black silk with a black fringed shawl tossed about her shoulders. It was the first time Jesse could ever recall seeing his great-aunt in anything but denim.

There were his cousins, tall, handsome, and, like Jesse, refusing to look at the casket standing beside a gaping hole dug in the earth.

"Who are all these people?"

Wyatt's muttered question had Jesse studying the crowd. "Townies."

"So many?" Wyatt exchanged a look with Zane. "When I left, Gold Fever consisted of a gas station, a grocery store, a movie theater showing last year's films, the fairgrounds..."

"That held one of the biggest rodeos in the area," Zane added.

"Yeah. And the Fortune Saloon."

"Just goes to show how long you've been away." Jesse frowned, realizing just how out-of-touch his cousins were. "In recent years they've built a high school and a medical clinic. That brought in teachers, doctors, nurses, who in turn needed new houses, which brought building contractors. There's talk that even more land could be developed to accommodate the number of people moving…"

Jesse's words died in his throat at the shock of recognition he felt when he spied Otis Parrish in the crowd.

Following his direction, Wyatt hissed out a breath at the sight of their nearest neighbor, in fact, their only neighbor. Knowing that Parrish had a long-standing feud with Coot that went back too many years to count, Wyatt whispered, "He's here for only one reason."

"Yeah. To gloat." Jesse continued studying the crowd.

He felt a nudge in his ribs and glanced over at Wyatt.

"Who's that?" Wyatt nodded toward a tall, slender woman whose mass of tangled red curls made her a standout in the crowd.

Jesse followed his direction. "Marilee Trainor."

"Married or single?"

Jesse felt a wave of annoyance. "In case you've forgotten, we're here to bury Coot, not play the dating game."

"Married or single?"

Jesse sighed. "Single. But don't bother. She's a no-nonsense woman who wouldn't be interested in a quick tumble with a rolling stone like you."

"Tell me about her."

"Lee's a medic with the town's emergency services. She was the first one here when she heard about Coot's fall, and she stayed with him until the helicopter arrived." Jesse felt a twinge of remorse when he saw her lift a handkerchief to her eye. "The truth is, she took it personally that she couldn't save him. From the looks of things, she's still beating herself up over it."

On the other side Zane gave him a nudge and nodded toward the old woman pushing her way to the front of the crowd. "Is that Delia Cowling?"

"Yeah."

Zane chuckled. "She was old when I was a kid. Now she must be old as dirt."

Jesse gave a snort. "Yeah. Our town historian."

Delia Cowling called herself that because of her collection of dusty books on the subject of the gold rush at Grasshopper Creek. Folks in town called her the town gossip. There wasn't much that happened in the town of Gold Fever that Delia didn't know about.

"I'm betting she's here to gather any information she can about the personal business of anybody in town."

Ledge Cowling, Delia's brother and owner of the Gold Fever bank, stood beside his sister, whispering behind his hand. Ledge had never married, and most of the folks in town believed it was because the woman hadn't been born that Ledge could love as much as he loved money. Money and his bank were Ledge's only passions. At least the only ones he'd ever admitted to.

Zane and Wyatt continued scanning the faces of so many strangers. There had been a time when they'd known almost everyone in the town of Gold Fever. Now, there were few who appeared familiar to them.

Zane studied a portly man, his gray hair cut close to his scalp, wearing a uniform. "Is that Ernie Wycliff?"

Jesse nodded. "Yeah. Our old football hero is now the sheriff."

"Good for Ernie."

Jesse frowned. "What was Aunt Cora thinking? What did these people care about Coot? Most of 'em are just here to gawk and gossip. Tonight they'll have themselves a good old time back at the Fortune Saloon over a couple of longnecks."

Reverend Carson stepped up beside the casket. His smooth preacher's voice carried out over the crowd. "I'm told this spot has been a burial place for many of the McCord family. Coot's father and mother are here"—He nodded toward the neat row of headstones around which a low, wrought-iron fence stood guard—"along with his baby brother, Edmond, who died in infancy, and Coot's wife, Annie, dead now for over thirty years. Coot's sister, Cora, told me that her brother considered this holy ground. So it seems fitting and proper that old Coot should rest here, now that his labors are over."

He took a paper from his pocket and read the instructions Cora had written, before looking up. "It says here that a couple of folks would like to say a few words." He glanced out over the crowd. "Mayor Stafford?"

Jesse couldn't prevent his eyes from rolling. Rowe Stafford had been the mayor of Gold Fever, Montana, for years, and kept getting reelected to office mainly because nobody else cared to run for the job. Though many enjoyed his speeches, Jesse considered him a windbag who loved the sound of his own voice.

Rowe looked out over the crowd. "Coot and I have been friends for more'n fifty years now. I've spent many a night defending him to those who called him crazy." He gave his famous lopsided grin. "But I'll tell you this. Coot might have gone a little overboard when it came to the search for his lost fortune, but he always said he was doing it for his family." The mayor nodded toward Cora and the three handsome young men standing beside her.

"It's good to see the McCords together again, if only for a day." He started to turn away before adding, "I'll be buying a round of drinks tonight in Coot's name. It's the least I can do for my oldest friend."

The preacher coughed before saying, "And now we'll hear a few words from Cal Randall."

Jesse swiveled his head in surprise and watched as the foreman stepped up beside the casket.

"I just need to say that"—Cal cleared his throat, looking like he'd rather be anywhere than here, baring his soul in front of all these friends and neighbors—"these years with Coot have been the best ever. He was fair and honest. His word was his bond. He was my best friend. I'm surely going to miss him." He jammed his hands in his pockets and walked back to join the others.

Reverend Carson turned to Cora. "Miss McCord?"

Cora stepped away from the others and paused beside the casket, running her hand along the smooth wood. "My brother didn't like fancy words, so I'll keep mine simple. Folks called him crazy for spending a lifetime searching these hills for our great-grandfather's gold. He never cared what others thought." She looked over the crowd, allowing her gaze to settle first on Jesse, then Wyatt, then Zane. "It just runs in the family, I guess. When your name's McCord, you have to do things your own way. I surely hope..." She gave a long, deep sigh. "I hope his dream doesn't die with him."

As she took a halting step away, Jesse hurried forward and offered his arm. She gave him a tearful smile, grateful for his quiet support.

Her voice quavered. "Did you want to say a few words, Jesse?"

He shook his head. "Whatever I've got to say to Coot is between him and me. It's not for here."

"I understand." She patted his hand.

The reverend glanced around. "Are there any others who would care to say a few words, or perhaps share a happy memory or two?"

Some of the wranglers shuffled their feet and coughed in discomfort. As the silence stretched out, Reverend Carson opened a book and began to read the words of a prayer.

As the words drifted over them, Jesse let his attention wander. What would happen to his grandfather's dream? Since Coot had been a young man of eighteen or twenty, he'd been consumed with finding something he wasn't even sure existed. Nuggets as big as a man's thumb. Some as big as a fist. The old man had been the butt of jokes for as long as Jesse could remember.

Maybe it was best if the dream was allowed to die with him. That wasn't the worst thing that could happen. Maybe then they all could have some peace.

There was land here. Rich ranchland. And thousands of head of cattle. Old Coot hadn't cared about the ranch. Had left the running of it to Cal and the ranch hands. And Cal did a fine job. No doubt about it. That old cowboy loved this place as if it were his own. Still, Jesse thought, maybe if he were to keep his attention focused on the ranch now, without the distraction of an imaginary fortune, he and Cal could take the most successful ranch in all of Montana and turn it into the most successful ranch in the world.

He had the prickly feeling that someone was watching him. Lifting his head he studied the crowd and felt his throat go dry when he caught sight of the young woman standing slightly behind Otis Parrish.

"Amy." He wasn't even aware that he'd spoken her name until he saw his cousins turn to glance at him.

He lowered his head and stared hard at the ground. When Amy Parrish had left Montana without a word, a mile-wide chasm had developed between them. And whatever feelings they might have shared had been washed away in a sea of anger and resentment.

Jesse was surprised when he sensed movement beside him and realized Cora was starting forward, taking him along with her. The casket had already been lowered into the ground, and Cora tossed a handful of dirt onto the lid. Jesse followed suit. His cousins, Zane and Wyatt, did the same.

They stepped away and watched as Cal and Dandy and the wranglers took turns tossing dirt and standing with bowed heads, bidding their final farewells.

The crowd had gone eerily silent. Out of respect? Jesse wondered. Or were they waiting for old Coot to rise up out of his casket and hold out a fistful of gold nuggets?

The minister said in his most funereal tone, "That concludes our service. The family asked me to invite all of you back to the house for a meal."

Just then Cora's voice rose with excitement and she pointed to the sky. "Oh, my. Look."

Everyone followed her direction, looking up to see a shimmering rainbow arched across the heavens.

A murmur went up from the crowd.

After watching for several minutes, Cora's voice trembled with excitement. "It's Coot's way of saying good-bye. I just know it." She turned to her nephew. "Don't you agree, Jesse?"

He nodded, too overcome to speak. Everyone in the

family had seen the rainbow keychain his grandfather had always carried in his pocket. When asked about it, old Coot had said it was a symbol of the fortune he intended to find one day. His personal pot of gold. It was now Jesse's good luck charm.

"You aren't just trying to console me, are you?" Cora's eyes glittered with tears. "You do believe, don't you, Jess?"

Jesse swallowed the lump in his throat and squeezed her hand. "I'm telling you straight, Aunt Cora. It's a sign."

CHAPTER THREE

———◆———

The sweeping front lawn of the ranch house had been transformed. Dozens of picnic tables were spread out beneath shade trees. Sawhorses supported rows of planks covered in white linen and groaning under the weight of enough food to feed the state of Montana.

Dandy Davis moved among the throngs of wranglers that had been pressed into service to slice the side of beef, the suckling pig, the smoked ham, and to serve the amazing array of side dishes he'd managed to prepare for the funeral lunch.

Despite the size of the crowd, it was quiet and orderly. The townspeople and the wranglers mixed easily, since the men who worked on the Lost Nugget ranch spent most of their off-hours in town, either drinking in the Fortune Saloon or eating the rubber that passed for pizza at the Grizzly Inn.

When the mourners caught sight of the car bearing

Cora and her nephews, the conversation faded to a hum. As she stepped out and started toward them, the wranglers whipped their hats from their heads, twisting them around and around in their hands and murmuring awkward words of condolence as she passed by.

Cora paused to speak a word to each person, since she knew them all by name. From the looks on their faces, they appreciated the time she took from her own grief to tend theirs.

The minute she took a seat at one of the picnic tables Dandy was beside her. "I fixed you a plate, Miss Cora. See that you eat something."

She gave him a gentle smile, though she knew she wouldn't be able to manage a bite. "Thank you, Dandy."

"You're welcome, Miss Cora." He turned to Jesse. "If you and your cousins tell me what you'd like, I'll fetch it."

Jesse shook his head. "No need, Dandy. We'll get our own." He walked to the rear of a long line of wranglers, with Wyatt and Zane trailing behind.

At once the wranglers began offering their words of sorrow and regret at Jesse's loss. Though it was painful to endure, Jesse preferred it to attempting to make conversation with his cousins.

He could get through this, he told himself. A few hours more and Wyatt and Zane would be gone. He and Cora could get on with their lives.

Without Coot.

The thought cut like a razor. So sharp and swift, he brought a hand to his stomach and had to suck in a breath on the pain.

"Zane?" One of the wranglers looked beyond Jesse to the young man behind him. "Is it really Zane McCord?"

Zane stepped closer, then gave a whoop as recognition dawned. "Jimmy? Jimmy Eagle?"

The two men clasped shoulders and shared a delighted laugh.

"Last time I saw you, boy, you were too young to shave."

"And you had hair down to your butt."

"Wore it in a braid," the older man said proudly. "Still do." When they stepped apart he turned to the others. "This is Zane, Wade's boy."

As Jimmy Eagle handled the introductions, Zane shook hands and turned to include his cousin. "This is Wyatt. His dad was my uncle Ben."

"You the one been around the world?" one of the men asked.

Wyatt chuckled. "I haven't seen it all yet, but I've been to a few places."

"More'n a few, I've heard."

Soon the men had completely surrounded them, eager to chat up Coot's grandsons, who'd been absent from the ranch for so many years.

"Jimmy taught me to ride," Zane explained to the others. "Dad said I was too young, but Jimmy trusted me enough to just stick me in the saddle and tell me what to do."

"Because you pestered me until I got tired of saying no." The weathered old wrangler shook his head. "You were way too young. Which is why you took that nasty spill that split your jaw. But you were jealous because your cousins were already riding, and you wanted to keep up."

"He was always trying to keep up," Jesse said with a laugh.

"With wild rascals like the two of you, I can't say I blame him. I guess that's why he was so wild and tough." Jimmy Eagle sobered. "Your pa was good to me, Zane. It wasn't easy for a full-blooded Blackfoot to make friends off the reservation, but your pa put me at ease and became a good friend." His voice lowered. "I heard he died in California."

Zane nodded.

"I'm sorry. But I wasn't surprised when he left the ranch. He used to say that one day he'd move to a place where it never snowed."

That had Zane smiling. "He hated snow. He said it was the one thing he never missed about this place." His smile faded a bit as he added, "Of course, he might have said that to appease my mother."

Jimmy ducked his head. "As I recall, she didn't much like it here. What'd she think of California?"

"She settled in." Zane tried to keep the bitterness from his tone. "Made a life for herself there after Dad died."

Jimmy Eagle helped himself to an empty plate and began loading it with food. "How long you plan on visiting?"

Zane shrugged. "I'll probably leave in the morning."

"That's too bad. I would've enjoyed a nice, long visit." The old wrangler stuck out a hand. "I have to be up on the south range in an hour. Great seeing you, Zane."

"You, too, Jimmy."

Zane stepped into line behind Jesse and Wyatt and filled a plate, then followed them to their aunt's table.

Cora looked up with a smile. "Did I see you talking to Jimmy?"

Zane settled himself beside her at the picnic table. "He used to call me his little shadow. I dogged that man's footsteps when I was a kid. I can't remember him ever losing patience with me. Not once. No matter how many times I pestered him with questions. He didn't just give me the answers, he'd tell me the why of things." He shook his head, remembering. "Nobody else except Coot ever took that kind of time with me."

Cora gave a dreamy smile. "Oh, Coot had a soft spot for his grandsons, all right. He just couldn't do enough for the three of you. It almost broke his heart when two of his sons moved and took you boys away."

"Water under the bridge, Aunt Cora." Jesse shoved away from the table.

She looked up. "Where are you going, Jess?"

He paused to press a hand to her shoulder. "I just need some space. I'll see you when the crowd thins."

She watched him walk across the lawn, pausing every now and then to speak to one or two of the wranglers before continuing toward the house. She knew him so well. Knew that tight, closed look. He was angry and hurting. And there wasn't a thing she could do about it. It was something he'd just have to work through by himself.

She turned to Wyatt. "Tell me about your life since you left Montana."

"Would you like to hear about Tibet, or India, or would you prefer something more exotic, like the luxury yacht I helped crew in the South Pacific?"

His rogue smile, so like his father's, had her spirits lifting at once. "Why not tell me about all of them?"

"I hope you have a few days." He sat back. "Why don't I tell you about my last job, wrangling horses in Texas."

"Texas?" Cora looked startled. "Is that where you were when you heard about Coot?"

He nodded. "I guess you wouldn't have known that. I travel around so much I use a service for my messages. No matter where in the world I am, they can always find me."

"If only Coot had known you were back in the country." Cora looked down at her hands, clasped in her lap. "Why didn't you offer to work here, Wyatt?"

He thought about evading the question. After all, she'd been through enough, losing her only brother. But he owed her the truth. "I guess I didn't know if I'd be welcome, Aunt Cora."

"Oh, Wyatt." She laid a hand over his. "Why would you think such a thing?"

"My dad didn't exactly part company with Coot under the friendliest of terms."

"No, he didn't. But that had nothing to do with you, Wyatt."

He looked down at his aunt's hand covering his. Even though the fingers had grown a bit knobby, they were still the long, tapered fingers of an artist. He'd always been amazed that this sweet and seemingly spacey woman could take a blank canvas and turn it into a blaze of color, form, and energy. Within this quiet, unassuming woman lay a depth of passion that was shocking in its intensity.

"It had everything to do with me, Aunt Cora."

"Why do you say that?"

"Dad told me he left because he thought I was too much of a dreamer. He said he could see me becoming infected with the same poison that was killing his father."

"Poison?"

"Coot's obsession with the lost gold." He lowered his voice. "You have to admit, Aunt Cora, that it colored his entire life."

She nodded. "It did. And who knows? Maybe he'd have been better off without it. But this much I know." She closed her other hand on his. "If Coot had ever found his fortune, he'd have gladly given it all away to his three grandsons. You boys meant everything in the world to him."

Seeing the crowd beginning to thin, she got to her feet. "Would you mind coming with me now? I need to say good-bye to our guests."

With Zane on one side and Wyatt on the other, she made her way to the wide porch where she stood, flanked by her great-nephews, thanking the wranglers and townspeople who were taking their leave.

In the kitchen Jesse loosened his tie and poured himself a tumbler of Irish whiskey. Like his grandfather, he wasn't much of a drinker. But every New Year, and at the annual roundup barbecue, Coot would pour a round of whiskeys for himself and the crew, and offer a toast to the future.

"Life's all about the road ahead. What's past is past. Here's to what's around the bend, boys."

Jesse could hear his grandfather's voice as clearly as if he'd been standing right there. There had been a boyish curiosity about the old man that was so endearing. He'd truly believed he would live to find his ancestor's fortune. The anticipation, the thrill of it, had influenced his entire life. And it was contagious. Jesse had been caught up in it as well. It's what had kept him here, chasing Coot's rainbow, instead of going off in search of his own.

Not that he had any regrets. He couldn't imagine himself anywhere but here.

He crossed the mudroom and stepped out onto the back porch, hoping to get as far away from the crowd as possible.

Just as he lifted the drink to his lips, a voice stopped him.

"I thought I might find you out here."

He didn't have to see her to recognize that voice. Hadn't it whispered to him in dreams a hundred times or more?

His tone hardened as he studied Amy Parrish standing at the bottom of the steps. "What's the matter, Amy? Make a wrong turn? Lunch is being served in the front yard."

"I noticed." She waited until he walked closer. "I just wanted to tell you why I came back."

"To gloat, no doubt."

"Don't, Jess." She pressed her lips together, then gave a sigh of defeat. "I'm sorry about your grandfather. I know you loved him."

"Yeah." Her eyes were even greener than he remembered. With little gold flecks in them that you could see only in the sunlight. It hurt to look at them. At her. Almost as much as it hurt to think about Coot. "So, why did you come back?"

"To offer some support to my dad while he had some medical tests done."

His head came up sharply. "He's sick?"

She nodded. "The doctor in Billings sent him to a

specialist at the university. The test results should be back in a couple of days, and then I'll be going back to my job, teaching in Helena."

"I'm sorry about your dad. I hope the test results come back okay." He paused, staring at the glass in his hands because he didn't want to be caught staring at her. "So, I guess you just came here to say good-bye before you leave. Again."

"I just..." She shrugged and stared down at her hands, fighting nerves. "I just wanted to offer my condolences."

"Thanks. I appreciate it."

The breeze caught a strand of pale hair, softly laying it across her cheek. Without thinking he reached up and gently brushed it away from her face.

The heat that sizzled through his veins was like an electrical charge, causing him to jerk back. But not before he caught the look of surprise in her eyes. Surprise and something more. If he didn't know better, he'd swear he saw a quick flash of heat. But that was probably just his pride tricking him into believing in something that wasn't there, and hadn't been for years.

He lowered his hand and clenched it into a fist at his side.

She took a sideways step, as though to avoid being touched again. "I'd better get back to my dad."

"Yeah. Thanks again for coming."

She walked away quickly, without looking back.

That was how she'd left in the first place, he thought. Without a backward glance.

Now he could allow himself to study her. Hair the color of wheat, billowing on the breeze. That lean, willowy body; those long legs; the soft flare of her hips.

Just watching her, he felt all the old memories rushing over him, filling his mind, battering his soul. Memories he'd kept locked up for years in a small, secret corner of his mind. The way her hair smelled in the rain. The way her eyes sparkled whenever she smiled. The sound of her laughter, low in her throat. The way she felt in his arms when they kissed. When they made love...

He'd be damned if he'd put himself through that hell again.

He lifted the tumbler to his lips and drained it in one long swallow, feeling the heat snake through his veins.

"What's past is past," he muttered thickly. "Here's to what's around the bend."

Cora stood, flanked by Wyatt and Zane, until the ranch hands had returned to their chores and the last of the townspeople had driven away.

Dandy and his helpers began the task of cleaning up the remains of the luncheon.

"You need anything, Miss Cora, you let me know." Dandy looked up from his work as she walked past.

"Thank you for everything, Dandy." Cora led the way inside the ranch house.

Vernon McVicker was seated at the kitchen table, sipping coffee. He picked up a briefcase from the floor. "Where would you like to do this, Miss Cora?"

"Coot's office. I'll just go find Jess and the others. Why don't you boys go with Vernon?"

As she walked away Zane and Wyatt glanced at each other with matching looks of puzzlement.

The lawyer led the way down a long hallway to a large room at the rear of the house, which was obviously a masculine retreat. A massive wooden desk and leather chair stood in front of a stone fireplace. Floor-to-ceiling shelves filled with books and ledgers occupied two walls of the room. The windows looked out over a spectacular view of green rangeland, with the peaks of Treasure Chest Mountain in the distance.

While Zane and Wyatt settled into comfortable leather chairs, Vernon McVicker walked to the desk and opened his briefcase. Minutes later Cal Randall and Dandy Davis arrived, looking annoyed at being taken away from their chores. By the time Cora and Jesse entered, Vernon had a sheaf of papers carefully spread out before him.

He waited until all were seated before settling himself in Coot's chair and steepling his fingers on the desktop. "It was Coot's desire that his last will and testament be read in the presence of his sister, Cora, and his three grandsons, as well as his two trusted employees, provided they were all in attendance. Since all parties are present, I'll begin by reading the will, which, as you'll be able to tell from the language, was dictated by Coot himself. Afterward, I'll have a signed, dated copy for each of you, in case there are any questions."

He picked up a document and began reading. "To my ranch foreman, Calumet Randall, I leave the sum of three hundred thousand dollars, for his years of dedicated service to my ranch. Cal, if you choose to retire and use this money to build your own spread, I'll understand. But I'd be beholden to you if you could see fit to remain on as foreman for as long as the work pleases you. I want you to know that you'll always have a home with us at the Lost Nugget."

Cal, caught completely by surprise, swallowed loudly, then stared down at his hands.

"To my friend Thayer Davis..."

Every head in the room swiveled to stare at Dandy. At last, they knew his given name.

Jesse coughed.

Annoyed at the interruption, Vernon continued, "To my friend Thayer Davis, I leave the sum of two hundred thousand dollars for his years of fine cooking. I know you really wanted to be a wrangler, Dandy. If that's still your dream, maybe this money can make it happen. But you're one hell of a fine cook. If you're so inclined, I'd like you to stay on as ranch cook for as long as the work pleases you."

Dandy blinked hard. One fat wet tear rolled down his cheek before he quickly brushed it aside with the back of his hand.

"To my sister, Cora, I leave the house, which has been in our family for four generations, and all the furniture therein, along with the sum of three million dollars in order to maintain it. I know the money doesn't mean a thing to you, Cora, honey. But humor me. All I ask is that you continue to love and cherish this place. Oh yeah. And keep on painting all those godawful things you've been painting. I may not have told you, but I'm really proud of you, little sister."

Though she'd been apprised of the terms of her brother's will, Cora was forced to bite hard on her lip to keep it from quivering. It all seemed so final somehow, hearing Coot's words read aloud.

Vernon picked up a second document and continued reading. "To my grandsons, Jesse, Wyatt, and Zane. If you're hearing this, it means you all got together for my big send-off. That makes me happy, boys. It's all I ever wanted. Now here's the deal. Jesse, because you've always loved the ranch, it's yours. Except for the house, which belongs now to Cora, I want you to have the herd and outbuildings. As for the land, which totals over two hundred thousand acres, I leave that equally to the three of you, provided each of you agrees to live on the ranch and continue the search for the treasure that has consumed my entire life. You know what that treasure means to me. I want it to mean the same to each of you. Don't misunderstand. If any one of you wants to leave, for any reason, you'll be given the sum of half a million dollars, with no hard feelings. Well, maybe a few. There's a catch. If you go, you'll have no claim to any part of the ranch, or any part of the treasure, if and when it should be found."

Vernon McVicker set down the document and looked up. "Are there any questions?"

No one spoke a word. In fact, no one moved.

Jesse looked mad enough to spit nails. And why not? He'd spent a lifetime here, working the land alongside the wranglers and putting up with his grandfather's obsession. He had to feel a little like the good son finding out that the prodigals had returned to share in the bounty he'd helped create.

And what a bounty. No one could have imagined just how much wealth old Coot had amassed.

Vernon got to his feet and began moving among them with the intention of handing out documents. Except for Cora, they behaved like robots, reaching out silently to accept the paper he thrust into their hands.

He returned to the desk and snapped the lid shut on his briefcase. As he walked to the door, Cora pulled herself together and walked with him.

At the doorway he paused and turned. "Miss Cora has my number, if any of you would like to call with any questions." He glanced around at the stunned faces. "Good day."

There was no reply.

Cora touched his arm. "I'll see you out, Vernon."

"There's no need." He patted her hand. "I think it best if you stay here and tend the shell-shocked, Miss Cora."

She stood in the doorway and listened to the sound of his footsteps receding. Then she took a deep breath and turned to study the faces of the men who had been so deeply affected by her brother's last will.

Dandy was gripping the rolled document firmly in his hand as he approached. "I'm...needed in the kitchen. Could we maybe talk later?"

She nodded and watched him walk away. When she turned, Cal was beside her, looking grim.

"You knew about this?"

"Some. Not all."

"Do you want me to stay, Cora?"

"You know I do, Cal. But the choice has to be yours. You'll need a little time..."

He was shaking his head. "I don't need time, Cora. What Coot did was generous. More than generous. I'm... speechless. But right now I need to get up to the range." As he started past her he paused and leaned close to whisper, "I'm real glad you want me to stay."

Before she could respond he was gone.

She turned to the three men remaining.

Wyatt had walked to the window to stare at the spectacular scenery in the distance. He had his back to the others.

Zane was pacing like a caged tiger. Across the room. A quick turn. Then a dozen paces in the opposite direction. He looked so much like Coot at that moment, Cora had to swallow hard.

Jesse was standing beside his grandfather's desk, running his hand around and around the scarred wooden top.

It was his voice that finally broke the silence. "I always knew he was a crazy old coot."

The others looked at him.

His eyes were hot and fierce, his voice edged with steel. "He's spent a lifetime searching for a treasure that doesn't exist. And now he's sucking us into it, too. Luring us in with the dream of a fortune. But if you guys have any sense at all, you'll take the money and run." He turned to Wyatt. "Isn't that what you want? To use the money to go off to some exotic South Sea island?"

Wyatt shrugged, his eyes glinting with sudden humor. "I can't say it didn't cross my mind."

"And you, Zane." Jesse fisted a hand in the document. "This ought to give you enough clout in Hollywood to produce your own documentaries instead of working on someone else's."

"It might."

"So." Jesse tossed aside his grandfather's will and leaned a hip on the desk before crossing his arms over his chest. "Does that mean the two of you are leaving?"

Zane merely shrugged. Wyatt turned back to stare out the window.

With a hiss of impatience Jesse started for the door.

Before he was halfway across the room Zane's quiet voice stopped him. "I'm thinking I might stay."

Jesse turned with a frown. "Why?"

His cousin shrugged. "There's a lot of material for a fascinating documentary right here." A smile flitted across his face. "Maybe I'll call it *The Search for the Lost Nugget.*"

Wyatt threw back his head and laughed.

Jesse turned to him. "What's so funny?"

His cousin shrugged. "You could call it *The Search for Fool's Gold.* Hell, maybe I'll stay, too. I've always loved an adventure."

Jesse looked from one to the other. "This isn't a dude ranch. The work is long and tedious. It doesn't matter how much money Coot left you. If you stay, you'll be expected to pull your own weight."

Wyatt's smile faded a bit. "You're not the only one who knows how to work, Jesse. You might have spent a lifetime doing ranch chores, but I've crewed a yacht during some of the worst storms ever seen in the Pacific. I climbed Mount Everest when it was twenty below. I shepherded a couple hundred fugitives halfway across Darfur. I think I can hold my own here in Montana."

Jesse turned to Zane with a scowl. "How about you, Hollywood? How long do you think you'll last driving a truck and shoveling manure?"

Zane's tone was deadly soft, but the heat in his eyes betrayed his temper. "I guess you'll have to wait and see, cousin. According to the terms of Coot's will, we've just become equal partners. And apparently that doesn't sit very well with you, does it?"

"You got that right. But let's see how it sits with the two of you a month from now, when you've had a healthy dose of the real world."

Zane turned to Wyatt. "I'm willing to stick around for a couple of months, just to see if it's a good fit."

Wyatt nodded. "Count me in, cuz."

Jesse slammed out of the room, his footsteps echoing in the empty hall.

CHAPTER FOUR

Jesse climbed into one of the ranch trucks and tore across an open field, tires spewing sand and grass in his wake. He didn't know where he was headed, but it didn't matter, as long as it took him away from here. The last place he wanted to be was anywhere near Wyatt and Zane.

"Why, Coot?" He hissed the words between clenched teeth. "All these years we got along just fine after they left. You and me. We didn't need anybody else. Why did you have to drag them back into my life?"

At the top of a hill he brought the truck to a halt and stared at the sweeping vista spread out before him. Acres of rich green pastures, studded with thousands of cattle. He knew every pond and stream and grassy meadow. He'd spent his entire life nursing sick heifers, dragging himself through muddy fields in the aftermath of a violent rainstorm, or trudging through waist-high snowdrifts caused by a sudden blizzard. Not because his grandfather had promised him a reward, but simply because he loved doing it. And now everything was about to change because crazy old Coot had made his grandsons an offer they couldn't refuse.

They'd stay. Oh, yeah. They'd stay, with visions of a fortune dancing in their heads. But they'd be nothing but dead weight.

"I'm not saving their lazy asses, Coot. I didn't ask them to be here, and I'm not going out of my way to make it easy for them to stay."

He gunned the engine and the truck careened down the hill, coming to an abrupt halt at the edge of the woods.

He slammed out the door and stopped dead in his tracks at the sight of the horse and rider heading toward him across a stream that snaked through the woods. The roan mare picked her way carefully through the water, managing to avoid the rocks and fallen trees that littered the path. But it wasn't the horse that had him staring. It was the rider.

Amy's hair streamed out behind her like ribbons of gold. She rode a horse the same way he imagined she taught her students. With that easy self-assurance that came from having been born for this. There was a smile of pure pleasure on her face. From her relaxed, contented look, Jesse knew that she hadn't yet spotted him.

He decided to simply savor the moment. To study her without having to school his features or hide his pleasure.

It wasn't just because she was so easy to look at. There were plenty of beautiful women in Gold Fever. But none who stirred him the way she always had. From the first time he'd seen her sitting in her father's truck, he'd been drawn to her.

Otis Parrish and Coot had been engaged in a shouting match. To spare his grandsons, Coot had waved the boys away. Wyatt and Zane had climbed onto their horses and hightailed it back to the house. But Jesse had brashly walked up to the truck where she'd been sitting, poked his head in the open window, and introduced himself.

Amy smiled and spoke her name, and he'd felt a flare of heat bursting inside him.

Unlike other girls, she hadn't blushed or stammered or flirted. And when her father had stormed back to his truck and climbed inside, gunning the engine, she'd turned to wave, leaving Jesse with his heart in his throat.

It seemed to be perpetually stuck there whenever he saw her.

He needed to remind himself that she'd been the one to leave without a word.

Even now, his heart was an open, gaping wound. He wasn't certain it would ever heal. But he'd be damned if he'd let her see him bleeding to death.

Spotting Jesse, Amy tensed and drew in the reins, slowing her mount to a walk.

"Didn't figure on seeing you out here." Jesse leaned against the hood of the truck and folded his arms over his chest.

"Just getting some air. We got a call, and Dad's test results are in. We're to meet his doctor late today. Then I'll head out tomorrow."

"You don't seem too worried about him."

She managed a faint smile. "I'm convinced he's too ornery to get bad news."

He couldn't help smiling. They had both tasted her father's temper. "I hope you're right. One last ride?"

She nodded. "Yeah. I've been missing Old Red." She leaned over to run a hand lovingly along the horse's neck. "And she misses me. She could hardly wait for the saddle."

He watched the movement of her hand and found himself sweating. There'd been a time when he'd felt those hands on him. Despite their time apart, he could still remember the way they felt. He could remember everything about her.

Resentment surged through him. The last thing he wanted was to remember anything about those times. About Amy. About the two of them.

"I saw Wyatt and Zane with your aunt at the funeral today." Amy slid from the saddle and stood watching as Old Red dipped her head to drink. "They haven't changed much. A little older, a lot taller, but I'd have known them anywhere."

"Yeah. Some things never change."

At his tone, she glanced over. "I'm sorry you have to go through this, Jess. I know how you felt about your grandfather. But he was their grandfather, too."

"Yeah?" He shoved away from the truck and jammed his hands in his pockets. "You'd have never known it by the way they treated him. Once they left, they never looked back."

"They were kids, Jess. They didn't have a choice."

"Last I saw, they were all grown up. And neither of

them bothered to visit the old man. Not once in all these years."

"They're here now. It's pretty obvious that once they heard about his death, they dropped everything to make it back for the funeral. Why don't you just concentrate on that, and make your peace with them before they leave?"

"I'd be happy to. If they decide to leave." He gave a grunt of impatience. "They're thinking about staying."

Her eyes widened. "Why?"

"Coot made them an offer that was too tempting to refuse. In his will he stated that they can leave with his blessing and a hefty sum of money, or they can stay, inherit a chunk of real estate, and continue his search for the lost fortune. They're both mulling over the option to remain here. I guess it's just too hard to pass up the chance to be a part of our famously crazy, dysfunctional family."

"Oh, Jess." Without thinking Amy put a hand on his. Squeezed. "I'm sorry you have to deal with so much on this sad day."

She looked up to see him staring at her in a way that had her throat going dry. She'd seen that look so many times, whenever he was about to kiss her. It always had the same effect on her, sending her heart into overdrive.

Annoyed by the feelings that rushed through her, she lowered her hand and took a step back before pulling herself into the saddle.

Before she could wheel her mount he caught the reins. Her head came up sharply.

"Thanks for your concern, Amy. I appreciate it."

When she said nothing, he added, "I hope your dad gets the good news he's hoping for. Safe journey."

He turned on his heel and climbed into his truck.

Amy watched as he gunned the engine and made a wide turn before heading back in the direction of his ranch.

She urged her horse into a run and wondered at the way her heartbeat kept time to the pounding of Old Red's hooves.

She'd thought, for just a moment there, that Jesse might haul her to the ground and kiss her. Or was it just wishful thinking?

She needed to get out of here. Out of the county and back to Helena where she wouldn't be close enough to Jesse McCord to be tempted to think about what might have been.

Jesse was doing plenty of thinking of his own. He'd driven out here to be alone, to deal with the pain of Coot's death. Amy's presence had brought another kind of pain—the pain of loss that had never been reconciled. And because they'd never dealt with what had happened between them, the wound had never healed.

She'd gone her way, without a word, and he'd been left to pick up the pieces of what passed for his heart. What kind of woman declared her love one night and was gone without a word the next morning?

There had been plenty of women since then, but none he'd allowed to get close. Once burned was enough. Only a fool would allow himself to get hurt like that again, and Jesse prided himself on being nobody's fool.

He wouldn't think about her. He'd had enough grief for one day.

He turned the truck into the barn and slammed the door hard enough to rattle the timbers as he headed toward the house.

"I made your favorite tonight, Miss Cora." Dandy set the platter of sliced meat loaf beside her plate before unloading the trolley containing mashed potatoes, gravy, green beans from the garden, and freshly baked biscuits.

The group seated around the table was subdued. Jesse made no attempt at conversation, keeping his attention fixed on his plate.

Across the table Wyatt and Zane directed their words to the ranch foreman.

"Thanks for the tour, Cal." Wyatt filled his plate before handing the platter to Zane, seated beside him.

"My pleasure. If you're going to be living and working here, I figured you'd want to familiarize yourself with the place."

"So many changes." Zane scooped potatoes from a bowl and made a crater in the middle before filling it with rich, dark gravy. "You've really gone high-tech on us."

"Some." Cal swallowed back a smile, remembering that it was Coot who'd taught his grandsons to do that so many years ago at this very table. His old friend had always enjoyed his potatoes smothered in Dandy's gravy. "Since you boys left the ranch, we've added computers and GPS, helicopters and all-terrain vehicles for the wildest stretches of land. But ranching is still hands-on, seat-of-the-pants dirty work best done by dedicated cowboys."

That had Jesse looking over at his cousins. "You two think you're up to it?"

Wyatt shrugged. "I guess we'll know soon enough." He grinned at Zane before turning to the weathered foreman. "You still planning on taking us up to the high country tomorrow?"

Jesse frowned at Cal. "You're sending them to Rafe?"

The old man nodded. "Zane and Wyatt said they'd like to jump in and lend a hand wherever they're needed. Rafe needs help with the herd."

"The last thing he needs is to babysit a couple of greenhorns."

Cora's jaw dropped. "Jesse…"

Before his aunt could say more, Wyatt held up a hand. "It's okay, Aunt Cora. Zane and I can fight our own battles." He looked over at Jesse and kept his smile in place, though his words were pure ice. "I get that you don't want us here. It must be a burr under your saddle to suddenly have to share what you've had all to yourself for so many years. But this was Coot's last wish. And I'm going to give it my best shot to make it my wish, too. For now, I intend to learn all I can about the operation of the Lost Nugget and see how I can fit in. *If* I can fit in," he added for emphasis. "Now if that sticks in your craw"—he gave a negligent shrug of his shoulders—"then you'll just have to swallow it or choke on it."

Jesse's scowl grew. He flicked a glance at Zane. "Does he speak for you, too, Hollywood?"

Zane set down his fork. "I don't need anybody to do my talking. I'm here by choice. I figure if I could survive three years of everything from the hottest stretches of desert to the frozen mountains tracking a herd of mustangs for our documentary, I can survive here. I'll stay or go on my own terms. And if you decide to try to push me out before I'm ready to leave, you'd better be prepared for a fight."

Jesse gave a bitter laugh. "A fight? You going to send for some movie extras to be your body doubles, Hollywood?"

Zane was on his feet, his hand fisted at Jesse's shirtfront. "Would you like to find out here and now?"

"I wouldn't want to mess up that pretty moviestar face." Jesse pushed away. "Excuse me, Aunt Cora. I think I'll head into town. I expect the company at the Fortune Saloon will be a whole lot more interesting than this."

As he slammed out of the house Cora took a calming sip of her iced tea before glancing at her nephews. "I know Jesse's hurting. But that's no excuse for his behavior."

"Don't worry about it, Aunt Cora." Zane reached across the table and caught her hand. "It's going to be a tough adjustment for all of us. I'm just sorry that it spoiled your supper."

She gave him a weak smile. "I really have no appetite tonight. But for Dandy's sake, I thought I'd try."

"I feel the same way." Zane nodded toward the doorway. "Why don't we give it up and take a walk outside before it gets too dark? Or would you rather just sit in the great room where we can talk?"

"The great room." Cora shoved away from the table. "It was always Coot's favorite room. We've been apart

too many years. I want to know all about the two of you."
She turned to Cal. "I hope you'll join us."

"Glad to." He nodded. "I'd like to do some catching
up of my own."

The four of them left the dining table and walked to
the great room, where a log blazed in the open four-sided
fireplace that dominated the center of the space. They
settled themselves comfortably in the overstuffed chairs
by the hearth. A few minutes later Dandy entered carrying a tray of frosty longnecks. After passing them around,
he made his way back to the kitchen, leaving the four to
their privacy.

Jesse drove like the very devil himself, leaving a trail
of dust in his truck's wake. By the time he reached town
the worst of his temper had evaporated. Still, he wasn't
ready to let go just yet. And so he nursed the simmering
anger, hoping to coax it back to flame.

He paused just inside the door of the saloon to allow
his eyes to adjust. A pall of smoke hung in the air. Added
to that was the smell of onions on the small grill behind
the bar, where burgers simmered in a lake of grease.
Violet Spence had her back to the door as she flipped the
sizzling meat patties before filling another drink order.

Through the smoky veil Jesse recognized the usual
patrons. Harding Jessup, owner of the hardware and plumbing supply store, was seated at the bar with Stan Novak, a
local building contractor. The two men were bent close,
deep in conversation, a set of blueprints between them,
which only confirmed to Jesse that the rumor he'd heard
about Harding's plans to add onto his store must be true.

Mayor Rowe Stafford was holding court in one corner with a cluster of the townsfolk who'd probably been there since returning from the funeral. By now they were well-oiled and hanging on his every word. Seeing Jesse, the mayor lowered his voice, and Jesse realized he was probably regaling the locals with one of his many tales of adventure with Coot. Though Rowe professed to be one of Coot's oldest friends, he was known to embellish his stories in order to make them just a bit more interesting than the original incident. And in most of the yarns that had been repeated to Jesse, it would seem that Rowe painted himself a hero and Coot nothing but an old fool.

At a table in the center of the room some of the wranglers from the Lost Nugget ranch were laughing and talking with several of the local women. When they spotted Jesse they beckoned him over, but he gave a quick shake of his head and sidled up to the bar.

"Hey, you sweet thang." Daffy Spence came up from behind and gave him a hard hug even before he'd parked himself on the bar stool.

Daffy and her twin sister, Vi, owned and operated the Fortune Saloon. Violet was as shy and sweet as her sister Daffodil was wild and crazy. The two women had bought the building when it was a grain and feed store in the 1970s. Once they'd turned it into a successful bar, they'd sold the grain and feed business to Orley Peterson, who relocated down the street.

The sisters took turns working the day and night shifts, except on the weekends when they worked together to handle the crowd. Both were stick-thin and wore their purple hair spiked, their eyes ringed with enough jet-black liner to give them the appearance of flirty raccoons. Their age was a source of constant speculation, though one thing was certain. Whatever their birth certificates said, they were still young and frisky enough to bed the occasional bartender or willing customer.

"You in need of a little sympathy, Jesse?"

"Just a beer, Daffy. And send a round to the guys over there." He indicated the table of wranglers.

"You bet." She rounded the bar and set a longneck in front of him before filling a tray for the others.

Violet hurried over to catch his hand. "I'm so sorry for your loss, honey." Her voice, whispery as a little girl's, trembled slightly.

"Thanks, Vi."

"Daffy and I were at the funeral, but we didn't stay for the luncheon. Had to hurry back and get ready for the afternoon rush."

"I understand." He glanced around. "Looks like business is good."

She nodded. "Most of 'em raised their first glass to Coot."

He lifted his bottle. "Then I'll do the same."

"We lost a good man."

Jesse saw her eyes tear up and prayed she wouldn't cry. He didn't think he could handle tears right now.

She sniffed. "Want a burger, honey? It's on the house."

"No thanks, Vi. But I appreciate the offer."

She patted his hand. "You want anything, Jesse honey, you let me know."

When she walked back to the grill he found himself

wondering if she and his grandfather had ever had a fling. Or would Coot have preferred her rowdy sister?

The direction of his thoughts had him scowling. He tipped up the bottle and took a long pull, hoping the taste of beer would wash away the bitter taste of loss.

"Hey, Doc. What'll you have?"

The sound of Daffy's voice had him glancing around. Dr. Frank Wheeler was just settling himself on the bar stool beside his.

"I'll have the same as Jesse." Dr. Wheeler's tufts of white hair and round, frameless glasses gave him an owlish look. He and Jesse exchanged a quick handshake. "Jesse. Sorry for your loss."

"Thanks, Doc."

When Daffy set down the longneck and walked away, Jesse shot him a sideways glance. "I saw Amy Parrish this afternoon. She said she and her father were seeing you today."

The doctor nodded gravely and took a long drink. "Just delivering the test results from the university hospital up in Billings."

"I guess Amy'll be halfway to Helena by noon tomorrow." He wondered why the words made his throat hurt.

Dr. Wheeler shook his head. "Doubt she'll be going anytime soon."

Jesse turned to study him. "Why's that?"

The older man shrugged. "Since Otis doesn't have any other family, he'll be depending on his daughter for support."

"Support?"

"Driving him to the clinic in town for his treatments.

Picking up his prescriptions. And pretty much holding his hand through this."

"How serious is it?"

Frank Wheeler stared down into his drink. "You know what the hardest thing about being a doctor is?" He looked up. Met Jesse's eyes. "Telling a man like Otis Parrish to get his affairs in order."

CHAPTER FIVE

Amy sat on the big porch swing, arms hugging her knees, staring into the darkness. Her father had gone into his room. A short time later she'd heard the creaking of his bed and knew that he'd retreated into sleep.

He hadn't said a word all the way home. Nor, for that matter, in the doctor's office. He'd listened in silence as Dr. Wheeler read the lab report and described the treatments suggested by the team of specialists in Billings. When Dr. Wheeler ended their meeting by telling him to get his affairs in order, she'd tried to take her father's hand. He'd shaken off her touch, but in that brief instant she'd recognized that it was as cold as the ring of ice that had begun to form around her heart.

How did others handle this kind of news about a parent? Did they cry? Get angry? Throw something? Some might urge a second or even a third opinion, or simply deny the truth. A few probably took a family trip around the world, hoping to store up memories for the harsh reality looming in their future. Did anyone else react like this? Or was she the only one in the universe to feel more like a statue than a human? She was numb. Her brain refused to function. She couldn't think. Couldn't even react. And so she sat, the swing motionless, staring without seeing the night shadows, the golden slice of moon, the glittering stars in the black velvet sky.

In her mind's eye she was four, teetering on a boulder to pull herself onto the back of her father's favorite stallion. While her parents watched in horror, she flicked the reins, sending the horse into a trot. She bumped up and down in the saddle, practically airborne, as the horse circled the corral. By the time her father managed to catch up with her and grab the reins, she was beaming with excitement.

"See, Daddy? I'm just like you."

He swore viciously, causing her smile to fade at his outburst. "Little fool. You could've been trampled."

"But I wasn't afraid, Daddy."

"You should've been. Fear's a good thing. It keeps us from jumping off cliffs."

"I didn't jump. I rode your horse. Just like you."

"Without my permission." He hauled her roughly from the saddle and swatted her backside before shoving her toward her mother, who was standing just outside the corral.

She wanted to cry, but even at that tender age she knew that it would add another layer to her father's anger. "You said I could ride when I was big enough." With hands on hips she faced him. "I'm big enough now."

"One more word and you won't be able to sit for a week. You hear me, girl?"

She looked up at her mother in confusion. "Daddy always says he wishes I was a boy. But then he gets mad when I try to be what he wants."

"Your father's going through a...difficult time." Her mother avoided Amy's eyes as she led the girl toward the house. "He fought with a neighbor, and I just gave him some bad news."

"Bad news?"

"You and I are going to stay with my sister for a while."

"Did Daddy cry?"

Her mother stopped, paused to kneel down, and managed a smile. "Your daddy doesn't know how to cry, honey. All he knows how to do is fight. Whether he's mad or sad or even when things are going fairly well, he just doesn't react like other men. But a good fight seems to clear the air."

"Did Daddy and I just have a fight?"

Her mother considered before she stood and hurried on toward the house, dragging Amy with her. "He'd have preferred a good knock-down, drag-out fight, but I suppose this was better than nothing."

At that, the little girl's spirits lifted. She hadn't completely failed. She'd managed to stay in the saddle. And she'd given her dad something he wanted.

That may have been the first fight Amy could recall. But it was far from the last.

She and her father had been butting heads almost from the day of her birth. She had long ago accepted the fact that she was fated to break every rule that Otis Parrish set, whether by accident or design. She'd lost count of the number and ferocity of their arguments.

But this time...this time, she thought with a sigh, all the fight seemed to have gone out of him, and she didn't know how to deal with it.

Her mother would have known just what to do. But ever since her mother's sudden death from a heart attack while Amy was away at college, nothing had been the same. She'd avoided coming home because it no longer felt like home. She and her father had grown more and more distant, and when, after graduation, she'd been offered a teaching job in Helena, she'd accepted with a sense of relief that it offered her the perfect excuse to stay away.

Now she was back, and she felt awkward and useless.

She looked up at the sound of an engine. Headlights momentarily blinded her. A truck door slammed and a tall figure bounded up the steps.

Amy sucked in a breath, then let it out in a whoosh when she recognized Jesse.

He was headed toward the front door but halted in midstride when he caught sight of her seated in the shadows. "You okay?"

Her heart was pounding again, but this time it wasn't because she'd been startled, but because of some other, deeper emotion. When she couldn't find her voice she merely nodded.

"Mind if I join you?" Without waiting for her reply, he settled himself on the swing beside her.

Their hips bumped and they both moved apart a fraction.

"You heard?" She studied his profile.

"I ran into Doc Wheeler at the Fortune Saloon."

"So much for doctor-patient confidentiality."

"The rules don't apply. This is Gold Fever."

"Yeah." She crossed her arms over her chest. "I should have known. Bad news and small towns."

"He wasn't spreading gossip. I asked and he told me." Jesse paused before adding, "How'd your dad take the news?"

"How should I know?"

He looked over. "Doc said you were there."

"Yeah. It was like watching a silent movie. All facial expressions and body language. But no dialogue."

"You two didn't talk? Not even on the long drive home?"

She shook her head.

"I'm sorry, Amy." She looked so defeated. He thought about taking her into his arms, but she'd probably slap him. "So, what're you going to do?"

"I don't know. I've been trying to sort things out. Dr. Wheeler said he didn't think Dad should be alone during the treatments. Since there's nobody else, I guess I'll take a leave of absence and ask the school district to get a substitute for me. After that, I'll just have to wait and see. If Dad responds to the treatments, I'll go back to Helena. If he doesn't..." Her words trailed off.

"Hey. He'll be fine."

"Don't." She covered her ears. "I'm not interested in empty platitudes."

"Then how about this?" He caught her hands. Held them fast when she tried to pull away. "Some people make it. Some don't. I'm betting your old man is ornery enough to survive anything."

That had her almost smiling, but the warmth of his touch

of her hands made her break contact. She didn't like the way her heart was pounding. To cover her feelings, she got to her feet and started pacing. "He is ornery, isn't he?"

"The toughest guy in the county." Jesse watched her stalk restlessly across the porch, then back. "If anybody can catch bullets in his teeth and spit them out, it's your father."

"Yeah." She released a long, slow breath. "I wish that were true. Oh, Jesse, when the doctor started talking about the series of treatments, I looked over at my dad and he looked so old and tired and beaten."

"Come on, now." Without thinking he stood and gathered her close. "This kind of diagnosis doesn't necessarily mean a death sentence. He's still breathing, isn't he?"

At his words she looked stricken. "What was I thinking? Here I am going on about my dad on the very day you've buried your grandfather. I'm sorry, Jess. At least Dad has a fighting chance." She touched a hand to his cheek. "You have to be reeling from the shock of Coot's death without any..."

The look in his eyes had her words trailing off. She recognized the smoldering heat. Had seen it often enough in the past to know exactly how unexpectedly it could build into an inferno.

Her heart nearly tumbled in her chest as his head lowered.

She braced herself, eager for his mouth to claim hers.

Instead, the moment seemed to freeze before he thought better of it and stepped back, clenching his hands at his sides.

"Guess I'd better be heading home. We've both put in a long day."

A breeze caught the end of her hair and he lifted a hand, tucking the errant strand behind her ear. His gaze held hers for just a moment longer before he turned away and bounded down the porch steps.

He opened the door of the truck and looked up. "If there's anything I can do..." He shrugged.

"Thanks."

She stood watching as the headlights receded. Within minutes the silence had returned, swallowing her in darkness.

Amy shivered. In that instant when his arms had encircled her, she'd had to fight a nearly overpowering urge to weep. She was so glad she'd managed to keep her composure. Especially since the expected kiss hadn't materialized. But she'd wanted, just for that moment, to allow him to be strong for both of them.

Fool, she thought with a rising sense of anger and frustration. He'd come here like a neighbor to offer her comfort, and she'd immediately begun to spin it into something more.

Whatever feelings had once been between them were dead and buried. Hadn't he made that abundantly clear years ago?

While she'd been feeling lost and alone in a brand-new town, struggling to get through crowded dorm rooms and confusing college classes, he'd been living the good life, dating every female within a hundred miles, according to the things she'd been told. And though she'd waited endlessly for him to contact her, he'd remained oddly silent, until, finally, she'd been forced to accept the message he'd been trying to send. Whatever feelings she'd had for him weren't returned.

The hardest lesson she'd ever had to learn was that Jesse not only didn't miss her, he didn't even think about her.

Out of sight; out of mind. At least on his part.

Just seeing him again had brought all the old emotions to the surface. It wasn't love, she cautioned. It was memory. Habit. Now that she was back in Gold Fever, she would have to remember to guard her fickle heart.

As she made her way inside she realized that now, after Jesse's visit, she felt even more desolate than ever.

Jesse let himself into the darkened ranch house and prayed he could make it to his room without running into anyone. He was in no mood to chat up his aunt or duel with his cousins.

He shed his boots in the mudroom and moved quickly through the kitchen. As he stepped into the great room he realized his mistake. In the glow of the fire two heads came up sharply.

Wyatt made a point of glancing at his watch. "Not even close to closing time yet. The Fortune Saloon run out of longnecks?"

"I decided to stop over at the Parrish ranch."

Now it was Zane's turn to glance meaningfully at his watch. "I guess this means you didn't get the warm reception you were hoping for." He chuckled at his little joke.

Jesse thought about ignoring Wyatt and Zane and heading off to bed without another word, but that would only give them a power over him they didn't deserve.

"Thought I'd pay a call on a neighbor who just got some bad news."

His cousins' smiles evaporated.

Wyatt spoke for both of them. "What was the bad news?"

"Otis Parrish got the results of his lab tests back late this afternoon, and he's facing some serious treatments if he hopes to live. Since Amy's his only kin, she's going to have to take a leave of absence from teaching to help him through the next few months."

"I'm sorry to hear that." Zane pointed to his beer. "Care to join us?"

It was on the tip of Jesse's tongue to refuse, but he found himself saying, "I guess I could use a cold one."

Zane left the room and returned a minute later with a frosty bottle.

Jesse took a long, slow pull before lowering it to his side. "Thanks. I was drier than I thought."

Wyatt glanced over from his position beside the fire. "How's Amy taking the news about her father?"

Jesse shrugged. "She's still in shock. Needs some time to sort through it."

Wyatt shook his head. "I don't blame her. When I heard about Coot, I felt like I'd been sucker-punched."

Zane nodded. "I know the feeling. I'd thought so many times about just packing up and driving out here, but the time never seemed right. Then, to get the news and know that I could never see him, never make it right between us..." He lowered his head.

Jesse wanted to remind his cousins that they'd had years to visit the old man if they'd really wanted to bridge the chasm left by old family feuds. Instead, he held his silence and took another long drink of beer.

Wyatt stared at the glowing coals of the fire. "It was the same when I heard about my parents going down in that plane. All of a sudden the most important people in my life were gone, and there was no way to bring them back. I spent years wandering the world, trying to make sense of it."

Jesse glanced over. "Did you? Make any sense out of it?"

"Some." Wyatt gave a dry laugh. "If I discovered anything, it's this: We have a certain amount of time, and we'd better use it wisely. When time runs out, there's no bargaining for more."

"That's profound." Zane yawned and drained his beer. "I wouldn't mind continuing this deep discussion another time, but right now, I need to get some sleep."

"You'd better both get some sleep." Jesse set aside his half-full bottle. "Rafe Spindler works his crew up in the hills like dogs."

"So I heard." Wyatt followed Zane toward the doorway before pausing and turning toward Jesse. "If you see Amy again, tell her that at least she's bought some time with her father. If there's anything they haven't resolved, now's the time."

"Yeah. I'll tell her." Jesse banked the fire before climbing the stairs to his room.

As he passed Coot's rooms, he resisted the urge to step inside as he often used to, just to talk over the day. He missed the old man with an ache that was so deep and physical, he held a hand to his midsection.

Upstairs he crossed the room and leaned a hip against the windowsill, staring at the canopy of stars in the midnight sky. He yanked his shirt over his head, intent upon tossing it aside. In that instant he became aware that it still bore the distinct fragrance of Amy.

On a moan he buried his face in the fabric, breathing her in, and felt a shudder pass through him.

He could lie to her, to his cousins, even to himself. But now, here, in the privacy of his room, in the dark of the night, in the depths of his own heart, there was no denying.

God, how he wanted her. Wanted her as much now as when he'd first held her in his arms all those years ago. In fact, since he was being completely honest with himself, he wanted her more. The need for her was a knife in his heart that nothing, not time, not distance, would ever heal.

On an overload of emotions he fell face-first across his bed, the shirt clutched tightly in his hand, praying for the release of sleep.

CHAPTER SIX

———◆◆◆———

Jesse tore open the driver's-side door of the truck and got slammed by a gust of wind and rain. He had to lean his weight against the barn doors to open them wide enough for the truck to pass through. He jumped back into the truck, drove it inside, parked it in a row of other vehicles, and then sprinted back into the rain to secure the barn door. By the time he made it to the house, his clothes were plastered to his skin. In the mudroom he levered off his muddy boots and hung his soaked hat and cowhide jacket on pegs by the door.

The weather this past week had been as surly as his mood.

Cora looked up from the table, where she sat sipping a steaming cup of tea. "I haven't seen you in a week."

"Been with Cal's crew mending fences." And putting as much distance as possible between himself and Amy.

"I missed you."

"Sorry." He felt a twinge of guilt. Her first days with her brother gone, and he'd left her all alone. Not that he'd have been any comfort to her, he thought with a trace of bitterness. He'd had his own demons to battle. Still, he wished he knew how to help his aunt get through her grief. God knew, he wasn't doing very well with his.

He spied the bulging travel case of paints and canvas standing in a corner. They always signaled another road trip for his aunt. "Where're you headed this time?"

"Treasure Chest."

At the mention of the distant mountain shaped like its name, Jesse arched a brow. "That's quite a hike, Aunt Cora."

"I'm not planning on climbing it. Just going to paint it. I think all those dark storm clouds will make an interesting background. Weather reports say they'll be around for at least three or four more days."

"Just what we need." He scowled. "More rain."

The old woman touched a hand to his sleeve. "You've been pushing yourself too hard, Jesse. With Wyatt and Zane up in the hills, why don't you take a few days off?"

"And do what?"

She smiled. He was so like Coot. Restless. Always on the move. "I don't know. Go for a walk or a ride. Maybe search for buried treasure."

"I'll leave that for the city slickers." He started toward the door. "Got to shower off all this range mud."

"Before you do that, would you mind helping me load my supplies?"

"You're leaving now? Before supper?"

"I asked Dandy to pack some food before giving him

the night off." She looked up suddenly. "Sorry. We didn't know whether or not to expect you."

"Doesn't matter about me." He shrugged. "I'll eat some of that glue Vi passes off as a burger at the saloon. When will you eat?"

"When I stop for the night." She laughed at her nephew's look of consternation. "After a lifetime with me, you have to know that I'm as crazy as my brother. Instead of gold, I keep chasing after art. I intend to be painting Treasure Chest by dawn's light."

Jesse picked up the box of supplies and paused to step into his boots before trailing her to her Jeep, buffeted by wind and rain. The back was loaded with a sleeping bag, a rifle, a cooler, a small cookstove, and enough supplies to see her through several weeks if necessary.

After loading the paint and supplies Jesse leaned in the open window. "You remembered your cell phone and charger?"

She nodded. "You sound like Coot. I'm fine, Jesse."

"Yes. You are. You're darned near perfect." He kissed her cheek. "Just remember to check in every day, or Cal and I will send the cavalry out after you."

"Yes, sir." She cupped his chin in one hand and gave him her sweetest smile. "While I'm gone, try to make peace with your cousins."

He stepped back, eyes steely. "Don't wish for miracles. Just stay safe."

"I'll be home in a week or two. Unless I run out of food or paint and canvas sooner." She put the Jeep in gear and pulled away, windshield wipers waging a furious war against the pounding rain.

Feeling as gloomy as the weather, Jesse trudged back to the house.

Up in his room he stood under the shower, letting the soothing warm water beat down on his head. After toweling dry he pulled on clean denims and rolled the sleeves of a well-worn shirt to his elbows.

In the mudroom he paused to slip into clean boots before heading for the barn. Minutes later he left a layer of mud in his wake as he drove the nearly hundred miles to Gold Fever.

Main Street was so littered with cars and trucks that Jesse had to drive to the very end of the line of businesses, alongside Harding Jessup's Plumbing Supply, to find a parking space. When he stepped inside the Fortune Saloon, he could see why. It seemed as though half the crew of the Lost Nugget was already there, eager to spend their paychecks.

"Hey, Jesse." Cal clapped him on the shoulder as he nudged his way toward the bar. "If I'd known you were coming into town, I'd've offered you a ride."

"No need, Cal." Jesse acknowledged the greetings from half a dozen men and women seated nearby before winking at Daffy behind the bar, who expertly flipped the cap off a longneck and handed it over the heads of several customers.

"You want a burger with that, honey?" Her rusty croak could be heard above the voice of Tim McGraw urging them to live like they were dying. The country-western singer was Daffy's latest crush, and her customers were subjected to marathon McGraw from morning to night.

"Yeah. Double onions."

"Double onions?" Burly Rafe Spindler looked up

from his seat at the bar. "I guess that means you don't figure on getting lucky tonight, McCord."

His words had everyone laughing, including Jesse, until he spotted Wyatt and Zane seated at the end of the bar. His smile faded as he ambled closer.

"Didn't expect to see you two in town."

Wyatt answered for both of them. "Couldn't pass up the chance to spend our first paycheck with the rest of the crew. We were told it was a rite of passage."

"It is. But I figured after a week up in the hills you two would be passed out in the bunkhouse. Or did you give up early so you could catch up on your beauty sleep before you went slumming?"

"I'll admit I'm a bit sore." Zane rolled his shoulders and grinned at the man beside him. "Jimmy here says I should be up to speed in a couple more weeks."

Jimmy Eagle nursed his soda. Even though he'd taken a lot of teasing over the years for choosing soft drinks over alcohol, he'd earned the respect of the wranglers for refusing to give in to their bullying. And while many of them had to drag out of bed for an early morning shift after a night in town, he was always clear-eyed and ready to face the day. "You keep working the way you did this week, son, and you'll have me thinking about retiring."

That had the wranglers from the Lost Nugget ranch laughing. They'd all heard Jimmy boast that he'd never slow down. His idea of heaven was to die in the saddle while bringing down one last herd from the high ground.

"It's going to take me a whole lot more months of wrangling to replace you, Jimmy."

"I'd say more like years." Stung by the easy camaraderie

between Zane and the weathered cowboy, Jesse tipped up his beer and took a long, steady pull.

"I don't know." Jimmy Eagle grinned at the two young men who had already begun to earn the grudging respect of the other wranglers. "You'd've been proud of your cousins, Jesse. Once they got the hang of it, the years melted away and they took to ranch chores like they'd never been gone."

Jesse gave a wry laugh. "You want me to believe our Hollywood pretty boy here was willing to get his hands dirty?"

Zane was halfway off the barstool when Wyatt's big hand pressed him down. His tone was low. "He's baiting you."

"Maybe I'm ready to take the bait."

Jimmy Eagle shot a quick glance at Jesse, who was rocking on his heels and staring daggers at his cousins. "Don't take it personally, son. He's been spoiling for a fight since Coot died."

"Oh, it's personal." Zane shoved aside his beer. "I'm more than willing to give him what he wants. He may have been able to beat me when he was twelve and I was nine, but that was too many years ago to count."

"You don't know..." Jimmy's head came up at a burst of raucous laughter from across the room.

Four strangers had been drinking steadily for the past couple of hours and their voices had grown progressively louder with every round of drinks.

"You know them?" Jesse nodded toward their table.

Jimmy gave a shake of his head. "Bikers, I'm thinking. I saw their motorcycles parked out back. Not from around here."

Vi turned away from the grill and held out a plate with a burger and a pile of her famous ranch fries, oozing grease. "Here you go, Jesse honey. Just the way you like it."

"Thanks, Vi." Jesse set aside his beer and lifted the burger to his mouth. Before he could take a bite one of the strangers, sporting a bushy beard and arms the size of tree limbs, strode across the room and snatched the burger out of Jesse's hands.

"What the hell?" Jesse looked more startled than angry. "What do you think you're doing?"

"We gave that old biddy our order half an hour ago. Since you just walked in the door, I figure this must be mine."

He started back to his table with Jesse's burger in his hand. Before he managed three steps Jesse spun him around and tore the food from his hand.

"Now you've gone and made me mad," the stranger said, then let loose with a string of oaths before throwing a punch.

Jesse ducked and managed to evade his fist. The burger slipped from his hand and landed on the floor.

Jesse looked down at the mess, then up into the cowboy's eyes. "Not nearly as mad as you've just made me. That was supposed to be my supper." His fist landed a direct hit between the stranger's eyes.

The biker, nearly a foot taller, barely blinked before jamming a fist into Jesse's midsection, leaving him grunting in pain. The man's buddies were on their feet now, cursing and egging him on.

One of them, with a beer belly hanging over the waist of faded denims, added to their laughter when he accused Jesse of fighting like a girl.

As they watched with the others, Zane turned to Wyatt. "Think we ought to lend a hand?"

Wyatt merely grinned. "Not our problem, cousin. Jesse was itching for a fight, remember? Now he's got one. I think he can handle this by himself."

The rest of the customers formed a circle around the pair. Some of them stood on their chairs, while others watched from barstools and tables. They gave the two men a wide berth, hoping for more action.

Jesse blew out a breath and straightened before landing a solid right cross to Bushy Beard's nose, sending blood gushing down the front of his shirt. The sight of all that blood had the crowd murmuring.

Before the stranger could recover, Jesse moved in with another blow to the man's jaw, snapping his head back.

For a moment the man looked dazed. He shook his head and staggered. That had his friends looking worried. Beer Belly was gesturing wildly to a beefy man in a ponytail and his remaining lanky friend. The three conferred, then moved in, circling Jesse.

Wyatt got to his feet so quickly he nearly kicked over his barstool.

Zane glanced up in surprise. "I thought you said this wasn't our fight."

"Those three just made it ours."

Beer Belly picked up his chair. Before he could lift it over his head, Wyatt tapped him on the shoulder.

He turned. "You want something, Surfer Boy?"

"Yeah. This."

The man found Wyatt's fist in his face. The chair clattered to the floor.

When Ponytail stepped up to help, fists raised, he found Zane directly beside him.

"Hey. Look at the pretty boy who came to join our party."

Zane landed a blow to his jaw that had him teetering backward.

The sight of the three McCords fighting the four strangers electrified the crowd. Even those who'd been trying to ignore the fight were now on their feet, watching avidly and calling words of encouragement.

"Behind you," Wyatt shouted.

Jesse ducked, and Bushy Beard's punch caught only air.

"Thanks." Jesse mouthed the word, then called to Zane, "Watch out."

Zane deflected the bottle that had come flying toward his head, then moved in to stop the lanky biker before he could toss a second one.

Without his friends to lend a hand, Bushy Beard realized he was in trouble. He'd picked the wrong cowboy to mess with. Desperate, he threw a punch that grazed Jesse's temple and was rewarded by a hard, stinging blow from Jesse's fist that sent him reeling.

Jesse turned to watch as Zane landed a solid punch to the lanky one's midsection. The man doubled up and hit the floor with a groan.

"Didn't know you had it in you, Hollywood." Jesse's grin faded when Zane pointed a finger. When Jesse turned, Bushy Beard had come back for more, landing a series of blows about Jesse's head that had his ears ringing.

When Beer Belly attempted to join in, taking aim with

a broken beer bottle, Wyatt caught the man's arm in a vicious grasp and began twisting until the bottle dropped to the floor, shattering into more pieces. Then Wyatt followed up with a fist to his jaw that rattled the man's teeth and caused his eyes to roll back in his head.

As he fell, Jesse threw a well-aimed punch at Bushy Beard that dropped him like a stone.

Both Wyatt and Jesse watched as Zane and Ponytail exchanged blows. Suddenly Zane took a fist to his eye and blinked furiously. He shook his head to clear it, then moved in with a series of blows. As the man brought his hands up to cover his face, Zane took advantage of the moment to take aim at his unprotected midsection. With a grunt of pain the man fell to his knees. Breathing hard, Zane waited, urging his opponent to get up so he could finish the job. Ponytail wobbled, then fell facedown on the floor.

After a few moments he lifted his hands in a sign of surrender. "I don't want to fight the three of you."

"You should have thought about that when you and your buddies decided to go four-on-one."

"We didn't mean anything by it. We had a few beers and just wanted to help a pal."

Jesse stared around at the mess. Broken chairs and bottles littered the floor, along with three unconscious cowboys.

"I expect you to pay the owners for the mess you made."

The man cowered before turning to Vi and Daffy. "Sorry for the mess, ladies." He reached into his pocket and withdrew a fat roll of bills. "I hope this will cover the cleanup."

Daffy accepted the money, then fixed him with a look of fury. "You owe my sister an apology."

"An...apology?"

"Your friend there called her an old biddy." In an aside she muttered, "Old biddy, indeed."

The man managed to choke out yet another apology. "Sorry, ma'am."

Anger gave Daffy's voice the rasp of a rusty gate. "Now take that"—she pointed to the three unconscious men—"trash out of our saloon. And see that you don't come back."

"Want to give him a hand?" Jesse turned to Zane and Wyatt, and the three of them began lifting, dragging, and nearly carrying the three cowboys toward the door. Once outside they dumped them unceremoniously in the mud and watched as Ponytail staggered off in search of their motorcycles. It took him nearly an hour to revive his friends enough to get them on their bikes.

When at last the rumble of their motorcycles faded into the darkness, the three cousins retraced their steps inside the saloon.

The crowd erupted into cheers before everybody returned to their beers.

Jesse wore a stupid grin on his face as he flexed his bruised, bloody knuckles. "That biker had the toughest hide I've ever encountered. I thought I'd broken my hand on his jaw."

"You think that's tough?" Wyatt leaned a hand on the wall until he could trust his legs. He gingerly touched his jaw and winced. "I'm lucky to have all my teeth."

Jesse turned to Zane, who had blood dripping from a cut over his eye.

"I think you're going to have a beautiful shiner by morning, Hollywood."

"Won't be the first time." Zane gave a short laugh.

"Yeah. I can see that."

Zane shared a grin with Wyatt. "Nothing like a good brawl to clear the air."

"Yeah."

Jesse looked from Wyatt to Zane, then surprised them both by dropping an arm over each of their shoulders. "Come on. Let's have a beer and some of Vi's awful burgers and fries."

"Better not let her hear you say that." Zane lowered his voice. "Poor thing's already had one insult tonight."

While the customers looked on with interest, the three cousins moved to a corner table, laughing like loons.

CHAPTER SEVEN

——◆◆◆——

Cora maneuvered her Jeep along the dirt road. The haunting strains of Debussy's "Clair de Lune" played by the London Philharmonic rose softly in the background. The soothing music seemed an odd contrast to the wild look of her. After a week of nonstop painting, her shirt and denims were spattered with paint stains. With Coot gone, she loved his cast-offs even more. They made her feel somehow closer to her brother.

She hadn't been to a beauty salon in years. These days she styled her own hair, which she'd allowed to go gray. In her younger days she'd gone through every color of the spectrum, from platinum blond to rich auburn to gothic black, hanging down her back almost to her waist. She'd been so proud of her crowning glory. Now, it all seemed too much trouble.

She knew how other people saw her. An oddball. A misfit. It never bothered her to be seen as a contradiction.

In her college years she'd traveled to France and Italy to pursue her love of art. Along the way she'd tasted the good life, had fallen in love a time or two, and had her share of heartbreak. And each time, through all the pain and heartache, she had found solace in her art.

She'd worked with some of the best and brightest in the art world, and had been offered apprenticeships that would have guaranteed her a grand life and a brilliant future. But she'd refused to accept the advice of the so-called experts. She needed to be here. Here on the land of her ancestors. It was a need so deep, so physical, she couldn't deny it. If some saw this land as raw and rough, Cora saw only the rugged beauty. And her great gift was the ability to convey that beauty on canvas.

When she'd first begun to paint the stark landscapes, she'd had no idea that so many would share her vision. After returning to Montana, she'd expected to live and die in obscurity. Then, when a local art dealer had seen her work and begged to be allowed to show it, she'd paid scant attention.

Her first show had given her such a thrill. It had been beyond her wildest dreams to see art patrons lavishing praise on her work and spending ridiculous amounts to own her paintings, while art critics around the world began raving about the rich, raw beauty of her work.

For Cora, it had never been about the money. Though that validated her success in art circles, it had always been about the need to express on canvas the rare beauty that she saw here, and then to share it with others.

She sighed. She'd needed this chance to reconnect with her work. To fill canvas after canvas with color and form and the vibrant life that was unique to her corner of the world. After the shock of Coot's death, and the arrival of her two nephews after so many years, she'd been feeling oddly disconnected.

"Oh, Coot." She veered off the dirt road onto the long dusty driveway that led to the ranch. "If only I understood men the way I understand art. I wish I knew what to do about our boys. I'm worried that the wounds are too deep, the chasm too wide, for them to ever be friends again."

As the ranch house came into view she slowed the vehicle to a crawl and let herself see it through the eyes of an artist. It was a handsome, sprawling building made of stone and aged wood that looked as though it had always been here. Rising to three stories, with tall windows to take in the breathtaking views of rolling meadows, evergreen forests, and soaring mountain ranges, it was an imposing sight. And yet, despite its size, it managed to be comfortable. Three generations had lived here together, and for a time, this house had been filled with love. Coot's three sons, their wives and children, had brought so much laughter to the old fortress. Then, one by one, his sons had left him.

Ben, the middle son, and his wife, Kelly, left first. They had craved a more adventurous lifestyle, and had taken their son, Wyatt, with them around the world, until the plane crash that had left a bitter son all alone, without the presence of his extended family. Judging from the places he'd been since then, Wyatt shared his parents' love of adventure. Cora wondered how long the spell of this place could hold him before he would have to once again cut himself loose from all that was familiar to explore the unknown.

Then Wade, Coot's youngest, had taken his wife,

Melissa, and son, Zane, to California, vowing to never again see snow or hear about the lost treasure. His untimely death left his son and young widow adrift. Melissa, who'd always hated the isolation of ranch life, had cut a wide swath through the smooth, slick Hollywood crowd before settling down with a famous director who had been, at the time, very married. Within a short time he'd moved on, leaving her for his young assistant. Through it all, poor Zane had been forced to deal with the loss of all that had once comforted him. Father, grandfather, ranch life. All denied him at a critical time in his life, while his mother ignored him to pursue her own pleasures.

Walker, Coot's firstborn, and his wife, Chris, had remained on the ranch with their son, Jesse. And although Walker never shared his father's passion for the treasure hunt, young Jesse's devotion to his grandfather more than made up for it. Walker's death, followed two years later by that of his wife, had brought Jesse and old Coot closer than ever. Theirs had been a bond forged out of desperate loneliness and need that nothing could ever break.

All the family ties had now been severed. Perhaps forever. And Cora could see no way to help heal the old wounds that had been festering for all these years. There was too much pain. Too much guilt. She found herself wondering if Coot had made a terrible mistake by tempting his grandsons with his vision of recovering the lost fortune. Look what it had already done to their family. The search for the elusive gold had completely consumed her brother, father, and grandfather. And now it looked as though it might destroy what little relationship was left between her remaining family members.

Was anything worth that price?

She circled the house and parked in the barn. Before she could exit the Jeep, Cal Randall approached, pulling a big wooden wagon that he'd made especially to transport her art supplies from her studio to her vehicle and back again.

"Cal." She gave him a bright smile. "With all you have to do, how could you see me coming?"

"I seem to have radar where you're concerned, Cora." He gave her a long, steady look. "You were gone so long I was beginning to worry."

She laid her hand on his arm. "You know I can take care of myself. I don't take foolish risks."

"I know." He closed a hand over hers. "But I worry all the same."

He began loading the freshly painted canvases, taking care to see that they were separated by tall wooden dowels.

The efficiency of his design never failed to please her. There was room for everything, from paints to finished canvases, with room to spare. Cal Randall had always been able to anticipate her needs and fill them before she could even express them. This wagon was no exception.

She lifted a sack of paint supplies from the passenger seat. "Lucky for me that you're here to unload all this. But if you're busy, I can handle it from here."

He caught her hand when she reached for the handle. "You go ahead, Cora. I'll see to this. Dandy's just getting ready to serve supper."

As he began hauling the wagon toward the house, she moved along beside him, matching her steps to his. Though she told herself she simply wanted to make conversation, it shamed her that she was reluctant to face her nephews. The tension between them made her feel so helpless.

Cal pulled the wagon into the mudroom and carefully hung his wide-brimmed hat on a peg by the back door before scraping the dirt from his boots. "You go ahead into supper and I'll set these in your studio."

"There's no need..."

"I don't mind. You may as well go ahead and get it over with." He gave her a gentle smile, and she realized that he'd been reading her mind.

She took her time washing at the big sink, using a brush to scrub the last of the paint from her cuticles. With a sigh she stepped into the kitchen.

Across the room Dandy was lifting a heavy roaster from the oven. The wonderful aroma of pot roast filled the air.

When he caught sight of her he beamed his pleasure. "Afternoon, Miss Cora. I was hoping you might get home in time for supper. I almost didn't make this, but Jesse's been asking for it for days."

"Then I'm glad, too, Dandy." She looked around. "Where's Jesse?"

He gave a nod of his head. "Great room, I'm thinking. He just got in from the north range about an hour ago."

"Wyatt and Zane?"

He shrugged. "They came down from the high country earlier today. Can't say if they're still here."

"Thanks, Dandy." She started toward the door, wondering if she and Jesse would be eating alone.

Even before she stepped into the great room, the sound of voices raised in a heated debate had her stomach clenching. Not alone, she thought. She'd stepped, once more, right into the thick of battle.

Zane and Wyatt were standing by the bank of windows, facing Jesse, who stood with his back to her.

Jesse's words had her stopping in her tracks. "...hate to admit it, but there's nothing as satisfying as a good down-and-dirty saloon brawl."

She studied Zane's black eye and her nerves started jumping. As if hateful words weren't enough, her nephews had now resorted to physical violence.

Oh, Coot. Where will this all end?

"Hey, Aunt Cora." Wyatt was the first to notice her.

As he hurried over, she saw the bruises on his cheek, the slight limp in his gait.

Her smile fled. "Who did this?" She touched a hand to his face when he bent to brush a kiss over her cheek.

"Never did hear his name." He pointed to a chilled longneck resting on a tray on the sofa table. "Care to join us in a beer while we rehash last week's donnybrook?"

"Fighting." She accepted the cold beer from his hand and took a long swallow before turning to Jesse. "Your cousins may not be aware of it, but you certainly know how I feel about that."

"Couldn't be helped, Aunt Cora." Jesse's face bore a bruise from cheek to jaw. "A guy's got to defend himself."

Zane nodded in agreement. "Especially since his attacker was the size of a mountain."

"His attacker?" She looked from Zane to Jesse to Wyatt.

"Some obnoxious biker who decided he'd help himself to my supper." Jesse drained his beer. "I figured I'd put him in his place and get back to my own business, but then his drunken buddies decided to join in. If it hadn't been for Wyatt and Zane, they might have wiped the floor with what was left of me."

Cora let out a quick breath. Not cousin against cousin, as she'd feared. "You three fought with strangers at the saloon?"

"Like I said, it couldn't be helped. We didn't start it, Aunt Cora."

Zane laughed. "But we definitely finished it."

For emphasis he raised his hand, and both Wyatt and Jesse slapped his palm in a high five.

Feeling a little dazed, Cora dropped into the nearest chair and studied the three young men, who were chuckling over their shared barroom brawl. She could still see three little boys who would come in from the fields covered in mud and laughing like loons over some silly adventure they'd shared. She blinked and saw them as they were now, three handsome, headstrong young men who had been on the verge of war.

And a battle with strangers had turned the tide.

They might not yet be the best of friends they once were, but a night's shared adventure had them stepping back from that impenetrable wall of anger. For now, she thought with a smile, she'd settle for a truce.

She stood and set aside the nearly full bottle.

"Where're you going, Aunt Cora?"

"I thought I'd shower. Will I see any of you at supper?"

"I'll be there." Jesse shot her a wink.

"Me, too." Zane tipped up his beer.

"I wouldn't miss it." Wyatt was grinning.

"I'll be right down." As she started up the stairs, her heart felt lighter than it had for many a day.

Oh, Coot. Maybe there's hope for us after all. At least they're all on the same team for now.

It may be true that she didn't understand men. But this much she knew. Their shared bruises had given them something in common. They were actually speaking to one another without bitterness. And wasn't that a wonderful thing to see?

"You throw a mean left hook." Over supper, Cal glanced at Zane. "Last week you didn't look like that was your first bar fight."

"It wasn't." Zane buttered another soft-as-air roll. He'd have paid a fortune for this meal at one of California's trendiest restaurants.

"Hard to believe you spent your time in seedy bars in Hollywood." Jesse grinned over the rim of his cup. "I figured you for fancy dinner parties and those pansy drinks with exotic names."

Zane was feeling too mellow to take offense. "I've had my share of those, too."

"Then where'd you learn to fight like that?" Cal was enjoying the new sense of camaraderie, and he could see that Cora was enjoying herself, too. The old cowboy wanted to keep the cousins talking, hoping they might find more common ground.

"From Jesse and Wyatt." Zane polished off the roll. "A good thing, too. My first day at middle school in Beverly Hills I came home with a black eye and was grounded for a month."

"Why'd you fight?" Wyatt's mouth watered when

Dandy stepped into the room and began passing around a plate of homemade chocolate chip cookies.

"It started with the usual bullying. Some kid made fun of my boots and jeans and got his friends to call me Cowboy, which soon turned into the whole class calling me Cow Patty."

"Ouch." Jesse winced. "Sorry I had to add to it by calling you Hollywood."

Zane shrugged. "Hey. I've been called worse. It wasn't worth fighting over. But if stupid name-calling wasn't bad enough, the same kid accused my mother of sleeping with his father."

That had everyone going quiet.

"I hope you gave as good as you got." Jesse was scowling.

"Oh yeah. I bloodied his nose and shredded the sleeve of his designer shirt."

"Good. Little liar had it coming." This from Wyatt.

Zane stared down at his plate. "Yeah. It was pretty satisfying. That is until I found out later he wasn't lying."

They all gaped at him.

"Not that she ever admitted it. But soon enough it was common knowledge. The next thing I knew, there was a very messy, very public divorce, and my tormentor was my stepbrother." He moved his food around without tasting it. "I learned to be damned good with my fists."

"Well." Feeling the weight of the sudden silence around the table, Cal cleared his throat and turned to Cora. "How was the weather up at Treasure Chest?"

"Cold and rainy." She shot Cal a grateful look. "But I got some great paintings."

"Good." He patted her hand before shoving back his

chair. "Sorry to run, but I promised to head on up to the north ridge before dark."

Zane scraped back his chair and stood. "Mind if I ride along?"

Cal studied the young man whose eyes bore a haunted look. "Not at all. I'd be grateful for the company."

Zane rounded the table and softly touched his lips to his aunt's cheek before following the old cowboy from the room.

Behind them, those still seated around the table had gone suddenly somber.

When the door closed behind Cal and Zane, Jesse let out a long, slow breath. "Guess I'll have to alter my view of life in sunny California. I figured my little cousin spent all his time lying around pools and ogling chicks in bikinis. Who knew he had to fight his way through middle school?"

He turned to Wyatt. "I hope you fared a little better."

Wyatt merely shrugged before scraping back his chair. "Maybe I'll tell you about it some time. For now, I promised to lend a hand out in the barn."

As he started away Jesse pushed back from the table. "Why don't I join you?"

They called out their good-byes to their aunt before heading for the back door.

Cora watched them leave, sipping her tea in silence. She carried her steaming cup to the great room, where she stood by the bank of windows watching a glorious sunset. But her mind wasn't on the beauty of the scene. Zane's words played through her mind.

How painful had it been for Zane to suddenly find himself alone and facing the taunts of strangers? He couldn't have been more than twelve.

Suddenly she felt an unmistakable presence next to her and a smile spread across her face.

"You know, Coot, it occurs to me that our boys are a lot more like you than I realized. You used to say there was nothing like a good fight to clear the air. I believe I see your hand in all this."

CHAPTER EIGHT

W ould you like to sit in the chair, Dad, or would you rather go in to your bed?" Amy helped her father from the truck and up the steps of the house.

Once inside he motioned toward the bedroom, and Amy hurried ahead to turn down the covers.

It worried her to see him moving so slowly, as though he'd aged ten years since leaving the local clinic after his first treatment. Dr. Wheeler had warned her that a side effect of the treatments was lethargy, but she hadn't been prepared to see her father asleep beside her during the entire ride home.

"I'll start some soup. It'll be ready by the time you wake from your nap."

"Thanks, Amy girl." He eased himself down on the edge of the mattress, kicked off his shoes, and fell back heavily against the pillows.

She watched helplessly for a minute before turning away.

In the kitchen she dragged out one of her mother's heavy stockpots and began assembling the ingredients for chicken soup. A short time later, while the soup simmered, she looked around for something to occupy her time.

She paused in the neglected family room and smiled as she studied the framed photographs on the mantel. There was her mother, Sarah Miller Parrish, as a young bride, standing proudly beside her tall, solemn husband. Amy studied another photo of a beaming Sarah holding her infant daughter. The joy of proud, new motherhood was evident in those laughing green eyes. Mother and daughter shared so much more than the color of their eyes. There was the shared dimple in their left cheek. A yen for pasta. A deep and abiding love of this ranch.

Amy picked up the family photo taken at her graduation. How could they have known it would be the last one of the three of them together? Scant weeks later her mother had taken the call from her beloved sister, Morgan, in Helena, begging her to come and tend to her during her illness. There was no way Sarah would have refused. Morgan had been Sarah's refuge during her stormy marriage, and was the only family she had. Amy and Sarah had packed hastily in the night and started the long drive to Helena, never dreaming that they would be gone the entire summer.

By the time her aunt Morgan had gone to her eternal rest and Sarah returned to Gold Fever, Amy started college in Helena alone.

Alone.

It was, she thought, the one word that best described her life. Even with Colin, a friend and fellow teacher who occasionally took her to dinner or to staff parties, she never really felt like part of a couple the way she had with Jesse.

Not that she minded. She was very good at being alone. And now, of course, she had her pupils. She missed the start of a new school year. This had always been her favorite time, setting up her classroom, greeting her students and their parents, seeing to it that newcomers were made to feel welcome. She had a real talent for teaching. She was one of those rare people who loved the challenge of making the lessons come alive. She thrived on the endless chatter. She took particular pride in seeing a student suddenly begin to shine because of her praise.

Amy picked up a load of laundry and headed for the small, enclosed room between the kitchen and the garage. It had once been an open walkway until, at her mother's urging, her father had added walls and a roof. Her mother had been delighted to move the washer and dryer from the damp basement to this sunny location.

Now the room had become a catchall for discarded newspapers and magazines, old clothing, and mismatched boots, all of which were piled on shelves and spilled over onto the floor, covering every available inch of space.

"Oh, Mom," she sighed. "You were always so neat. Too bad Dad lacks that gene."

With the first load of laundry in the washer, she picked up an empty box and began filling it with junk. While she worked she thought about Jesse. She'd thought of little else since his visit that night.

Was it just because she was back staying in her

childhood home that she was unable to shake the image of Jesse McCord? His presence had unleashed a tide of buried feelings. His arms around her, making her feel safe and protected. His strength that made her want to let go of all her worries and trust him to be strong for both of them. His tenderness that brought her to the verge of tears.

That potent male energy simmering just below the surface had always been her downfall. Even in her teens, when her father had made it abundantly clear that the McCords were to be avoided at all costs, she'd been drawn to Jesse and he to her. Though she'd been forced to sneak around behind her father's back, making her feel like a cheat, she hadn't been able to resist any chance to be with him.

His visit the night of her dad's diagnosis was no exception. She'd wanted him to kiss her. To crush her in his arms and kiss away all the tears and fears. Instead, he'd chosen to walk away, leaving her confused and frustrated.

The old Jesse would have taken what he wanted. And she'd have gladly given. She paused in her work. Maybe, she thought, they had both done some growing up while they'd been apart.

She tossed another pile of newspapers into the box and was reaching for more when a handwritten slip of yellowed paper caught her eye.

She read the words: ...*trail to the treasure points to*... The rest of the page had been torn away. At the bottom were more words, but these were blured, as though the paper had been water-soaked: ...*going to try that next chance I*...

She turned the paper over and saw the doodles.

Squiggly lines that could have been a child's drawing of a mountain peak or a crude graph of sorts.

"Coot." Like everyone in Gold Fever and the surrounding area, Amy had seen examples of old Coot's journal. Pages had been turning up for years, ever since the old man had begun keeping a record of the places he'd searched for the lost treasure. Like an absentminded professor, Coot would make notes to himself on scraps of paper, along with his own personal directions, before putting them in his pocket to copy when he returned home. Except that the slips of paper often fell from his pocket along the trail and were lost or retrieved by strangers. Some people, recognizing them as Coot's property, would make it a point to return them to their rightful owner. Many more simply tossed them away or, like her father, added them to the junk pile.

Had it been an accident on her father's part? Or had it been deliberate?

The thought had her pausing in her work. In her mind she went back to the day when she'd watched her father face off against Coot McCord, fists raised, voice a roar of fury.

"If you or your sons set foot on my land again, I'll blow your heads off. You hear me, McCord?"

"Wade told me what you saw, Otis, but it wasn't the way it looked."

"I know what I saw. His telling you different doesn't make it so."

"Your wife fell off her horse. Wade happened to be nearby and helped her, is all."

"And kissed her in the bargain."

"So you say. According to Wade, she was crying after

the fall. He used his handkerchief to dry her tears. He swears he would never touch another man's wife."

"I'm not a fool, McCord. Your youngest son has a reputation for chasing the ladies. All ladies. But what's mine is mine." A vein throbbed at his temple and his face had grown red with rage. "So be warned. You so much as set foot on my land, you'll pay. Now get out of my sight. And if your boy ever comes near my wife, I won't be responsible for what happens."

"You're a damned fool, Parrish." Coot's fury was more than a match for Otis's.

Amy had sat frozen in the truck, listening to every hateful word. Then, without warning, Jesse had been there, peering at her through the open truck window, introducing himself. In that instant she'd been utterly charmed by that rogue smile, that boyish bravado, and more than a little relieved to have a distraction from the ugly scene playing itself out before them.

When her father had slammed back into the truck and taken off, laying down a trail of dust as he drove away, she'd seen Jesse in the side-view mirror lift his hand to wave. She'd turned and waved in return.

The child she'd been hadn't understood the significance of what she'd witnessed. But as she grew older she realized just how long and deep that festering anger lay.

She'd heard the rumors that her mother once had been wildly in love with Wade McCord, Coot's youngest son, and he with her. But like so many young lovers, they had drifted apart, and each had married someone else.

Apparently, Otis wasn't willing to let a long-dead romance die in peace. To save face, he later attempted to sue over infringement of water rights, which the judge had disallowed as a frivolous lawsuit. But it had been a cover for her father's jealousy. That long-ago incident had been the actual trigger. And it went a long way in explaining why he'd refused to allow Coot to buy him out, as Coot had purchased the land of many others in the area whose poor ranches had stood in the way of the old man's search for the lost treasure. What was worse, that had been the cause of the chasm that had grown between her father and mother, continuing long after it should have been dead and buried.

Dead and buried.

Like her mother. Like Coot and his sons. Like the feelings she and Jesse had once shared.

Amy glanced at the slip of paper in her hand. She had no doubt that her father would have tossed this in the trash rather than pass it along to Coot's family. She read the blurred words again before tucking the page in her pocket. This belonged to the McCords. It was only right that she return it to them.

As she continued cleaning, her heart felt suddenly lighter. It wasn't, she told herself firmly, because she now had an excuse to see Jesse again. It was simply because she felt better knowing she was doing the right thing.

She would head out after her dad was awake and comfortable. Old Red needed the exercise. The ride would be good for both of them.

Jesse wrestled the fence post into the hole he'd dug, then took a pair of pliers from his hip pocket and began tightening the wire that he'd cut from the rotted, discarded original post.

Hearing the sound of hoofbeats, he paused to glance up, squinting against the glare of sunlight.

"Hi, Jesse." Amy hoped her voice didn't reveal her nerves. All the way over to the Lost Nugget ranch she'd rehearsed a casual conversation. Now, seeing him, shirt damp, muscles rippling, she felt tongue-tied and jittery.

"Amy." He reached up and removed his wide-brimmed hat, slapping it against his thigh as he wiped sweat from his brow.

"Looks like hard work." She slid from the saddle, keeping hold of Red's reins.

"Somebody's got to do it."

"I thought you had a machine for this."

"We do. If there's a line of fencing down. But for one broken fence post, it's just easier to do by hand."

He moved closer to run his open palm down Red's muzzle. The mare whickered, causing him to smile. "She remembers me."

"Of course she does. You always brought her a carrot."

"With good reason. It kept her from whinnying and alerting your dad that I was around."

They both grinned at the memory.

"Speaking of Dad..." Amy reached into her pocket. "When I was cleaning house, I found this."

Jesse read the slip of paper, then turned it over and studied the doodles.

"Coot's." His voice was little more than a whisper.

She nodded. "I recognized it as his and figured you'd want it."

He stared at the torn yellowed paper, studying each word with a look of naked pain that had her heart breaking for him.

"I'm sorry, Jesse." She laid a hand over his. "Maybe I shouldn't have brought it."

"No. You were right to come. I appreciate it." He tore his gaze from the paper and looked at her. "I'm just a little...bruised, and still missing him. How's your father?"

She was touched that he could think of her troubles at a time like this. Touched and grateful. She had a desperate need to talk to someone. "He had his first treatment today, and it really knocked him down."

"Is he in the hospital?"

"No. The doctor said it was safe to drive him home. He slept for nearly two hours. When I brought him a bowl of soup, he barely managed a few sips before he threw it up."

"Is that a normal reaction to these treatments?"

She shrugged. "A nurse at the clinic gave me a list of things to expect. Weakness, lethargy, extreme fatigue, and nausea are just some of them. But it scares me to see him down like this. He's always been so tough."

Jesse saw the fear in her eyes. Without thinking, he reached a hand to her cheek. "Your dad's a scrapper, Amy. Tough as nails. But right now he's dealing with a new opponent, and he's going to need some time to figure out his best strategy for fighting the battle."

"What if he never figures it out? What if he just gives up?"

"Hey." He drew her into the circle of his arms, sensing that she was struggling to hold back the tears. "You're scared. He's scared. But you've got each other."

"I feel so alone. He doesn't talk to me. He won't confide in me, Jess." Her voice vibrated against his throat, sending a thrill all the way to his toes.

He caught her chin, forcing her to meet his look. "You just have to give it time, Amy."

"What if time is running out?"

He ran a thumb over her trembling lips. "Then you'll have to be strong enough for both of you. But I'm betting, once these treatments take over, he'll come out of this stronger than ever."

She drew in a long, unsteady breath. "Oh, I hope you're right." She gave a toss of her head. "I miss our fights."

That had Jesse grinning. "Now that's something not every daughter could say."

She managed a shaky smile. "I guess it does sound silly. But at least when we were fighting I could say what was on my mind. Now I find myself monitoring every word so I don't add to his misery."

"Maybe you should try a little tenderness."

She flushed. "I don't know how. Besides, we've spent a lifetime arguing. If I start to go all mushy on him now, he'll figure he's been given a death sentence."

Jesse chuckled, and Amy realized how much she'd missed the sound of it. He had a warm, rich laugh that wrapped itself around her heart and squeezed until she felt her throat go dry.

"Know what you need?" He caught her hand and started toward the house in the distance.

She felt the jolt of electricity that shot along her spine when he kept her hand in his. "What?"

"A cup of Aunt Cora's tea."

Amy dug in her heels. "I don't want to interrupt her if she's working."

"You couldn't if you tried. When she's painting, she's in another zone." He tugged her along, and she picked up her pace to match his long strides, the roan mare following close behind. "But most afternoons she takes a break from her studio. We'll just see if she's around."

At the back door he took the reins from Amy's hand and tied Old Red at the hitching post before leading the way inside.

Like everyone who'd ever visited the Lost Nugget, she knew the routine, scraping her boots in the mudroom and pausing to wash at the big sink before stepping into the kitchen.

Dandy looked up from the stove. Spotting Amy, his face was wreathed in smiles as he wiped his hands on a towel before hurrying over to catch her hands in his.

"How good to see you, Amy. It's been too many years."

"Yes, it has, Dandy. It's good to see you, too. I saw you at the funeral, but I know you were too busy to notice me." She breathed deeply. "Something smells wonderful."

"Beef stew. If you'll stay for supper, you can see if it tastes as good as it smells."

"I wish I could." She took a step back. "Dad will be expecting me to get home in time to make his supper."

"I heard about his illness. Tell him I send my best."

"Thanks, Dandy." Amy felt herself relaxing in this courtly man's presence. He'd been part of the McCord ranch since she was a kid. Despite her father's nasty temper and harsh treatment of the McCord family, they'd never held it against her. She had always been warmly treated by everyone here.

Jesse spied the China teapot on the counter. "Aunt Cora's tea?"

Dandy nodded. "I was just about to add a sugar bowl and creamer to the tray before taking it in to her."

"I'll take it. I invited Amy to join us."

"Then you two go ahead, and I'll bring the rest. Your aunt's in the great room."

Amy held the door while Jesse carried the tray with the tea service. Cora stood by the bank of windows, staring out at the mountain peaks in the distance.

"Aunt Cora, look who's come to visit."

At Jesse's words Cora turned and hurried across the room to embrace the young woman. "Oh, Amy. How good to see you."

Amy poured herself into the hug, knowing this woman's words came from the heart. "It's good to see you, too, Miss Cora."

The older woman held her a little away. "How is your father?"

"I'm not sure. He had his first treatment today, and he slept all the way home. Then he napped for another two hours or more."

Cora led her across the room, where they settled side by side on a comfortable sofa. "From all I've read, that's to be expected."

"He looks..." Amy lifted her palms, then folded them nervously in her lap. "He looks defeated."

"I'm sure that's how he's feeling right now. In a battle for his life, and it seems the illness is winning. But as his strength returns, I think you'll see a significant improvement in his attitude."

"Oh, I hope you're right."

Cora watched as Dandy entered carrying a second tray, on which rested additional cups and saucers, as well as a plate of cookies still warm from the oven. When he'd filled three cups with tea, he passed them around and placed the plate of cookies on a coffee table.

"If you need anything else, just let me know," he called as he took his leave.

"Thank you, Dandy." Cora sipped and sighed with pure pleasure. "Nobody makes a more perfect cup of tea than Dandy."

"Not to mention his cookies." Jesse reached for one, ate it in three bites, then took a second one and forced himself to eat it more slowly, savoring every bite. "Mmm. Chocolate chip. The chocolate is still hot and melting." He held out the plate to Amy. "Come on. You know you could never resist Dandy's cookies."

She took one and ate it slowly. By the time she'd finished, she was smiling. "I'd forgotten how good these really are."

Jesse pulled the yellowed slip of paper from his pocket. "Amy found this and thought we'd want it."

He handed it to Cora, who studied it in silence. When she'd turned it over, she smoothed out the wrinkles and continued holding it in her hand, as though unwilling to let go of something that had once been held by her brother. It took several moments before she was able to compose herself.

"I wish we had a bit more. It's so vague, it could be just about any mountain peak in the area."

Jesse nodded.

Amy set aside her tea. "I found it among a pile of old newspapers. Before I toss any of them away, I'll go through each one carefully to see if there's more."

"That would be grand." Cora continued to hold it as

she gently led the conversation back to Amy's father. "How often will you need to drive Otis to the hospital?"

"Twice a week until the doctors can determine how much he's capable of tolerating. They'll add as many treatments as possible until they feel they have this under control."

Cora studied the young woman. "That's a lot of responsibility to handle alone."

Amy managed a weak smile. "I'll be fine."

"Yes, you will." Cora placed a hand over Amy's. "I hope you'll remember that we're not just neighbors, we're friends. Please let us know what we can do to help."

Amy was shaking her head. "I wouldn't..."

Cora interrupted. "I know. The feud. That's all in the past."

"Not in my father's mind."

Cora held up a hand. "You know, I've always felt a bit sorry for your father."

"Sorry for Dad?"

The older woman nodded. "Think about it. For three generations your land belonged to your mother's family. With no sons, your grandfather was considering selling it to Coot rather than let it fall into the hands of strangers. But then your mother came home with her new husband, and Otis agreed to farm his wife's property. Even now, there are old-timers in Gold Fever who refer to your ranch as the Miller place."

Amy went very still, absorbing her words. "I knew all this, of course, but I never considered the fact that my father may have felt like nothing more than a caretaker of Mom's land. Thank you, Miss Cora. I guess I never gave it enough thought."

"Then think about this, too. At times like these, old feuds need to be put aside. Any one of us would be more than happy to drive Otis to town when you're not able, or to sit with him if you need a break."

Amy met her look and read the concern in her eyes. "Thank you, Miss Cora. I appreciate that." Not that her father would ever permit it. But it helped to know that these good people could look beyond the past to the future.

She stood. "Now I'd better get home and start supper."

Cora got to her feet and gave her a hard hug. "Don't be a stranger, Amy. You're always welcome here."

"Thanks. You'll never know how much I've needed this."

Amy quickly turned away, hiding the tears that sprang to her eyes.

Jesse followed her from the room.

As they stepped into the kitchen, Dandy pointed to a linen-wrapped package on the counter. "I hope that'll fit in your saddlebag."

At Amy's arched brow he said, "Beef stew. And some of my cookies."

"Oh, Dandy." Amy crossed the room to give him a big hug.

Before she could reach for the parcel, Jesse picked it up and led the way to the back door. Once outside he tucked it into her saddlebag and untied the reins.

"I'm glad you came, Amy."

"I knew you'd want Coot's note."

"It means a lot to me. And even more to Aunt Cora."

She nodded. "I could see that." She paused, considering

her words before asking, "Are you thinking about continuing the search for the treasure?"

He shrugged. "Some days I think I want to, and other
days I figure I'll leave that to the city boys."

She heard the disdain in his tone. "Still not friends?"

"Things are better, but there's a lot of baggage
between us."

She met his eyes. "You could be talking about us,
instead of Zane and Wyatt."

"I guess I could be."

He stepped closer, keeping his eyes steady on hers.

Her heart started racing.

A breeze caught her hair and he lifted a hand to
smooth it back. "But, except for the ending, our baggage
was all good." Instead of pulling away he kept his hand
there. His thumb stroked her temple and he could feel the
way her pulse leaped. "Maybe some time we could talk
about…"

"Hey, Amy. Long time."

At Zane's voice both their heads came up sharply and
they stepped apart with matching looks of guilt.

Zane and Wyatt came striding from the barn, crossing
the distance between them to give Amy a quick hug.

"Zane." She embraced him before turning to Wyatt.
"How good to see you both."

"You look fantastic." Zane gave her a long look that
had Jesse doing a slow burn.

"How's your father?" Wyatt asked.

"Not good today. He had his first treatment at the town
clinic. Ask me again in a week, and maybe I'll have better news."

"Good. You'll let us know?"

She nodded and pulled herself into the saddle.

To Jesse she said, "Thank Dandy again for the food. Even if Dad can't enjoy it, I know I will."

With a wave she urged Old Red into a leisurely trot.

Feeling frustrated, Jesse stood watching until horse and rider disappeared over a ridge.

When he turned, he found Zane and Wyatt grinning like conspirators.

"I think," Zane said with a laugh, "our timing was just about perfect."

"Yeah." Wyatt slapped Zane on the back. "One minute more and the poor fool would have been right back where he started years ago."

"It's a good thing you've got us here to save you, cuz." Zane dropped an arm around Jesse's neck.

Before Jesse could shove him away, Wyatt chimed in. "Oh, no. Don't thank us. We're only too happy to save you from temptation."

The two slipped their arms around his shoulders, dragging him toward the house and laughing.

CHAPTER NINE

J esse?" As she moved about her bedroom, Amy hoped her tone sounded sufficiently businesslike over the cell phone. It had been three days since she'd been to his family ranch. Three days of replaying in her mind every word he'd spoken, every look they'd shared. Three days of regretting the arrival of Zane and Wyatt at the very moment when she'd been certain that Jesse intended to explain about their abrupt parting. And maybe kiss her in the bargain.

She'd swallowed bitter disappointment on the ride home and reminded herself over and over that she was behaving like one of her students with a first crush.

"Hey, Amy."

She caught the note of surprise laced with pleasure in his voice. "Hey, yourself. I've been going through my dad's stuff, and I've found a few more bits of paper that you might be interested in seeing."

"That's great. I can't stop over right now." Amy could hear a truck's horn sounding and the whoosh of passing traffic in the background. "I'm on my way to town."

"If you're going to be there awhile, I could meet you somewhere. I'm just about to drive Dad to the clinic."

"Do you have to stay with him during his treatment?"

"No. I'll have about two hours to be on my own."

"Great. Why don't we meet at the saloon at noon? We'll see if the daily special is edible."

That had Amy laughing. "All right. I'll see you there."

She dropped her cell phone into her purse and went off in search of her makeup. Not that she was going to fuss just because she was seeing Jesse, she reminded herself. But it wouldn't hurt to take a few extra minutes before she headed to town.

When she walked out to the truck, her father was already in the driver's seat and waiting impatiently, engine idling.

"What kept you, girl?"

She shrugged. "I just had to get a few things." She swallowed back her surprise at seeing her father at the wheel.

Before she could fasten her seat belt he put the truck in gear, the wheels spitting gravel as he headed along the winding driveway.

He glanced over. "I'll need you to pick up some supplies at Orley Peterson's. I wish I could handle it myself, but…"

"I've got the list."

He handed over a blank check. "No more credit. Fill in the amount and get a receipt."

She studied the familiar signature before tucking it into her pocket. "Why don't you want to buy on credit? Isn't that the way we've always done it?"

"I don't want to leave you with any debt."

Her heart did a quick plunge, all the way to her toes. "Dad, I don't think..."

"No need to think. I've done enough of that for both of us. Tonight, if I can keep my head out of the toilet long enough, we'll go over the books so you have a handle on how things stand with the ranch."

"I have a pretty good..."

"You don't have a clue. But it's time I laid it all out so you won't have to deal with any surprises."

Amy bit back any further protest. This was the first time her father had opened up even a tiny crack in that wall he'd built. If it got him talking about his illness, his fears, it would give her a chance to do the same.

"Okay." She turned to stare out the side window. "Tonight's fine with me."

They drove the rest of the way into town in silence.

Amy hauled a four-wheel, flatbed cart along the aisles of Orley Peterson's Grain & Feed, wrestling sacks from shelves. Because their ranch was too small to qualify for free shipping, Otis Parrish had opted to haul his supplies himself rather than pay the additional fee. Though her muscles protested, she reminded herself that it was an excellent workout. If Violet and Daffy had anything decent on today's menu, she could eat her fill without a thought of the calories.

"Morning, Amy." Orley Peterson stood behind the counter, checking a packing slip while a trucker waited for approval. "Be with you in a minute."

Orley was as round as he was tall, his plaid shirt stretched tautly over his bulging middle. His bald head glistened with sweat, and his double chin jiggled with each movement as he checked the figures, scrawled his signature on the paper, and handed it to the trucker before turning to Amy. "How's your dad?"

"Fine. I left him at the clinic for another treatment."

Orley walked around the counter and began scanning each sack with a handheld device. "How's he tolerating the treatments so far?"

Amy shrugged. "They leave him weak and sick. Just when he starts to feel a little better, it's time for another one."

"Yeah." He circled back behind the counter and rang up the sale. "My wife's sister had the same reaction."

"How's she doing?" The minute the words were out of her mouth, Amy regretted them, but it was too late to take them back.

Orley didn't quite meet her eyes. "That'll be three hundred and seventy-five."

He seemed surprised when she took the check from her pocket and filled in the amount, but he accepted it without a word before handing her a receipt.

As she started to pull the cart he stopped her. "Where's your truck?"

"Out front."

"You got anything else to do in town?"

She nodded.

"Then you go ahead, and I'll load this stuff in your truck later."

She smiled. "Thanks, Orley. I appreciate it."

"No problem. And Amy?" he called to her retreating back.

She turned.

"My wife's sister is in remission. They're not calling it a cure, but she's got her hair back, and her strength. For now, that's more than enough."

She wanted to hug him. Instead she just flashed him a smile. "That's good to hear. Thanks again, Orley."

The Fortune Saloon was doing a standing-room-only business. Their nearest competition was a tiny diner at the other end of town. Despite the good food, the surly owner of the Grizzly Inn, Ben Rider, drove away as many customers as he attracted. Most folks would rather eat the greasy burgers offered by Vi and Daffy, just for the chance to enjoy their bawdy humor. These two sisters, with their outrageous style and brash demeanor, were the darlings of the town of Gold Fever.

Jesse, seated at a corner table, spotted Amy the minute she stepped through the doorway. She paused to look around before spying him and giving him a bright smile.

He resented the fact that his heart rate shot up at that exact moment. He set down his coffee and sat back, enjoying the look of her, hair wind-tossed, cheeks pink as she started weaving her way among the tables.

She paused to speak with Mayor Rowe Stafford, and the two exchanged a laugh before she moved on to talk to Stan Novak, who was having lunch with Ledge Cowling. The way the two men had been huddled over a sheaf of papers, Jesse figured Stan was angling for another loan. It was common knowledge in town that the construction business was down.

At the next table Amy was flagged over by Delia Cowling, who was lunching with Harding Jessup.

"You alone? If so, you can join us." Delia indicated the empty chair at their table.

"Thanks, but I'm joining someone."

Amy tried to move on, but Delia already had a firm hold on Amy's sleeve. "I hear your daddy's not doing so well."

"He's fine. Just a little weak. Thanks for asking." Amy resisted the urge to tug her arm free and waited until the older woman lowered her hand before making her escape.

Amy passed only two tables before stopping yet again, to speak to Rafe Spindler and Cal Randall, on a break from their ranch chores. The two were close enough for Jesse to hear Amy's response to their questions about her father's health.

"...doing fine. He's at the clinic right now having another treatment."

"You be sure and give him our best," Cal said as she thanked him and moved on.

Jesse got to his feet when she reached his table and held her chair. She sank down gratefully.

"Thanks." She gave a long, slow sigh.

"I never gave a thought to the number of times you must be called on to answer the same questions about your father."

She smiled. "I don't mind. Really. It's nice to know so many people care. But sometimes I feel like I'm climbing a mountain."

"Yeah." He started to reach for her hand, then stopped as Daffy approached.

"Hey, Amy." The older woman wrapped her arms around Amy and gave her a warm hug, which Amy returned. "How you doing, girlfriend?"

"Fine now. I always love your hugs."

"That's what I'm here for. Your mama was the first friend Vi and I made when we came to Gold Fever. And she remained our best friend until she was gone. So now you're stuck with us whether you like it or not."

"I love both of you." Amy waved to Vi, who was standing over the grill behind the bar.

"The feeling's mutual." Daffy pulled a pencil from her purple hair. "Something to drink, honey?"

"Iced tea, please, Daffy."

"You got it. Know what you want for lunch yet?"

Jesse shook his head. "What's the special today?"

"Vi and I are calling it the Fortune Five. Turkey, ham, pastrami, corned beef, and cheese in an onion roll, drizzled with our special dressing. The deluxe comes with fries or slaw."

Jesse winked at Amy, who nodded.

"We'll give that a try, Daffy. And slaw on the side."

Daffy glanced at Amy. "You letting him order for you, honey?"

"He knows what I like." The minute the words were out of her mouth she felt her cheeks grow hot. Especially since Delia Cowling, who was staring at their table, was close enough to overhear every word. Whatever they said, Amy knew, would be repeated all over town by tonight.

"I just bet he does." Daffy slapped Jesse's shoulder. "This good-looking cowboy sure does know how to please the ladies." Still cackling at her little joke, she hurried away to call their order to her sister, Vi.

A short time later Jesse and Amy were devouring their lunch like two starving ranch hands.

Midway through, Jesse glanced over. "You forget to eat breakfast again?"

Amy flushed. "Yeah. Too many ranch chores to see to."

"You ought to have help."

"I can manage."

"I know. But between running the ranch and driving your father into town for these treatments, you have to be running on empty."

She shrugged. "I'm okay with it."

"I could loan you somebody from our ranch."

"I said I'm fine." She instantly hated the edge she'd let creep into her voice.

He sat back and sipped his coffee, knowing better than to push. "You bring those papers that you found?"

"Yeah." She reached into her pocket and handed over the discolored slips of paper. "They were stuck between a bunch of newspapers and magazines. If I hadn't been looking, I'd have never spotted them." She watched the way Jesse studied each word, each line and squiggle. Wouldn't she do the same, if someone found an old note of her mother's? "Do they make any sense?"

"No."

"I thought this was interesting." Amy leaned close and pointed to a torn scrap of paper with the words *possible cavern beneath rock ledge.*

Jesse breathed in her scent and struggled to concentrate. It wasn't easy, when she was this close. He remembered that she used to dab some kind of light floral perfume between her breasts. The mere thought of it had him sweating.

"Yeah. Fascinating. But not much help. There are so many rock ledges in these hills, it would be impossible to know which one he meant."

Their heads came up sharply when Delia Cowling swooped down on their table. "Those look like some of crazy old Coot's notes. Where'd you find them?"

Before Amy could respond Jesse shot the old woman a grin. "Now how'd you see them from where you were sitting, Delia?"

"I recognized that yellow paper. Folks have been finding Coot's notes for years now. In fact, I've found a few of my own."

"You don't say?" Jesse arched a brow. "I don't recall Coot ever telling me you'd turned in some of his notes."

"Well I have. Now and then."

"Now and then? Where'd you find them?"

She took a step back. "Here and there. They used to fall out of his pockets and blow all over Montana."

"Well, if you find any more, I'd appreciate it if you'd return them to me. For sentimental value, you understand."

"Sentimental? I hear Coot promised your cousins a share in his estate if they'd stay and join in the treasure hunt."

"Who told you that?"

"I can't recall. Is it true?"

"They're still here, aren't they?"

The old woman shot him a knowing look and quickstepped back to her table.

"Now you've done it," Amy whispered. "You know she'll tell the entire town that you and your cousins are still interested in finding Coot's treasure."

He grinned at her. "You mean she isn't going to buy my claim of being sentimental?" He gave a casual shrug of his shoulders. "It doesn't matter what gossip she spreads. Half the town already knows. And the other half will hear all about it by tomorrow."

They shared a laugh before returning their attention to the strips of paper and the faded words.

"Does the drawing on the other side help?"

Jesse turned the paper over, studying the crude lines before giving Amy a quick grin. "No help to me. But then, most of Coot's notes never made any sense, except to him. He had his own secret code."

"Maybe Miss Cora can decode them."

"Worth a try." He shoved the papers into his pocket and picked up his cup, staring into the coffee as though searching for answers to all life's questions in its depths. "Coot was so sure he'd find the treasure."

"And now he has you and your cousins in on the hunt."

He gave a grunt that could have been a laugh or a sneer. "Aren't we a fine bunch to go treasure hunting? A surfer, a Hollywood pretty boy, and a hotheaded cowboy."

Hotheaded and hot-blooded, she thought. "But what if you find it?"

He looked over and saw the spark of excitement in her eyes. "Hey. Don't tell me you're getting caught up in this?"

To his amazement, instead of denying it, she fell silent.

He shook his head. "I'll be damned. Coot just got himself another convert."

"I'm not saying I believe. Well…" She chuckled. "I'm not saying I don't believe either. But think about it, Jess. All that gold, just lying somewhere out there for more than a hundred years. Doesn't it seem reasonable that the ancestors of the man who found it originally ought to be the ones to find it again?"

"Reasonable." He gave a rough laugh. "Now what makes you think anything in this life will have a reasonable ending?"

"Some things do."

"Name me one."

She saw the heat in his eyes and felt her cheeks color. He wasn't thinking about the lost treasure now. They both knew it. They had a history together. Because of Jesse, she'd defied her father's rules, had lost her heart to the enemy, and had eagerly joined him in planning a future together. But their story had ended badly, because he hadn't cared enough to contact her even once through the years she'd been away at college. He'd cut her off without a word. No explanation. No sugarcoated apology. Just stony silence, making it abundantly clear that he'd had a change of heart.

So much for all those sweet dreams she'd spun around him.

"Can't think of one, can you?" Jesse's tone hardened. "While you're looking for a happy ending, all I'm seeing is twists and turns along the way."

Hearing him, Daffy paused beside their table to refill Jesse's coffee and drop the bill for their lunch beside his plate. "Honey, my philosophy is this: Life is supposed to take all these twists and turns so that we're forced to slow down and enjoy the passing scenery instead of just racing along a boring, straight, narrow stretch of highway to get where we're going. Some folks may want to cruise a fancy new highway. Me? I'll take twists and turns along a rutted country road any old time."

Jesse surprised her by getting to his feet and planting a kiss on her cheek.

She touched a hand to the spot. "Now what's that for?"

"For being your absolutely brilliant self. I love your philosophy, Daffy."

Looking slightly dazed, she walked away.

Jesse dropped some money on the table before catching Amy's hand. As he led her from the saloon, he continued holding her hand, while every customer turned to stare and then to whisper.

Talk about twists and turns. She was having a hard time keeping up with his mercurial moods.

Amy hoped his unexpected gesture hadn't left her looking as dazed as Daffy.

CHAPTER TEN

W here're you parked?" Jesse continued to hold
Amy's hand as they walked away from the Fortune
Saloon.

Was he just doing it to taunt Delia Cowling and the
other gossips in town? Amy wondered. Or had he, in his
haste to escape the saloon, just forgotten what he was
doing? Though she was puzzled, there was no denying
that she liked it. And that annoyed her, since she considered it a silly weakness on her part. Did she need a man
holding her hand to make her feel special?

"End of the street." Amy pointed.

If half the town had been in the saloon for lunch, the
other half seemed to be milling about the sidewalk on their
side of the street. Jesse was forced to let go of her hand and
trail behind her when they met up with a cluster of people
just entering the courthouse after their lunch break.

"Hey, Jesse. Amy." Judge Wilbur Manning, toting his

ever-present attaché case, paused. "I heard about your father, Amy. How's he doing?"

"He's just started his treatments. But so far, he seems to be doing fine."

"You give him my best, you hear?"

"I will. Thanks." Amy nodded.

The judge turned to Jesse. "How're your cousins adjusting to life in Gold Fever again?"

"So far, they seem to be enjoying the chance to play cowboy."

"This is the place to do it." The judge chuckled before starting up the steps of the courthouse.

As Jesse walked beside Amy he muttered, "So much for trying to keep any secrets in this town. Especially from the judge, who knows everybody's business."

"These people care about us."

He grinned. "And they feel that it entitles them to know every little detail of our lives."

When they came to Amy's truck, she nodded toward the sacks loaded in the back. "Thanks to Orley, I only have to wrestle these one more time."

"I could follow you home and unload them in the barn for you. It'll only take me a few minutes."

"I can handle them, Jess." She paused. "Besides, there's no reason to add to my dad's guilt about not being able to do things himself."

Jesse could see her point. A man like Otis Parrish was used to handling his own chores. As hard as it would be seeing his daughter struggling to do his work, it would be twice as painful to see a McCord lending a hand. Her old man could hold a grudge better than anybody else Jesse could think of.

"What time do you have to get back to the clinic?" Jesse leaned a hip against the door of her truck, reluctant to end their time together.

Amy glanced at her watch. "The treatment is over by now, but Dad always needs a few minutes to rest before tackling the ride home."

He reached a hand to an errant strand of her hair, tucking it behind her ear.

At the familiar gesture, heat spiraled all the way to her toes, annoying her yet again. Jesse McCord had always had an easy way with the ladies. She had to keep reminding herself that the gesture meant no more to him than breathing.

Jesse's tone softened. "I wish there was a way to make this easier for you. I wish I could..."

"Hey, Jesse." Rafe Spindler's voice had them looking up.

The husky cowboy was standing on the sidewalk, squinting against the noon sunlight.

"Cal wanted me to tell you that I need to beef up my crew on the north range. I thought maybe, seeing that you're"—his voice was heavy with sarcasm—"all one big happy family now, you'd like to join Zane and Wyatt for a couple of days." His look turned sly. "That'll give me a couple of nights to win back the stallion you won from me in last night's poker game. He was the best saddle horse I've ever..."

Jesse gave a quick shake of his head. "Can't do it. I've got too much to do in the next couple of days. Call Jimmy Eagle and see if he can spare some hands from the south pasture."

Rafe glanced from Amy to Jesse with a knowing

smirk. "Yeah, I can see you're going to be real busy in the coming days. And nights."

"You've made your point, Rafe. Now beat it."

"Yeah. Wouldn't want to crowd you."

As he sauntered away, Jesse clenched his hands into fists in silent fury. Rafe was another one who knew everybody's business and enjoyed letting them know it.

Huffing out a breath, he turned back to Amy. "Is this some kind of conspiracy?"

She merely shrugged at the absurdity of it. The interruptions were endless, but so was Jesse's flirting.

"I swear this is some evil plot to keep us apart. A few days ago, back at the ranch, it was Zane and Wyatt. Today, it's all these well-meaning citizens who keep interrupting. All I wanted to do was"—he leaned close—"say a proper good-bye."

"Oh, Amy. Glad you're still here." Orley Peterson came rushing out of the store, holding a parcel in his outstretched hand. "Be sure to give this to your father."

Amy couldn't help laughing at the look on Jesse's face as he jerked back. "Thanks, Orley. What is it?"

"An antibiotic he ordered for his heifers." He grinned at Jesse. "Hey, Jesse. Good to see you."

"You, too, Orley."

Jesse watched the older man waddle away.

When he turned back, Amy had already opened the truck door and slid into the driver's seat before dropping the parcel beside her.

She turned the key in the ignition.

Before she could put the truck in gear Jesse stuck his head in the open window. His voice was a low growl of frustration. "Would it be okay if I stop by later tonight to see you?"

"I guess so." She nodded. "I'd like that."

He felt a sense of relief. "Good. So would I." He'd had no intention of taking no for an answer. If she'd refused, he'd have found an excuse to see her anyway.

He stepped back as she checked for traffic, made a quick U-turn, and headed along the street toward the clinic.

Jesse jammed his hands in his pockets, watching her truck move along Main Street. It was a good thing she'd agreed to see him tonight, or his head might have exploded.

He was happy to let his cousins cool their heels on the north range, babysitting a herd of cattle. As for him, he had a challenge of a different sort in mind.

He needed to sort out just what was going on inside his head. Not to mention his heart.

He'd thought he could live without her. He'd learned all kinds of tricks to keep himself from dwelling on what he'd lost. He managed for years to throw himself into the tough, demanding ranch chores, working killer hours alongside the wranglers so that he could sleep. But even in sleep his mind refused to give him peace. She was there in his dreams, taunting him, teasing him.

Now she was back and he found himself wanting to see her again. In fact, if he was to be perfectly honest, it was more than just a want. These feelings for her were a need. He needed to see her, even though he knew there was a chance that she'd be gone in a short time, back to the life she'd made for herself in Helena. A life that didn't include him.

It was the risk he was willing to take.

That probably made him the biggest fool in the world.

Amy stepped out onto the porch, her head still spinning from the rows of figures she and her father had gone over in his ledgers. Though he may not have wanted to talk about his illness, it was plain that he'd given it a lot of thought. Aware of his mortality, he'd taken great pains to arm his daughter and only heir with as much information as possible. To that end they'd discussed the exact acreage owned, the number of buildings and the repairs that would be needed in the coming year, and the amount of county, state, and federal taxes owed, as well as expected income from the sale of cattle.

Amy now had a handle on their income, expenses, and maintenance fees. And though money would be tight, she was comforted by the knowledge that she wasn't in any danger of losing all that her father had worked so hard to manage through the years.

Besides discussing their finances, he'd said something that had caught her by surprise.

"You realize this ranch was never mine, girl."

She'd looked up at him. "What's that supposed to mean?"

"When I married your mother, she made it clear that she intended to see her family's ranch passed along to the next generation. Whether you return to teaching or stay on the land, it's still yours to do with as you please."

"Don't be silly, Dad. You worked it alongside Mom for more than thirty years. That makes it yours."

"I had no illusions about it ever being mine. Long

after I'm gone, the land will remain your legacy. I know it would please your mother if I kept it as a working ranch. But the future of this place will be squarely in your hands."

In her hands.

There seemed to be way too much in her hands these days.

Amy lifted her head to study the full moon rising above the peaks of Treasure Chest in the distance.

It was one of those perfect autumn evenings. Though the day had been warm, there was a chill in the air as the last of daylight faded, bringing a hint of what was to come.

Amy draped her mother's faded old afghan around her shoulders. It gave her such comfort to have something of her mother's.

She loved autumn here in Montana, just as her mother always had. Loved the burnished gold of the aspens. Loved watching the mist rise up off the lakes as late-morning sun began to heat the chilly waters. She felt energized by the thought of a solitary morning of fishing when the cooler water brought walleye and trout up from the depths to practically leap onto her hook.

Though she missed her students, she had to admit that she was beginning to appreciate the chance to leave the daily routine behind and return to her roots. Especially since it meant a return to...

She looked up at the sudden flash of headlights in the distance. Jesse. The mere thought of him had her heart doing cartwheels. Damn him for having this effect on her after all this time.

Long before she heard the crunch of tires, she'd

discarded the afghan and was down the steps, waiting at the end of the driveway as he stepped from his truck.

"How's your dad?"

"He only got sick twice on the ride home this time. He was able to keep down some broth when we got here and then slept for an hour. So that's all good."

While leading Jesse up the steps to the porch swing, she paused. "Isn't it strange how quickly things can change in our lives? I can't imagine another time when I would consider any of this as good news. Not long ago it would have been impossible to imagine my father spending one day tired, nauseous, or weak. He was so strong. So confident. Now he seems to grow a bit more frail every day. For supper he managed a couple of bites of a grilled cheese sandwich, and he had just enough energy to stay awake for a while before calling it a day."

"He's asleep?" Jesse sat beside her, giving the swing a nudge with his foot.

She nodded, struggling to ignore the press of his shoulder and hip to hers. "Those treatments really knock the wind out of his sails. But the nurse at the clinic assured him this was only temporary, and that he'd bounce back."

"Hold on to that thought." He squeezed her hand and absorbed the quick rush of heat he always felt when touching her. Instead of letting go, he continued holding it lightly in his as the swing rocked gently back and forth.

"I will. I'll take all the assurances I can get." She looked up at the canopy of stars. "It's funny how a life-and-death situation puts everything in perspective."

"Yeah. I guess the little things just fall by the wayside."

"Most of them." She sighed. "Before Dad went to bed, he went over the ranch accounts with me."

"Is that good or bad?"

She gave a shrug of her shoulders. "He's been so silent, so distant, I was convinced that he was in complete denial about the seriousness of his illness. Now I realize he's been doing some heavy-duty thinking."

"That sounds good to me."

"It is. But the poor guy had to figure out how to talk to me, how to bring me up to speed on his finances, how to plan ahead on keeping the ranch going without his help. And all without Mom here to act as mediator." She looked over. "It was always Mom who kept the two of us from ripping each other into shreds."

Jesse sandwiched her hand between both of his. "The main thing is, he did talk to you. And I take it he did it without fighting."

"He did." She studied their joined hands, enjoying the connection. She'd missed this. Missed him more than she'd ever allowed herself to admit. "And now that he's opened that door, I intend to keep it open, even if I have to pester him with questions on a daily basis. I'm not going to let him shut me out again."

"I know just how you feel." Jesse's words, though spoken softly, held a thread of steel.

She looked up to see his eyes, hot and fierce, fixed on hers, and felt the jolt to her heart.

"Whatever happened between us is in the past, Amy. We can't undo it. But I don't want to be shut out again."

"Jess . . ."

He touched a finger to her lips to still her words. "Hear me out."

The press of his finger against her mouth had her heart stammering. She couldn't have managed a word if she'd wanted to.

"I'm sorry that it was bad news that brought you back. I wouldn't wish that on anyone. But I'm not sorry you're here now. The minute I saw you at Coot's funeral, I had the sense that you and I had been given a second chance."

She gave a wry laugh. "Is that why you were so warm and inviting that day?"

"I deserve that." He swore under his breath. "I was trying to deny what I was feeling, what I am feeling. I'm hoping you feel the same way."

He waited, staring into her eyes with a look that implored even while it challenged.

She hadn't expected such honesty. But now that he'd been forthcoming, how could she be less so?

"I didn't know what to expect, Jess. I guess I still don't know exactly how I feel about being back here. I've made a life for myself in Helena. I love my work. Have some good friends..."

"Any in particular?"

She shrugged. "A couple."

"Any marriage proposals?"

She shook her head. "Not so far." She thought about Colin, the history teacher. They'd been spending a good deal of time together, and she knew it was getting serious, at least on Colin's part. As for her, she'd been holding back, and she didn't even realize it until now. Was Jesse the reason?

"But you don't hate me?" His words sent her thoughts scattering.

"I came close." She sighed. "But I couldn't hate you, Jesse."

"Then why did you...?" He paused, considering his words carefully. He wanted desperately to know why she'd left him without a word. But he worried that if he brought up the past, he would end up right where he'd been stuck these past years. Hurt, angry, and distant. He was sick and tired of such feelings.

Instead, he drew her close. Against her temple he murmured, "For now, I'll be satisfied that you don't hate me."

With no warning he lowered his head and touched his lips to hers. He hadn't planned this, but now that he'd started, there was no way he could stop.

Dear God. She tasted even better than he'd remembered all these years. Wild and sweet and as cool, as fresh as a mountain stream. This reality was far better than any of the memories he'd stored up. And there'd been enough of them to rob him of too many nights of sleep to count.

Amy responded with the same shocking hunger, wrapping her arms around his waist and throwing herself fully into the kiss.

She'd always loved kissing Jesse. Those firm, practiced lips. That hot, clever tongue that could tease and tempt until she forgot everything else. And those hands. Those rough cowboy's hands that could stroke and soothe and coax until she was mad with need. Hands strong enough to break her, but when they went all soft and easy, as they were now, moving over her slowly, carefully, as though afraid she might break, they had her flesh and bones melting like hot wax. These same hands had always been there to hold her and keep her from falling.

He kissed her long and slow and deep, until they both were fighting for air. The heat between them felt as though they'd been thrust into a furnace.

The need for her was so sharp and deep, he found himself sucking in a breath on the pain. "God, Amy. I've never stopped wanting you."

"I…" She broke free, filling her lungs, struggling to calm her ragged breathing. "I need a minute."

"Time is the last thing we need. We've wasted far too much already." He drew her close and touched his lips over hers. "I just need you."

"Wait." She pulled a little away, her head spinning, hating the way her body strained toward his. It shamed her that with a single kiss all the old feelings were back, and stronger than ever. "I don't even know how long I'll be here. It could be months or just a few weeks. And then I'll be leaving again."

Not if he had anything to say about it.

Aloud he merely said, "Let's not think about the future or dwell on the past. Let's just think about today. Tonight. Now."

When she opened her mouth to argue he stopped her. "Life doesn't pass out guarantees. But for whatever time you're here, Amy, let's make the most of it."

He cradled her face between his big hands, kissing her eyelids, the tip of her nose, the corner of her mouth, drawing out each butterfly kiss until her heartbeat pounded in her temples, drowning out any negative thoughts she might be harboring. "I've missed you so much, it's like one big ache in my heart."

She knew a thing or two about aching hearts. She sighed and wondered that hers didn't burst clear through her chest. "Damn you, Jesse. You always could win me over with tenderness."

He grinned. "I was counting on it."

"You're one cocky cowboy. Think you're smart, don't you?" She stared into those laughing eyes and felt her heart do a slow dip.

Why did Jesse McCord have to be her weakness?

He caught her hand, drawing her up from the porch swing. "We could go out to the barn. For old time's sake."

His words were like a dash of water.

Her smile faded, and a sad, haunted look crept into her eyes.

"I don't make love for old time's sake, Jess. Not even with you. I think you should go."

He knew he'd crossed the line and cursed himself for his foolishness. "Let me stay awhile."

Before she could refuse he whispered, "Please, Amy."

She stared into his eyes. "No pressure?"

He shook his head. "No pressure." He sat back down and was relieved when she reluctantly sat beside him.

He nudged the swing into a gentle motion and stared up at the moon.

"Oh, Jess." Her sigh seemed to rise up from some-where deep inside. "I'm so worried about my dad. I wish I had more family to share this with. There are times when I feel so alone."

"You're not alone, Amy." He wrapped a big arm around her shoulders and tucked her up against him.

They fit together like two pieces in a puzzle. Perfectly.

Against her ear he whispered, "I want you to know that you can count on me."

"Thank you." She closed her eyes, breathing him in, loving the feel of him beside her.

They sat that way for long, silent minutes, while the swing moved back and forth, and the stars winked above them.

Though he wanted her more than he'd ever wanted anyone or anything in his life, he knew that he would have to bank his needs in order to tend hers. And what she needed right now was tenderness, trust, and a feeling of safety. If those things were all he could give her for now, he would have to be satisfied with that.

As the minutes ticked by, he glanced at her head resting lightly on his shoulder, eyes closed, breath warm against his neck. She was so exhausted by her father's illness and the never-ending ranch chores, she'd fallen asleep.

Jesse realized that, though he should have been feeling really frustrated, he was, instead, feeling almost content.

Just holding her, watching her sleep, he thought with a smile, was bringing him more happiness, more peace, than he'd known in years.

Maybe, when her life became more settled, they could resolve whatever had gone so wrong between them and move on. Or maybe it would all end as it had before.

He just hoped he didn't go slowly mad while he waited.

CHAPTER ELEVEN

J esse awoke with a start and realized that both he and Amy had fallen asleep on the swing. He glanced down at her head, still resting against his shoulder.

She looked so peaceful here. The worry about her father, the million and one ranch chores, all were forgotten as she lost herself in sleep.

Careful not to wake her, he reached for the afghan lying at their feet. Drawing it over them, he tucked it around her shoulders.

She sighed and snuggled closer. His pulse did a quick dance. He was fully aroused. The thought of waking her with a slow, easy kiss had the blood pounding in his temples. He had no doubt he could wake the slumbering passion within her while she was still in the throes of sleep.

Though he was sorely tempted, he drew back, watching her. It wouldn't be fair to take advantage of her in this state. She was exhausted by the burdens she was being forced to carry these days. Besides, though he wanted her desperately, he wanted the decision to be hers alone. If they made love... *when they made love,* he mentally corrected, he wanted her fully engaged, as eager and hungry as he would be.

This time, he thought with a little frown, there would be no second thoughts. No regrets.

No regrets.

Hadn't he lived with regret every day since Amy had left Gold Fever without a word?

They would get past that, he vowed, or he'd die trying. He wanted her to want what he wanted.

What he wanted. He sighed and lifted his head to study the path of a shooting star. He knew from his childhood here on the ranch that it wasn't possible to get everything he wanted in this life. As a boy he'd lost his cousins, who were also his best friends. He'd lost both his parents. And now Coot. Still, he realized that he'd been lucky to have a chance to grow up as he did, surrounded by so many caring people.

Right now, he would give up everything he had for the chance to get back the years he and Amy had lost.

"Jesse." Amy jerked awake and lifted her head from his shoulder, staring around in confusion.

In that brief instant she'd seen the way he'd been looking at her with a strange, almost haunted look. It was unsettling to realize that he'd been studying her without her knowledge. "How long have I been asleep?"

He glanced at the moon. "Most of the night, I'd say."

Despite the warmth of the afghan tucked firmly around

her, she felt a trickle of ice along her spine at the thought of having spent the night in his arms. "Sorry."

"I'm not."

She looked over, expecting him to say more. Instead he continued watching her with that wary look.

"You work so hard all day, Jess. The last thing you need is to spend the night on my porch swing."

"There's no place I'd rather be."

He smiled then, and her heart actually fluttered.

"I should get inside."

"In a minute." He closed a hand over hers. "I want to be with you, Amy. But I need to know what you want."

She looked away, unable to meet that steady gaze. "I'm not sure what I want, Jess."

"Then you take your time until you're sure."

"You don't understand. My first concern has to be my father."

"I know that. I'm not pushing for your answer right now. I'm not going anywhere. When you're ready, I'll be waiting." He looked up, watching the first faint light of dawn beginning to streak the sky. "Want to catch a few more winks before you start your day?"

She chuckled, but seeing his warm invitation, she moved closer and laid her head on his shoulder. Knowing there was no pressure on her to make a decision had her sighing with relief. "This is nice."

He nuzzled her hair. "Yeah."

"Your arm ought to be numb by now if it was around me all night."

"My arm's just fine. Never better."

She closed her eyes, loving the feel of his calm, steady

heartbeat. "Good. Maybe, since you offered, I'll just take a few more minutes before I think about those chores."

"I'll call you later, Amy, just to see how your father's doing." Jesse dropped his cell phone into his shirt pocket.

Beneath a spectacular sunrise, they stood beside his truck.

She touched a hand to the dark stubble at his cheeks and chin, which only added to his appeal. "I have to get inside. Dad will be awake soon."

"You realize that sooner or later you'll have to tell him that you're seeing me."

She lifted her chin. "Am I? Seeing you?"

He caught her chin between his thumb and finger and met her questioning look. "Damn right you are."

She grinned. "I guess that answers my question. But I'm not ready to tell Dad yet. He has enough to deal with. I can't add to his problems right now."

"I understand." He bent his head to give her a quick kiss. Then, thinking better of it, he gathered her into his arms and lingered over her lips until they were both struggling for breath. "That's so you'll think about me from time to time."

She managed a shaky laugh over the tightness in her throat. "You kiss me like that too often and I won't be able to think of anything else."

"Promise?" He hauled her up against his chest.

"Oh, yeah."

"Good. That's my plan."

She lifted her face for another kiss and wasn't disappointed.

When at last he climbed into his truck and closed the door, she stepped back and waved as he backed the truck away and turned it in the opposite direction before heading down the long gravel drive.

She waited until he was out of sight before walking to the house. As she climbed the steps she thought about the night they'd spent together. Together and yet not together. Strange. But she felt at peace knowing that he'd been content to just hold her.

She didn't like the fact that all the old feelings were back and, if possible, even stronger. How would she deal with them? It was too soon to act on those feelings. She just wasn't sure that anything could ever come of them. There were too many barriers between them. Not just her father's resentment against anyone in the McCord family, but also because of their past. Neither of them had spoken about their long separation, or the reason for it.

They were tiptoeing around things. Neither of them had wanted anything to spoil the mood, and so they'd deliberately avoided bringing it up. Still, it was there between them. And sooner or later they would have to deal with it if they hoped to move forward.

Forward?

What was there for them as they moved forward? Great sex in the barn? Wasn't that what Jesse had suggested last night?

She paused on the front porch, staring at the fiery ball of sun rising above the mountain peaks in the distance. Sex with Jesse would be great. Better than great. Fantastic. Earth-shattering. And the truth was, she wanted it. Wanted him.

But for now, while she dealt with her father's serious

health issues, there wasn't room in her life for any thoughts about the future. She'd have to think about it later. Much later, when her life was more settled.

She hurried inside and started the coffee before heading back to the barn for morning chores.

Jesse swore as he drove his truck into the barn and caught sight of Rafe Spindler talking to a cluster of cowboys. He'd expected them to be gone by now.

Their heads came up sharply and they turned to watch as he stepped out of his truck. He recognized Cal Randall, Jimmy Eagle, Zane, and Wyatt among them and cursed his lousy timing.

"Catching an all-nighter?" Rafe sauntered over, his big, beefy face wearing a mean grin.

Ignoring the question, Jesse turned to the others. "I figured you'd be up on the north ridge by now."

"I bet you did." Rafe wasn't about to let this go. "Now I see why you couldn't lend a hand with my crew."

Enjoying the flare of anger in Jesse's eyes, he decided to push a little harder.

His eyes glittered. "I could've made myself a fortune taking bets on how long it would take you to score with Amy Parrish. I could tell by the look on both of your faces at the old man's funeral that it was just a matter of time."

Jesse's hand was at his throat before he had time to blink. With a fistful of Rafe's shirt he dragged him close, his eyes hot and fierce. "That old man was my grandfather, and he had a name. You want to talk about him, you call him by name, you hear?"

Rafe tried to pull away, but Jesse's hand tightened.

"I asked if you heard me."

Rafe swallowed hard. "I hear."

Jesse twisted the fistful of shirt, drawing Rafe's face even closer. "As for Amy Parrish, I don't see that she's any of your business. Not now. Not ever. You got that clear?"

Rafe gave a barely perceptible nod of his head, all that he could manage in that tight, choking grip.

Jesse lowered his hand and spun away.

"Let's get moving." Rafe's shouted order had the cowboys scrambling to climb into a line of trucks that were idling in the barn.

As Jesse started to walk away, Zane and Wyatt followed him to the door of the barn.

When Wyatt dropped a hand on his shoulder, Jesse spun around, fire in his eyes, until he realized that it wasn't Rafe.

"What?" His voice was a snarl.

Wyatt lowered his hand and his voice. "There's a rumor going around town that Amy found some more of Coot's notes."

"I guess it's like Amy said. There are no secrets in this place."

Zane glanced at Wyatt before turning to Jesse. "Is it true?"

"Yeah." Jesse dug his hands in the pockets of his jeans and pulled out the crumpled slips of paper. "They were mixed in with some old newspapers, just like the others."

"Do they make any sense?"

He shook his head. "No more than any of the dozens of others that have been found over the years. A few words, a couple of doodles, but no clear pathway to anything. But even though they don't make any sense, both Amy and I are feeling pretty good about this latest discovery. In fact, we're thinking of joining forces to continue Coot's search."

The two cousins shared a long, speculative look.

It was Wyatt who finally spoke. "We've been talking about it. We both decided that we'd like to study the papers. If you and Aunt Cora have no objections."

Jesse surprised himself and them by giving a negligent shrug of his shoulders. "I'm sure Aunt Cora will welcome your input."

"And you?" Zane shot him a challenging look.

Jesse met his look. "I won't object. Hell, Coot invited you in. Who am I to say otherwise?"

As he started to turn, Wyatt lifted a hand to Jesse's hair, smoothing out the clumps of bed-head.

"Next time you sleep over, you might want to at least give your head a shake before you drive home." He shot Jesse a wide grin. "So long, cuz. When we get back in a day or two, we'll take a look at Coot's old journal and notes and see if we can make any sense of them. Maybe, if we all put our heads together, we can come up with a plan."

"Fine." Jesse watched as his cousins sauntered away and joined Cal Randall and Jimmy Eagle in one of the ranch trucks.

He should have been glad that they were heading up to the north ridge, where they'd be out of his hair for a couple of days. But he couldn't help wishing he'd arrived home a little sooner, or a lot later. With little to occupy the cowboys except cattle and weather, they enjoyed every little bit of gossip they could uncover. Word of Amy's papers was proof of that. It was already spreading like wildfire. Jesse had no doubt that Rafe Spindler would spin out this latest tidbit as far as he could, enjoying every little minute of his self-importance while he told and retold his story of Jesse's nightly romp with the daughter of his grandfather's sworn enemy.

Because he wasn't about to take any more chances, he tossed his head like a shaggy dog and ran his hands through his hair before heading to the house. No sense broadcasting his night to Aunt Cora and Dandy, too.

It occurred to him that he wasn't nearly as angry about being caught sneaking home at dawn as he ought to be. And, wonder of wonders, he wasn't even upset about the fact that his cousins had decided to intensify the search for Coot's fortune.

Maybe all this warm, fuzzy mellowness had to do with the fact that he'd spent the night with Amy in his arms.

Just sleeping beside her made him feel better than he'd felt in years.

He couldn't wait to do it again.

CHAPTER TWELVE

"This is nice." Cora looked around the dinner table at her three nephews. Cal had gone into town with some of the crew. "I believe this is the first time we've all been together in a week or more."

Earlier in the day Zane and Wyatt had returned, bewhiskered, weary, and caked with mud after their stint with the wranglers from the north ridge. Jesse had ridden in at nearly the same time after lending a hand with a crew mending fences on the south ridge.

Now, freshly shaved, showered, and dressed in clean clothes, they were enjoying a meal of Dandy's best stuffed pork chops and garlic mashed potatoes.

Cora set aside her napkin. "How about taking dessert in the great room?"

"Good idea, Aunt Cora." Jesse pushed away from the table.

Dandy, busy spooning chocolate sauce over devil's

food cake topped with ice cream, looked up. "You folks go ahead and I'll bring it, along with a pot of coffee."

Jesse held the door for his aunt, who was trailed by Zane and Wyatt.

They settled on two facing sofas in front of a roaring fire. The three men stretched out their long legs, enjoying the warmth and peace after the frantic pace of these last few chore-filled days.

After Dandy delivered a tray of desserts and coffee, they sat for long minutes in companionable silence enjoying the rich confection, washing it down with strong, hot coffee.

Wyatt glanced at the others. "This might be a good time to start sorting through Coot's journal."

If Cora was surprised at his remarks, she was even more surprised when Jesse agreed. He left the room and returned minutes later carrying an old shoe box, then dumped the contents on the coffee table between them. Besides the yellowed slips of paper, there was a small, pocket-sized notebook bulging with handwritten notes.

At Wyatt's raised eyebrow, Jesse grinned. "This was Coot's idea of a file cabinet."

"Yeah. I'd say that suits old Coot."

At Zane's words, the others burst into laughter.

They looked up when Dandy knocked before opening the door. "You have a visitor. Amy Parrish is here."

"Oh, Amy." Cora was on her feet and hurrying across the room as Amy entered.

"Is this a good time?" Amy returned the warm hug from the older woman.

"There's never a bad time for a visit, my dear. Come." Cora caught her hand and led her toward the sofas.

Jesse stood back, staring at her while his cousins offered their greetings.

"Good to see you again, Amy." Zane kissed her cheek.

"Hi, Amy." Wyatt kissed her other cheek.

"Hi to both of you." She looked across at Jesse and held out her hand. "I just found another slip of paper that looks like the others. I thought since Dad is asleep for the night, I'd bring it over."

"And just in time." Instead of taking the paper, Jesse caught her hand in his.

Amy wondered if the others could see her heart in her eyes, or the sparks that seemed to flare at their simple touch.

Jesse winked. "We were about to start sorting through Coot's journal. Want to join us?"

She began to back away, shaking her head. "This should be a private, family thing. I'll just go."

Jesse wasn't about to let go of her hand just yet. "Didn't you tell me just the other day that you were starting to believe in Coot's treasure hunt?"

She flushed. "I did. But..."

"Stay. Please." Cora laid a hand on Amy's shoulder and guided her to sit beside her on the sofa.

Without further protest Amy sat and was soon as caught up in the puzzling array of papers as the others.

"What a mess." Jesse sat back, studying the mountain of paper, then glanced over at Wyatt. "What are you doing?"

Wyatt was already turning each slip of paper faceup across the length and width of the coffee table. "I thought we'd treat this like a picture puzzle."

"What a fine idea." Getting into the spirit, Cora joined him in setting out each slip of paper, laying the pieces end to end until they filled the entire coffee table.

While they worked, Zane stood a little away, his trusty camera recording every word and movement.

Since moving in, half a dozen shipments of equipment had arrived for him. Video cameras, movie cameras, filters, lights. His suite was beginning to look like a Hollywood soundstage, complete with editing equipment and a soundboard.

Jesse looked annoyed. "I can't think while that camera is stuck in front of my face."

"Then stop thinking and just smile. You wouldn't want to be edited out of my documentary, would you?"

Jesse gave the camera an exaggerated grin before returning his attention to the puzzle.

Amy was studying a torn piece of paper, when suddenly she reached across the table and held up a second one. "Look. These torn edges match exactly. They have to be from the same note."

Everyone stared as she held the two pages close and read, "Finished with...buttes." She looked up. "He may have meant the Gold Rush buttes. They're the closest buttes to your ranch."

Jesse nodded. "You're right. And it sounds as though he meant to say there was no further need to search there. At least that's what 'finished with' means to me."

"I agree. Let me try something." Wyatt left the room. Minutes later he returned carrying a much-folded, oversized map of the ranch and the surrounding area.

At their questioning looks he explained, "While I was traveling the world, I wanted to remind myself of the place where I'd been born. So I've carried this with me."

He wasn't aware of the looks that were exchanged by the others as he smoothed out the map on the floor, then marked off the Gold Rush buttes. "If we agree that this area has already been searched and yielded nothing, we'll mark it off so we can concentrate on other areas."

Zane peered over his camera. "I could make a clear plastic overlay on my computer and print it out. That way we could see at a glance where Coot finished searching and what areas he missed. It would certainly simplify our hunt."

After a moment of charged silence, there was a renewed sense of excitement as they began searching through the papers for more matching edges.

Jesse looked over at Wyatt. "What made you think of a puzzle?"

His cousin shrugged. "In my travels around the world I've always been fascinated by primitive stick drawings. No matter what the culture, the people found a way to communicate. And those left behind to sort through those drawings have usually had to rely on piecing them together to form the big picture." He shrugged. "It just seemed to make sense to set out all of Coot's papers and then sort through them." While he spoke, his gaze searched the jumble of papers on the coffee table.

"Like these." Jesse held up two pages smeared with dirt and badly wrinkled in an identical fashion. "This one goes with this. I'm sure of it." He studied them. "The only words here are *north cliffs*."

Cora's eyes sparkled. "Oh, my. I wonder if Coot

meant that he wanted to search those cliffs? Or if he'd already searched them and found nothing?"

Jesse laid a hand over hers. "We won't know unless we find another piece to this page telling us what he meant. But at least we can see a pattern beginning to form."

"Yes. Oh." Cora touched a hand to her heart. "If only Coot were here to show us the way."

Zane, taking a close-up shot of the map and papers, aimed his camera at her. "He is here, Aunt Cora. He's here in every word and drawing. In every torn scrap of paper. Once we figure out his shorthand, he'll show us all the places he's already searched, so we won't have to duplicate his trail. And maybe, just maybe, when we put them all together, he'll show us the way to the treasure."

"I don't believe I've ever seen your aunt so excited over anything other than her art." Amy stepped out into the darkness and walked beside Jesse to her father's truck.

"Yeah. I'm feeling a little excited myself. Of course"—he shot her a sideways glance—"that could be because of the pretty woman next to me." He caught her hand. "I wish you could stay."

"Now that could prove interesting. Let's see. How would I greet your family when I walked downstairs in the morning? Hi, Miss Cora. Zane. Wyatt. My…um… truck wouldn't start, and I thought rather than tinker with the engine, I'd just sleep with Jesse. Oh, good morning, Dandy. What's for breakfast?"

Jesse burst into laughter. "Yeah. They might not buy your story. But you know what? They wouldn't say a word. You'd be as welcome in the morning as you were tonight."

Though she had joined him in laughter, she sobered. "They did make me feel welcome. I'm so grateful for that. Through all the troubles between my dad and your family, they've always been kind and considerate where I was concerned. I only wish my dad could make an effort to do the same for you."

Jesse dropped a hand on her shoulder. "Don't push, Amy. Give him time. Right now he's dealing with some major issues."

She nodded, relieved that Jesse was willing to be patient. "As for the treasure hunt, I never really gave it much thought before. But now that I've seen your grandfather's papers, and watched the enthusiasm grow between you and your cousins, I have to admit that I find it really exciting. No wonder Coot spent a lifetime searching. The thought of finding lost treasure is so tantalizing."

"Almost as tantalizing as your lips." He brushed his mouth over hers and they both absorbed the flare of heat.

Was it just the excitement of this night, with all the talk of lost treasure and the thought of taking up Coot's search? Or was there something else going on here?

He'd thought that once he'd made the decision to slow things and allow Amy time to chart her own course of action, some of this wildfire raging inside him would cool. But if anything, it was burning hotter than ever. Maybe he'd just try to nudge her along.

Against her mouth he muttered, "I'd give up a treasure for you, Amy."

"Oh, sure." Despite her thrill at his admission, she drew away a little, determined to keep things light. "You say that now. If you and your family ever find that treasure, I'll remind you of those words, cowboy."

"I've never meant anything more." He gathered her close and lingered over her lips until they were both sighing.

Reluctantly Amy pulled away, keeping a hand at his chest. "I'd better get home. Will I see you soon?"

"You bet." He kissed her one more time for good measure before holding open the door of her truck. "Wild horses couldn't keep me away from your door."

Though she was thrilled at his remark, she was determined to remain composed.

"Night, Jesse." She blew him a kiss and started away.

Jesse watched until her taillights were just a blur before turning back to the house.

Inside he made his way to his room. He pried off his boots and kicked them aside before unbuttoning his plaid shirt and tossing it over the arm of a chair. Barefoot and shirtless, he walked to the bank of windows that looked out over the foothills of Treasure Chest Mountain. He loved the look of it, silhouetted against the night sky, its peaks gilded by the light of a half-moon. These mountains and hills and this glorious land hid a million secrets. And somewhere, they hid a fortune in gold that had once, for a few precious hours, belonged to his ancestors.

Though he'd never shared old Coot's hunger for the lost treasure, he could understand the desire to retrieve what was rightfully his. After all, that treasure had cost the lives of Coot's father and grandfather. To be perfectly honest, Jesse thought, it had cost all of them a great price. Coot's sons, weary of their father's obsession, had abandoned him. Coot had been denied watching two of his grandsons grow to manhood, and Jesse had been denied his cousins and closest friends at a critical time in all their young lives. And all because of a lost treasure that could possibly remain lost for another century.

Though they were a long way from regaining what they'd once had, this late-night session had been a pleasant interlude. An uneasy truce in their family feud. Maybe, he thought, old Coot hadn't been as foolish as he'd first appeared when the will was read. At the time, they'd all recognized his clumsy attempt to entice them to stay. But maybe there was more to it. Maybe the sly old man had hoped that the search for the treasure would be a catalyst for them to learn how to be a family once more.

Yawning, Jesse lowered the shades and turned off the light before kicking off his jeans and stretching out on the bed.

He found himself wishing that Amy could be here in his arms.

He should have followed her home.

Could've. Should've. Would've.

The thought had him alternately smiling and frowning as he drifted into sleep.

CHAPTER THIRTEEN

———◆◆◆———

The town of Gold Fever was buzzing with the gossip that the McCord boys had decided to follow in their grandfather's footsteps and chase the elusive dream.

"Are they so foolish they've forgotten the curse?" Delia Cowling was holding court in the Fortune Saloon while many of the lunch crowd gathered around.

Delia's brother, Ledge, nodded. "Took the lives of three generations of McCords. I guess that's not enough for them. They'd like to gamble away what's left of 'em. But what the hell. It's their lives to risk."

Rafe Spindler and Cal Randall, in town to pick up supplies, couldn't help but overhear as they shook the dust from their hats and ambled toward their table.

Rafe hung back, letting Cal walk ahead while he remained beside Delia's table. "From what I've seen, it looks like Amy Parrish has agreed to join forces with them."

Rafe's words had everyone muttering as they gathered around him.

"You sure of that?" Delia's eyes were as big as saucers.

Rafe ignored Cal's scowl of disapproval. Cal Randall was a stickler for keeping ranch gossip away from the town. The old man knew the rumors about Amy and Jesse were all over the Lost Nugget. Why shouldn't they be repeated in town? Too bad if Cal didn't like it. Rafe might work for the McCord family, and Cal might be his boss on the ranch, but here in town, Rafe reasoned, he was his own boss. And this town was his lifeblood. Besides, it wasn't often he found himself the center of attention. He puffed himself up, enjoying his moment of fame.

He raised his voice a fraction, so everybody could hear. "From what I've heard, Amy found some of Coot's old notes and drawings in her family's trash."

Delia snorted. "Trash, is it? I'm not surprised. Her pa made no bones about the fact that he hated the whole pack of McCords. What better way to show his true feelings than to hide Coot's precious notes? Why would he hand over any papers to them? Especially if the papers would prove helpful in their foolish search."

Rafe nodded. "Exactly. Amy found them and turned them over to the McCords. But then, I'm not surprised." His tone lowered for dramatic emphasis.

Everyone bent close to hear.

"She and Jesse have been getting really cozy, if you know what I mean. I saw him coming back from her place at dawn."

His words brought the desired reaction. Delia hissed out a breath. Ledge rolled his eyes and his lips thinned into what was the closest he ever came to a smile. A couple of the others exchanged knowing looks.

"And Amy's truck has been at the McCord ranch a couple of nights, too."

Delia crossed her arms over her chest. "If Otis Parrish knew about this, he'd pack his daughter off to Helena without another word."

"Seems to me he did that once." Harding Jessup grinned. "But she's not a teenager now, Delia. She's all grown up and in charge of her own life. Plus, she's become a mighty fine teacher, I hear."

Delia clucked her tongue. "She's still living under Otis's roof. He has every right to expect her to respect his feelings. This is a fine way for a daughter to behave while her father is dying."

"Now, Delia." Orley Peterson patted her hand to silence her. "You don't know that Otis is dying."

"He's in treatment, isn't he? Has anybody asked Doc Wheeler what his chances are?"

"Not my business." Mayor Rowe Stafford turned toward another table, having heard enough to pass along to any and all who would listen. And he had no doubt there were plenty willing to listen when it came to news concerning the McCord boys. "I don't think you ought to make it yours either. Besides, Doc wouldn't tell you even if he knew."

Delia watched him and Orley leave, then gathered the others closer to whisper a few choice words before breaking up the crowd and leading the way toward her table.

Daffy approached, pencil in hand, and fixed Delia with a hawk's stare. Her rusty voice lowered a notch.

"You folks going to eat, or are you already filled up on gossip?"

Delia looked as though she'd sucked a lemon. "I suppose you're going to claim you're above a little gossip?"

"Not at all. I hear enough of it every day to make my ears bleed. But most of it's like that old greasy stuff we scrape off the grill. When it's fresh and clean, it cooks a heap of chicken and fries, and we love sharing. When it gets old, the only thing it's good for is the critters out back. The stuff you're talking about is old as the hills, and too rancid for my taste. I doubt even the critters would care for it."

"If you're through spouting your folksy words of wisdom"—Delia cut her off with a wave of her hand—"I'll have the special."

"Make that two," her friend said.

"Two specials," Daffy shouted to her sister, Vi, manning the grill. "With a side of our best fries, cooked in… fresh oil."

She walked away, humming to herself, while many in the room struggled not to laugh out loud.

Still, with the seeds of gossip sown, it was only a matter of time before speculation, jealousy, and outright lies would begin to blossom.

"You doing okay, Dad?" Amy helped her father from the truck and up the steps of their house.

"Fine. Just help me to my room, girl." Every word was an effort, and he was sweating profusely despite the cold wind that swirled around them.

Once he was settled into bed, Amy headed toward the

barn to finish her chores. A glance at the distant field had her puzzled. The hill that should have been dotted with cows was oddly empty.

She started across the field at a run, spotting a section of fence that was down. There was no sign of the cows.

Frantic, she raced back to the barn and saddled Old Red.

Horse and rider followed a creek that ran between the Parrish property line and that of the McCord ranch. Several miles distant Amy came upon her cows, some standing leisurely in the stream and drinking, others grazing on a nearby hillside, mingling with the McCord herd.

Cal Randall spotted Amy and drove his truck across the field.

In a courtly gesture he whipped his wide-brimmed hat from his head. "Afternoon, Amy. Something I can do for you?"

"I'm sorry, Cal. I just found a section of my fence down and"—she waved a hand—"my herd wandered down here while I was in town seeing to my dad. I'll get them home as fast as I can."

"I'll get some of the wranglers to give you a hand."

She slid from the saddle. "There's no need..."

He stopped her with a hand on her arm. "No sense herding them home until that fence is mended, or you'll just have to do it all over again tomorrow. First let me see that fence. When it's properly repaired, I'll have my men bring your herd back. In the meantime, why don't you just head home and tend to your pa."

When she realized that she couldn't win the argument, she let out a long, deep sigh. "Thanks, Cal. I owe you."

He gave her a smile. "Not at all. That's what neighbors are for."

As soon as Cal pulled up to the Parrish fence line, Jesse, Zane, and Wyatt clambered down from the truck and began assembling their tools.

Zane pulled his ever-present video camera from his pocket and began filming each word and movement.

Jesse looked over at him. "Okay. I get that you're going to document every damned thing we do, but can you lend a hand first?"

Zane gave one of the famous McCord grins. "I figure you two are doing such a great job, I'll just sit this one out."

"Like hell." Jesse tossed a pair of leather gloves, hitting Zane in the face. "Put these on and get to work."

"Yes, sir." Laughing, Zane joined them.

Cal tucked his cell phone into his shirt pocket before exiting. "I told Rafe to start rounding up the Parrish herd. This isn't much of a break. We ought to have this done in an hour or two, and by then he can have those cows back. We'll have this wrapped up before dark."

It occurred to Cal that these three cousins worked well together. Despite the years apart, despite the teasing banter, they still shared a similar work ethic. The minute he'd phoned Jesse about Amy's problem, Zane and Wyatt had volunteered to help. Now the three dropped to the ground, examining the length of fencing that was lying in the dirt.

"Look at this." Jesse's voice was sharp as he turned to the ranch foreman. "Cal. Take a look. What do you think?"

The old man knelt beside him and ran a hand along the surface of the metal links. "These don't look broken to me."

Behind them, Zane grabbed up his camera and began recording everything.

Jesse's eyes narrowed. "Yeah. These don't look like they were pulled apart by a surge of cattle, or eroded by weather. The links aren't jagged or worn. They're too smooth, the pattern at either end of the break too similar."

"Cut?" Zane spoke the word they were all thinking.

"Looks like." Cal continued running his hand over the edges, as though hoping to prove his theory wrong.

"But why?" Wyatt looked around. "Who would benefit from this?"

"Nobody that I can see." Cal sat back on his heels. "This kind of thing is usually done when somebody wants to free a herd worth stealing. Lure them far enough away from the ranch so nobody can hear the trucks pulling up in the night. The Parrish herd is too small to be worth stealing. Besides, the only place the cows could wander is onto McCord land. And anybody hoping to rustle cattle has to know that we have cowboys keeping watch day and night."

Zane looked from the old cowboy to his cousin. "So, the Parrish herd would actually be safer on our land than they would be here?"

"Exactly."

Jesse turned to Cal. "Why don't you drive up to the house and tell Amy what we found. While we get this fence mended, she'd better phone Sheriff Wycliff and make a report. Even though it isn't exactly a crime, it looks a lot like harassment. Either this is the result of an old grudge, or it's some kind of cruel prank. Poor Amy. As though she doesn't have enough on her mind right now."

Cal hesitated. "Don't you think you should be the one to tell her?"

Jesse gave a weak smile. "Her father might be awake. He's apt to toss me off the property without even bothering to ask why I'm here. I don't think he's ever had a beef with you, has he?"

Cal shrugged. "We're civil whenever we meet."

"That's good enough for me."

When Jesse said nothing more, the old cowboy gave up the argument and climbed into the truck.

Even before the dust had settled, Jesse, Zane, and Wyatt were hard at work mending the fence.

Whenever Zane and Wyatt glanced over at Jesse, his eyes were narrowed, his look grim. It was obvious that he had a lot on his mind. And none of it pleasant.

A raw, bitter wind, dubbed an Alberta clipper by the locals, blew in from the north, reminding the ranchers of the winter they would soon be facing. What few leaves had clung tenaciously to the aspens were now torn loose to fly through the air like golden snowflakes.

Amy pulled on a parka and headed toward the barn to begin the morning chores. After gathering a basket of eggs in the henhouse, she mucked out stalls and forked dung and straw into a wagon before tackling the milking.

Outside, the wind rattled the big door and whistled against the windows of the hayloft.

The barn creaked and groaned, complaining like an

old woman. The sound sent shivers along Amy's spine. She could actually feel the old structure bending and swaying.

She picked up the heavy buckets of milk and started toward the door. Just as she opened it, a gust of wind blew her nearly backward. She heard a crash as loud as a freight train and turned in time to see a massive timber beginning to fall.

As if in slow motion she saw the main rafter separate from the roof and swing downward.

Dropping the buckets, she stumbled backward through the open doorway just as the timber came crashing to the ground. It smashed the walls of an empty stall, barely missing the row of cows at a trough as it landed with such force it sent a shudder through the old barn that rattled the walls and windows.

For long moments Amy was too stunned to react. She sat numbly in the dirt, staring at the destruction, seeing it all through a haze of disbelief. Then, realizing the enormity of what had just occurred, she got to her feet, and, despite the nerves that sent a trembling through every part of her body, she ran as fast as she could to the house. By the time she reached the back door, the breath was burning in her lungs, and tears of anger and confusion filled her eyes.

"I'm really sorry to bother you with my problems." Amy met Jesse, Wyatt, Zane, and Cal at the door to the barn. "But I didn't know who else to call."

"You did the right thing." Knowing they had an audience, Jesse contented himself with a hand to her shoulder.

He pulled open the door. As they crowded inside, they surveyed the damage in silence.

Zane plucked the video camera from his pocket and began recording.

Wyatt walked closer to the smashed trough. "It's lucky that this happened when you were almost out the door. Any closer, and you could have been crushed."

Amy nodded. "That timber has been here since my grandfather built this barn. Who would have believed that a gust of wind could topple it?"

Cal and Jesse knelt to examine the ancient wooden beam, and both looked up at the same instant.

In a low voice that only Jesse could hear, Cal muttered, "I'm no carpenter, but I know one thing. This was no accident. Anybody with half a brain can see that this was sawed nearly all the way through. Feel how clean this break is."

While Jesse ran his palm over and over the wooden beam, his mind was working overtime.

He got to his feet. "Amy, I know you have to take your father into town for his treatment. We'll stay here and check on any structural damage."

"You think the barn might collapse?"

He gave a quick shake of his head. "I hope not. But we'll need to check it out. I'll call you later with a report."

She glanced at her watch and turned away reluctantly. "I'm sorry to leave you with all this."

"That's what we're here for," Cal assured her.

When she was gone, Jesse's forced smile fled as he plucked his cell phone from his pocket and called the sheriff.

CHAPTER FOURTEEN

Hours later, after Sheriff Wycliff had gone over every inch of the scene, he walked outside, trailed by Jesse and his cousins.

He paused beside his truck. "This doesn't look like an accident. And now, coupled with the damaged fencing, I'm inclined to agree that somebody is out to do Otis Parrish harm. I'll go through my records to see if I can find anyone who has had a problem with him." He shifted his gaze to Jesse. "You realize, of course, that the McCord family will be at the top of that list."

Jesse nodded. "As far as I'm concerned, that feud between Otis and Coot died with Coot."

"Maybe. Maybe not. I can appreciate that you don't want Otis upset right now, while he's going through these treatments. But we all know he's a hothead. He's probably made plenty of enemies over the years. After I go through my files, I'm going to need to speak with him, even if it upsets him. He and his daughter have to be made aware of any danger."

Jesse shrugged. "You do what you think is right, Ernie."

When the sheriff's truck disappeared in a cloud of dust, Cal walked from the barn, wiping his hands on his pants. "It doesn't look like there's any structural damage, but I asked Stan Novak to bring his construction crew over for a better look. They'll be here within the hour. I'll have them go over this place with a fine-tooth comb."

"Thanks, Cal." Jesse looked back at the barn. "Who would want to hurt Amy or her father?"

Wyatt turned up the collar of his parka against the wind. "You heard Ernie. Otis Parrish is a hard man to like. I'm betting he knows a dozen people who wouldn't mind seeing his ranch fail, and Otis along with it. It's just a shame that Amy has to be painted with the same brush as her father."

"We're making headway." Wyatt added another flag to the clear overlay on his map, while Jesse filed the notes they'd already matched into a manila folder.

Zane recorded the action with his newest addition, a tiny handheld video camera small enough to carry in a shirt pocket. It was the size and thickness of a credit card. He'd tested the quality of the pictures and sound and was pleased with the professional results. It was, he decided, well worth the outrageous sum he'd paid.

Amy and Cora sorted through the rest of the slips of paper that littered the tabletop.

They had agreed to work together to whittle down the number of places Coot may have hunted for the treasure, in order to chart a path for future searches.

It was Jesse's suggestion that they meet one or two evenings a week, schedules permitting, to keep Amy's mind off her father's illness. They gathered in the great room around a roaring fire and struggled to identify as many of Coot's notes as they could.

The pile had already dwindled, though there were still a dozen or more slips of paper that made no sense whatever. They decided to place all those slips in an envelope for future reference, while they concentrated their energy on the facts at hand.

"You can see where Coot was headed." Wyatt ran a finger along the map, showing a definite trail from the Beartooth Mountain Range, across the Gold Fever River that crisscrossed their land, snaking ever closer to the foothills of Treasure Chest. "If we're correct, Coot had already scoured this part of McCord land, and was narrowing his search to this."

"That's a mighty big 'if,' " Jesse said with a chuckle. "Even when he was alive, nobody could fathom old Coot's mind. How're we supposed to believe that we can figure him out now?"

"It does seem logical," Cora mused aloud. "I agree with Wyatt that there appears to be a direct line from there to here."

"I'll trust your artist's eye, Aunt Cora. But that still leaves a couple thousand acres of McCord land to search." Jesse looked up. "A pretty daunting task for the five of us."

"At least we're five times as many as Coot. There was only him searching." Cora's eyes grew dreamy, as they always did when she spoke of her brother. "And he never doubted that the fortune would be found one day."

"One day could be in the twenty-third century." Jesse winked at Amy. "When some multinational megacon-glomerate comes in here and decides to blast through all these mountains and rivers. Of course, they might find nothing but gold dust."

That had everyone laughing, lifting their moods considerably.

Amy got to her feet. "Time to head home and check on my dad."

Jesse stood. "I'll follow you."

"There's no need." She touched a hand to his arm. "You and your cousins put in a full day."

She bent to brush a kiss over Cora's cheek before heading to the door, with Jesse trailing behind.

Outside, she paused beside her truck. "It's nice to see you and Zane and Wyatt working together on this."

"Yeah." He gathered her close and softly kissed her lips. "But this is a hell of a lot nicer. This is what really charges my engine."

She laughed before climbing behind the wheel of her father's truck. "Will I see you tomorrow?"

He shrugged. "Hard to say. With weather coming in, we need to get the rest of the herds down from the hills." He reached inside the open window and caressed her cheek. "If I had my way, I'd leave the ranch chores to the others and just spend all my time with you."

"That might be hard to do right now." She sighed. "Dr. Wheeler called and said he thinks it's time for Dad to increase the treatments."

"How often will you need to go to town?"

"We're adding a day next week, to see how Dad tolerates that. If he does well enough, they may add yet another. That would mean driving to town four times a week instead of only two."

"That's bound to raise hell with your ranch chores."

She sighed. "I'll just have to manage."

Jesse stepped back. "Let me know what happens."

"I will. Night, Jesse." She put the truck in gear and headed into the darkness.

Jesse watched until she rounded a curve in the long driveway before heading inside and up to bed. He'd put in fourteen hard hours today, and his body was screaming for rest. He was asleep as soon as his head hit the pillow.

It took five rings of Jesse's cell phone to break through his sleep-shrouded mind. Eyes closed, he fumbled for it on the night table. In the dark he snapped it open, without bothering to see who was calling. "Yeah?"

"Jesse?"

Amy's voice sounded breathless. He sat up and switched on the light, studying the clock. Not even midnight. No wonder he was so addled. He'd been asleep less than an hour. "What's wrong?"

"My tire blew."

"Where are you?"

"A couple of miles from home. Just over Gold Strike Pass. I hated waking you. I know I could leave the truck here and walk home, but..."

He was already across the room, retrieving his clothes. "It's too cold to walk that many miles, especially in the middle of the night. Stay in your truck. I'll be there to pick you up in no time."

"Thanks, Jesse."

He rang off and fumbled into his clothes and boots. Minutes later, shrugging into a sheepskin jacket, he raced to the barn and climbed into his truck.

Amy stepped out of the truck to survey the tire. A blast of frigid air had her hunching into her parka. Though the calendar said October, this was a sample of what was to come. Folks had a saying around here: Winter came to visit early in Montana, and it always overstayed its welcome.

With her hands jammed into her pockets, she fingered her cell phone and thought about calling Jesse back. She'd hated waking him, knowing the hours he was putting in on ranch chores lately. Maybe she would tell him to go back to sleep. If she jogged at a steady pace, she'd be nearly home by the time he got here anyway. What was the point of both of them losing sleep?

She smiled in the darkness, thinking about the sound of his voice, husky with sleep. She could picture him in her mind, dressing too quickly and fumbling around for his keys.

When the clouds of sleep had cleared, he'd sounded genuinely concerned about her. It was comforting to know that she had someone to rely on. Someone she could call on, even at this hour, and trust that he would keep his word.

There was no way she would have called her father for help. The last thing she wanted was to add to his worries.

She decided not to call Jesse back. By now he was probably dashing to the barn to retrieve one of the ranch trucks. Besides, just thinking about him had her wanting him. Maybe, as long as he was awake anyway, they could make the most of the night. Why keep fighting what they both wanted?

She was chuckling when she heard the sound of an engine racing at high speed.

It was way too soon for Jesse to be here, even if he could fly.

"What...?" She turned.

There were no headlights piercing the gloom, but even as she watched, a truck came roaring at her in the darkness.

She leaped out of the way, falling over rocks that lined the road and tumbling down a slight embankment. Behind her, up on the road, she could hear the sound of metal scraping metal, and the distinct sound of shattering glass. From the impact, it would appear that a vehicle had smashed directly into hers.

For a moment all the breath was knocked out of her and she lay still, wondering what had just happened.

She got to her knees, breathing deeply, struggling to clear her mind.

Was this a random drunk who'd made a wrong turn and ended up on this desolate stretch of road? Was the driver hurt? Dead?

"Oh, my God. Hang on."

She made it to her feet and was just about to scramble back up the embankment when she heard the sound of a vehicle door opening. A tiny slice of light split the darkness before the door was slammed shut. In that instant she caught sight of a man's silhouette on the road above her. A man holding a rifle.

Her heart nearly stopped.

Most folks around here carried a rifle in their vehicles, and had several more in their houses and barns. It was as natural as having a tractor, or a spare can of gas close at hand.

But why was this guy carrying a gun while checking out a crash he had caused? Did he see her as a threat?

She remained very still, hearing the crunch of footsteps on gravel. A beam of light flashed and she could see someone peering through the windows of her shattered truck.

He hadn't yet spotted her. Maybe over the sound of his truck's engine, he hadn't heard her calling out. And just maybe, that was a good thing.

Her heart was racing like a runaway train. The fall had left her feeling dazed, but she was suddenly alert. And terrified.

If he was drunk...if he saw her as a threat...he might be tempted to shoot first and ask questions when it was too late.

She couldn't take a chance on showing herself. Not in the presence of this unknown.

Turning away, she set out across the barren hills toward home.

She'd gone no more than a few hundred yards when she heard the slam of a car door and an engine roar to life. From the sound of it, the vehicle was picking up speed, and still there were no headlights to tell her exactly where it was. She knew only that it was closing in on her.

She began running in a zigzag pattern, but the truck continued to draw near.

Was this some drunk's cruel game? Or was this threat somehow connected to the things that had been happening at her ranch?

How could the driver pick her out in the darkness? Yet, she could tell, by the way the sound was growing closer, that he was deliberately trailing her, and he would soon overtake her.

She ran until her breath was burning a path of fire down her throat, but like a laser, the vehicle continued to close in on her.

Not a game. A deadly reality. This was no accident. He was chasing her in the hope of running her down. And by the way he was weaving and gaining, he was very determined, and very familiar with the area.

Amy veered to her left and raced down a dry gully, with the vehicle roaring in the darkness behind. When she knew that it was too close to outrun, she waited until the last second, then twisted to her right, ducking behind a huge boulder.

She heard the screech of brakes and felt a wave of earth and stones rolling over her as the driver stood on the brakes to keep from crashing into the boulder. Before the vehicle had even come to a stop she was racing across a flat stretch of land and up an incline, desperate to escape this madness.

She was halfway to the top when a truck came roaring over the hill, heading directly toward her, its headlights blinding her.

She let out a cry and flung an arm over her eyes. Now she would be caught in the cross fire of two crazed drivers.

As she turned to flee, she heard the truck's door slam and Jesse's voice calling, "Amy. Wait."

Hurried footsteps had her heart hammering as a hand clutched her arm, spinning her around.

"Oh, God. Jesse. Thank heaven it's you." She couldn't say more over the terror that had her by the throat.

"What's this about?" He could feel the erratic tattoo of her heart. Could feel the tremors that rocked her, while she struggled to calm her ragged breathing.

"He tried to run me over."

"Who?"

"I don't know. I need a minute." She sucked in deep draughts of air, fighting for calm.

They both looked up at the roar of an engine as the other vehicle took off in the darkness.

When the sound of the engine faded away, Jesse led her to his truck and helped her inside.

By the interior light he could see how pale she was, and the absolute terror in her eyes.

Though Jesse's first instinct had been to follow the vehicle and try to overtake it, he had to think about Amy and what she needed. And so he gathered her into his arms and held her until the tremors faded. And though he wanted to swear and pound his fists in frustration, he merely listened in silence as she told him what had just happened.

His eyes narrowed with fury when she looked up at him.

"At first I thought it was just some drunk who'd made a wrong turn and was lost. When I saw his rifle I was afraid that, in a drunken haze, he might try to shift the blame onto me for the accident because he plowed into my disabled truck. But then he began chasing me across the hills…" She struggled for calm. "I don't care how drunk he is, he can't possibly think this is all my fault."

Jesse clenched his jaw. "There are some pretty mean

drunks in this world. I've been forced to fight my share of them."

Amy drew in a ragged breath. "You don't understand. It was scary enough when he crashed into Dad's truck. But when he started after me..." She gave a shudder. "This was deliberate, Jesse."

Jesse lifted her face, pressing soft kisses to her mouth, her cheeks, her tear-filled eyes. "The main thing is, you kept your wits about you and got away."

"I hate to think what would have happened if you hadn't gotten here in time."

"Shh." He kissed her mouth and could taste her fear. "Don't think about that now. You're safe. He's gone."

He enfolded her in his arms, staggered by the depth of emotion that swamped him.

He'd thought, when he'd found her truck damaged and had seen those deep gouges in the dirt, that she'd been injured in an accident and the other party was taking her for help. But then he'd heard that far-off engine and a sea of endless blackness, and he'd feared that someone had taken her against her will.

If he hadn't made it here in time...

He shoved aside the thought and concentrated on the only thing that mattered. Amy was safe.

By now the drunk was no doubt halfway across the wilderness, and would probably wake in the morning so hung over he wouldn't even be able to remember what had happened or how he'd damaged his vehicle.

If, in fact, this had been the actions of a drunk. Amy thought it was a deliberate act. He had no reason to doubt her.

Jesse gathered Amy close, needing to feel her safe

beside him. Safe. Maybe, if he'd been here sooner, she could have been spared all this. He'd lost her once before, and he couldn't bear the thought of losing her again. They'd been given a second chance at something rare and precious.

As he drove toward her ranch, he whispered a prayer of thanksgiving that he'd been in time to save her from a stranger's wrath.

CHAPTER FIFTEEN

W hoa." Zane looked up from his morning coffee as Jesse stepped into the kitchen. "You look like hell."

"And a cheery good morning to you, too." Jesse straddled a chair and scowled into the steaming cup Dandy placed before him.

Cal Randall, having learned years earlier to gauge the moods of the various family members, kept his thoughts to himself. Across the big kitchen table Cora wisely watched and listened without comment.

Zane dug into his pancakes. "I thought I heard a truck leave last night after Amy was gone. Did you go into Gold Fever to party?"

"This was no party." Jesse shot a look at his aunt. "Amy had a blowout on the way home last night. She called for help, but before I could reach her somebody plowed into her truck, then chased her clear across hell's half acre."

His statement had everyone's attention. Around the table, they all sat up straighter, staring at him with worried eyes.

Cora touched a hand to her nephew's arm. "How is Amy?"

"Scared, but otherwise fine."

"She has a right to be scared." Wyatt's eyes narrowed. "If some idiot chased me in the dark, I'd be pretty freaked. I can't believe you left her alone with only a sick father for company."

"She ordered me to leave. So I spent the night in my truck at the end of her driveway. With all that's been going on at the Parrish ranch, I'd say this can't be considered the random work of some drunk. Although we can't rule it out until we see what the sheriff thinks." Jesse sipped his coffee, hoping to chase away the cobwebs of sleep that lingered.

Zane pushed aside his coffee. "We need to figure out who has a grudge against Otis Parrish."

Jesse frowned. "As Ernie Wycliff said, our family would be at the top of that list."

Zane and Wyatt exchanged a look before Zane said, "I'm betting the list is a long one. Over the years, Amy's father hasn't exactly endeared himself to a lot of people in Gold Fever."

Jesse nodded. "Look, I know Otis Parrish is a tough old bird. But nobody with half a brain would blame Amy for the sins of her father."

Wyatt thanked Dandy for the plate of bacon and eggs before glancing at Jesse. "At least nobody you know of."

Jesse drained his cup and got to his feet.

"Where are you going?" Cora called to his retreating back.

"To town. My first stop will be to see if Vi and Daffy saw any drunken cowboy stumble out of their place last night with murder in his eyes."

As he started toward the door Zane shoved aside his half-eaten breakfast. "I'm coming with you."

Jesse turned. "Why?"

Zane shrugged. "Sometimes a second pair of eyes and ears can come in handy."

Wyatt smashed his bacon and eggs between two pieces of toast, making a messy, oozing sandwich he could carry with him, before shoving away from the table. "Make that three pairs of eyes and ears."

As they left, Cora exchanged a look with Cal and Dandy. "Poor Amy. No wonder Jesse is so furious. But I'm worried about that anger of his. If he doesn't control it, he could find himself in trouble."

Cal gave her a gentle smile. "He has a right to be angry. And worried. Whatever's going on, the threat to Amy and her father is real."

Cora nodded.

Cal added, "But I wouldn't worry about Jesse, if I were you. He'll be just fine. And look at the bright side of this incident. Just weeks ago he was ready to take on both his cousins and wipe the floor with their hides. Now he and Zane and Wyatt are chasing a common enemy. I'd say those three working together make a pretty formidable team."

Cora sat back, her breakfast forgotten as Cal's words sank in.

She nodded. "They were awfully quick to come to Amy's defense, weren't they?"

"Just like their grandfather," Dandy added. "The McCord hasn't been born who could resist a challenge."

By the time Cora returned to her studio, she'd put aside her fears and was humming a little tune, buoyed by the fact that her nephews seemed to be growing closer with each passing day.

"I know it isn't much, Coot." She paused, her hand holding the artist's brush in midair. "But every day that our boys work together brings them closer to the way things used to be." She sighed. "Oh, how I hope they can find their way back to that happy, joyous place of their childhood."

"Well now." Daffy, wearing a T-shirt that read HELP WANTED: ONLY SEXY COWBOYS NEED APPLY, and a pair of jeans two sizes too small for her skinny hips, looked up when Jesse, Zane, and Wyatt stepped into the Fortune Saloon. "You boys get tired of Dandy's fancy food up at your ranch?"

While Zane and Wyatt chuckled, Jesse got right to the point.

"Somebody tried to run Amy over last night, after hitting her parked truck on the side of the road."

Hearing him, Violet left the grill, wiping her hands on a big apron as she approached. "Oh, honey, that's just awful. Was Amy hurt?"

"Just scared. The driver roared away when he spotted my truck heading toward him."

Vi sucked in a breath. "Thank goodness you were there to scare him off."

Daffy frowned with concern. "And you're wondering

if we had any cowboys here last night that could've been drunk enough, or mean enough, to do this?"

"Yeah."

She gave a quick shake of her head. "No strangers. We had the usual. Ledge Cowling was in, along with Harding Jessup and Orley Peterson. The doc was here, and Mayor Stafford. A couple of others. But nobody got drunk or disorderly. Nobody sulking or brooding. Though your names did come up a time or two."

At Jesse's arched brow she added, "Just the usual speculation on whether or not the three of you really intend to take up where Coot left off." She gave them each a probing look.

Wyatt chuckled and lifted his hands in a sign of surrender. "Guilty."

Vi gave a little gasp of surprise. "It's true, then?"

Daffy turned to Zane. "You, too, Hollywood?"

He shook his head at the nickname that Jesse had flung in anger. It would take time and hard work before this town would forget his years in California. "Guilty as charged."

"It runs in the family." Daffy gave a shake of her head, sending purple spikes fluttering. "You're all crazy as loons."

She turned to Jesse. "I may as well tell you that there were bets being made on you and Amy, too."

"Bets?"

"On whether the two of you will hook up or crash and burn like last time. Odds are in favor of crashing and burning, by the way."

At the look on Jesse's face, Wyatt slapped him on the back. "Now this is the town of Gold Fever that I remember as a kid. No secrets here. Everybody not only knows your business, but knows it better than you do."

Jesse unclenched his jaw long enough to say, "Thanks for that wealth of information, Daffy. If you think of or hear about anybody who has a grudge against Amy or her father, I'd like you to call me."

"You know I will, honey." Daffy touched Jesse's cheek. "For all our teasing, you know that Vi and I love that girl like our own. Ever since her mama passed, we've worried and fretted over how she'd survive her daddy's temper. Oh," she added with a grin. "We love you, too. Almost as much as we love Amy."

He closed a hand over hers. "Thanks, Daffy." He kissed her sister's cheek. "Vi."

As the three cousins strolled out of the saloon, Violet and Daffy stood watching, wearing matching looks of appreciation at their tight, sculpted backsides in those faded denims.

Jesse climbed into the truck and waited while Zane and Wyatt crowded into the passenger side.

"What now?" Wyatt asked.

Jesse shrugged and put the truck in gear. "I'll stop at the sheriff's office. See if he has anything to go on. When I drove Amy home last night I asked her to phone Sheriff Wycliff first thing this morning and file a report. Maybe he can think of something that I've overlooked."

An hour later, after an uneventful meeting with the sheriff, they realized they had no more information than when they'd left the ranch.

Wyatt broke through the somber mood that had settled over them. "At least you've notified the law. As Sheriff Wycliff said, by now the predator driver of that truck is

awake and aware that he messed with the wrong woman.
If he has any sense, he'll be long gone by this time tomorrow. And if he was just an angry drunk, it'll be an even
longer time before he gets behind the wheel of a truck
after he's been drinking."

"I'm still not sure that Amy was the real target."

At Zane's remark, Jesse looked over. "Otis?"

"It has to be." Zane nodded. "He's probably insulted
more people in Gold Fever than any other citizen. I'm
betting there's a laundry list of people who wouldn't
mind seeing him and his ranch fail."

Wyatt nodded. "I'm with Zane on this. If someone's
holding a grudge against Otis, there's no better way to
hurt him than by hurting the person he most loves."

His words, spoken casually enough, had Jesse reeling
as a new thought struck.

Wyatt studied Jesse's ashen features. "You look
like you've just been struck by lightning. What're you
thinking?"

"It's something you just said. What better way to hurt
someone than to threaten the person they love? What
if the object of all these threats isn't Otis, or Amy, but
somebody else who cares about her—like me?"

"Okay." Wyatt gave this some thought. "So, who in
town would want to hurt you?"

Jesse shrugged. "The only people I can think of that
I've had any real trouble with are those bikers."

Wyatt shook his head. "Strangers."

"Strangers to us. But they could have learned my
name from anyone in town."

"Do you think they're angry enough to want to get to
you through Amy?"

"I don't know yet. But I intend to find out everything I can about them. Who they are, where they live and work, and what they were doing in town the night of the fight."

Jesse plucked his cell phone from his pocket and dialed the sheriff's office. After filling the lawman in on his thoughts, he listened before saying, "Thanks, Ernie."

He turned to his cousins. "The sheriff will see what he can find out about those bikers." He braked, turned the wheel sharply, and headed the truck in the direction they'd just traveled. "We need to go back to the saloon and see if Daffy or Vi can remember anything about them." He hissed out an impatient breath. "I wish now I'd filed a complaint against them the night of the fight. At least Ernie would have their names, addresses, maybe even where they work."

Wyatt was shaking his head. "I don't know, Jess. This just doesn't look like the sort of thing a couple of angry strangers would do. Why would they go to all the trouble of finding out about Amy and then set up these accidents? If they wanted to even the score, they could just follow you from the Fortune Saloon some night and leave you dead along the highway."

Zane shrugged. "Maybe they're afraid of facing him in another fight."

"As I recall," Wyatt said with a grin, "they'd have wiped the floor with him if you and I hadn't stepped in to help."

"I was doing fine."

At Jesse's offended tone, Wyatt and Zane grinned.

"Okay, Superman." Zane slapped Jesse on the back. "Next time we'll just stand back and let you rid the world of all the evil villains."

That had Jesse joining in the laughter. "Okay. I'll admit I was glad to have you guys lending a hand."

"You mean a fist," Zane said, still laughing.

"Not to mention a jaw." Wyatt touched a hand to his jaw and pretended to wince.

That only made them laugh all the harder.

It was, Jesse realized, good to be able to laugh, considering all that was going on in his life.

And for that he had Coot to thank. Though he wasn't quite ready to believe that his cousins could ever become his best friends again, there was no denying that it was nice to have someone to share his concern over all the strange things happening.

Jesse adjusted his sunglasses. "Since we're going to be quizzing Daffy and Vi about what they know about those bikers, we may as well have lunch there."

Zane nodded in agreement. "Especially since I passed up Dandy's breakfast. Wyatt was smart enough to bring part of his along for the ride, but right now my stomach's so empty, it wouldn't matter if Vi was serving raw steer, I'd order a plate of it."

"Now this is much better'n raw steer." Zane took a big bite of his burger.

"You mean it isn't raw?" Jesse studied the red meat oozing blood.

Zane took another bite. "I like it rare."

"Rare is one thing. That looks like Vi never even bothered to kill it before serving it."

Zane ignored him and polished off his lunch in a couple of satisfying bites.

When the three were finished, Vi and Daffy approached the table.

"You wanted to talk to us about those nasty bikers?" Daffy glanced around to make certain that no one at the nearby tables was in need of a coffee refill.

"Just to see if there's anything you can recall. Something they might have said that would give a hint as to where they work or where they were headed that night."

Daffy gave a shake of her head. "Honey, the only thing I know for certain about them is that if they ever show their faces in our place again, I'm calling Sheriff Wycliff right away."

Jesse patted her hand. "That's what I'd recommend, Daffy. And after you phone him, phone me. I'd relish a chance to ask them a few questions."

When he got to his feet Vi said, "folks in town have already heard what happened to Amy."

Her sister nodded. "I heard Delia Cowling telling some folks that now that Amy has aligned herself with the McCords to hunt old Coot's lost fortune, she'll have to expect to deal with the curse. Most folks around here figure she brought this on herself."

"Brought this..." Jesse stared around at the familiar faces. "Where is Delia? I'll give that old gossip a piece of my mind."

"Now, honey." Violet laid a hand over his. "If you confront her, you'll just add to her self-importance."

He was beyond hearing. When he spotted the self-proclaimed town historian sitting with Rowe Stafford, Harding Jessup, and Orley Peterson, he stormed over to their table. The four looked up.

"Well." Delia sipped her tea before saying, "We were just talking about you."

"I'll bet you were." His tone was low with anger. "Let's get something clear. I don't believe in the curse. What happened to Amy Parrish is neither supernatural nor accidental."

"You don't say?" Delia set down her cup with a clatter.

"You heard me. This was no accident. It was a deliberate attempt to hurt her. And I mean to find out who's behind it and why."

The mayor pushed aside the last of his lunch. "If I were you, I'd be very careful about saying such things without proof."

"Oh, I'll have proof."

"Don't you think that ought to be Ernie Wycliff's job?"

"I do. And I've already told the sheriff how I feel. But I intend to do what I can to lend a hand."

"As mayor, I must advise you to step aside and let the law handle this, Jesse."

"As a...friend of Amy's, I'm afraid I can't do that, Rowe."

Delia hadn't missed that slight hesitation. Her black-bird eyes looked sharper than ever, while her tone was sugar-sweet. "My, my. Does Otis Parrish know about your...friendship with his daughter?"

"I'm sure he'll hear about it before I'm halfway home." Jesse turned and headed toward the door, where Wyatt and Zane stood waiting and watching.

He could feel every pair of eyes in the room following his movements. His jaw was clenched so hard his teeth ached.

Before he was halfway to the truck, the saloon was buzzing about the latest proof that quick-tempered cowboy Jesse McCord was building up a head of steam and headed toward a satisfying no-holds-barred fight with someone, anyone, in order to clear the air.

CHAPTER SIXTEEN

———◆◆◆———

Jesse?" Sheriff Wycliff's voice was punctuated with static over the cell phone. "The state police sent an investigative team to the Parrish ranch to check out that beam. While they were at it I asked them to check that section of fencing that was down. They won't have any conclusive evidence for a couple of weeks, but one of the inspectors told me privately that it certainly looked deliberate rather than accidental."

"Thanks, Ernie. I appreciate the call. I know you'll relay their findings as soon as you can."

"You bet. In the meantime, I sure wish I could spare someone to keep an eye on Amy and her father, since I don't have anything at all in my files on those bikers. But with only Harrison helping me days, and his daughter, Charity, manning the phone at night, there's just nobody left."

"I understand. My crew and I will keep a close eye on things."

"I know you will. You call if you see anything out of place."

When the sheriff hung up, Jesse stood a moment, staring at the foothills of Treasure Chest in the distance. Then he made his way to his truck.

"Jesse." Amy stepped out onto the porch, carefully closing the door behind her. "We just got home from the clinic." She glanced over her shoulder. "Dad's asleep. He's having an awful reaction to the latest treatment."

"I'm sorry." He motioned toward the path leading to the barn. "Let's walk and talk."

As she moved along beside him, Amy kept her gaze averted. "Sheriff Wycliff talked to us about the accidents. Dad said he doesn't know anybody who would want to hurt us or scare us."

"I talked to Ernie, too." Jesse stuck his hands in his back pockets to keep from reaching out to her. The need to hold her, to protect her, was almost overpowering. "He feels that the threats are real, and that you have to take steps to stay safe."

"I promised him that I'd be careful, and call him the minute I see anything out of the ordinary."

"I don't think that's enough."

At Jesse's words, she stopped. "What do you suggest?"

"That you and your father come and stay at our place." Seeing her mouth open to protest, he added quickly, "I know. It would be awkward for your father, but I think if you persuade him that it's what you want, he'll go along."

She gave a vehement shake of her head. "You know

how stubborn he is. My wanting something wouldn't change his mind. Besides, knowing his pride, I'd never put my father in a position of having to accept help from your family."

"To hell with your father's pride." Without thinking he caught her arm and felt the current of electricity that shot between them. He fought to keep the anger from his tone. "Listen to me, Amy. This wasn't meant to just hurt or scare. You could have been killed by that beam. Then there's that nighttime incident. We both believe it was deliberate. It could have been deadly."

She shook off his hand, though it cost her. "I won't deny that I'm afraid. And I don't want to fight with you, Jess. I know you care about us. But this just isn't going to happen. I'm not asking my father to leave his home. He's fighting for his life. And we're finally starting to bridge a chasm that's been between us for years. Now you're asking me to push him into accepting help from your family. It's all too much. I can't do it."

His eyes narrowed. "Can't? Or won't?"

She saw the hard, tight line of his mouth and wished with all her heart that she could find a way to reconcile the differences between them.

"I won't ask it of him, Jesse." Seeing his quick flash of temper she struggled to soften the blow. "But I do thank you for your offer."

He looked as though she'd just slapped him. The sorrow in his eyes had her fighting to keep her voice from breaking. "Now I'd better see to my chores before my dad wakes up."

Jesse watched her shove open the barn door. He wanted, more than anything, to drag her into his arms and tell her everything would be all right. But how could he say the words to her when he didn't really believe them?

Someone wanted to hurt her. He was certain of it. And though he wanted to toss her over his shoulder and drag her kicking and screaming to a place of safety, he was helpless to do more than watch her walk away.

Damn her father's stubborn pride. And damn the daughter who was just as tough. They were two of a kind.

He strode back to his truck, more determined than ever to find out what this was all about.

The woman he loved was in trouble, and he was feeling helpless to do anything to help her.

The woman he loved.

He stopped dead in his tracks and absorbed the shock to his system.

Yes, by God. It was time to stop denying the truth. The woman he loved. Hadn't he loved her for years while grieving the loss of her?

Well, she was back now. And in harm's way.

He didn't need the state police or Sheriff Wycliff to hold things together.

He'd do it himself.

He drove away in a cloud of dust, mulling a plan of action.

Amy poured herself a mug of spiced tea and carried it to the front porch. With the afghan around her, she sat and sipped and tried to let the cares of the day slip away. It wasn't easy. She and her father, though not close, had declared a sort of truce. He still refused to discuss his illness, but he had become resigned to allowing his daughter to see his weakness. He permitted her to help him to bed, to feed him when he was too weak to feed himself, to lay out his clothes. Beyond that, their only common bond was the ranch. And the memory of the woman they'd both loved.

"Oh, Mom." She closed her eyes.

Though her father had danced around these frightening, annoying incidents, declaring them more a puzzle than a danger, he was willing to discuss any problems she had with the operation of the ranch. So they discussed milk production, and the cost of feed from Orley Peterson, which offset what they had harvested. They talked about replacing the weatherstripping on the doors and windows, and how much they would pay Stan Novak each month for the repair of the damage from the fallen beam. It would take them six months to completely pay off that debt.

More than that, her father had spoken about her mother. She'd waited so long to hear him express any feelings of love for the woman who held such a special place in her heart. He hadn't said much.

"I miss Sarah." He'd said it with a sigh, and then, realizing what he'd admitted, he'd added, "You know, girl, I never really appreciated her until she was gone."

Hearing it, Amy had fought back tears.

Why had it taken him so long to say those words?

She was relieved that her father had finally fallen asleep. He'd had a really tough afternoon after his latest treatment.

She drained her cup and tipped her head back with a sigh. A sliver of moon gleamed in the night sky. A canopy of stars looked close enough to touch. She wished she could just drift among them, high above this world of worry and work.

A silly, foolish wish.

She hurried inside and deposited her cup in the sink, then pulled on a warm parka before hurrying out to check the barn before turning in for the night.

Ordinarily she wouldn't bother. The cows and horses weren't going anywhere. Nor the barn cats. But she'd promised Jesse that she would take extra precautions.

Jesse.

She hated that she'd sent him away hurt and angry. But what he was asking of her was impossible. She'd meant what she'd said to him. She had no intention of asking her father to put aside his pride and take help from the McCords. This illness was enough of a blow to his dignity.

Still, it rankled that she and Jesse had parted in anger.

It wasn't the first time. But right now, when they'd been working so hard at repairing the rift, it was even harder to bear.

She absorbed a quick blow to her heart at all the turmoil whirling inside her mind as she slid open the barn door and stepped inside. In a purely reflexive manner she glanced toward the high, steepled roof, where a new beam had been installed by Stan Novak's crew. Just then, out of the corner of her eye, she saw movement in one of the empty stalls. Her head swiveled in time to see the tall figure of a man getting to his feet.

"No!" She let out a yelp and reached for a pitchfork. Before she could wield it like a weapon Jesse closed the distance between them and caught her wrist.

"Jesse." His name came out in a whoosh of air. "Oh, God, Jesse."

"Sorry." Seeing her distress, he tossed aside the pitchfork and gathered her close, running his hands over her hair in an effort to soothe. "I didn't mean to frighten you."

"Frighten me?" She pushed free of his arms to look into his eyes. "You scared me half to death. My poor heart nearly stopped. What are you doing here?"

He was wearing that cocky grin that always did such strange things to her heart. A grin, and not much more. He'd shucked his shirt and boots, and was barefoot and naked to the waist. His faded denims rode low on his hips. A lifetime of ranch chores had left him more toned than any physical fitness expert. Just looking at him made her mouth water.

"Since you wouldn't move over to my ranch, I thought I'd just settle in here and keep an eye on things."

"Settle in...?" She huffed out a breath. "You were planning on sleeping in the barn?"

"It wouldn't be the first time." His smile grew. "I seem to remember you sleeping here with me a time or two."

Her heart gave another quick jolt. If the sight of all that muscled flesh wasn't enough, the reminder of what they'd shared had her breath backing up in her throat.

"You're..." She was at a loss for words. "You're crazy. You can't just give up your bed and move into the barn permanently."

"I never said it would be forever. Just until we find out who's trying to get our attention, and why."

"That could take weeks. Months. In the meantime, do you expect to just commute back and forth between your ranch and mine?"

He kept his eyes steady on hers. "If that's what it takes to keep you safe."

"Oh, Jesse." She felt a lump growing in her throat, and she knew if she wasn't careful she might find herself weeping at any moment. "You can't do this."

"Who's going to stop me?"

She took a step back and stiffened her spine. "I am. I'm ordering you to leave."

"Just like that?"

"Just like that."

There was a moment of silence, and Amy watched a flicker of emotion cross his face. In the gleam of moonlight, she caught the half-smile that curved his lips. She recognized that look. Not just humor, but determination. He was digging in his heels. How could she have forgotten that Jesse liked nothing better than a challenge? And she'd just tossed down the gauntlet.

"All right, Amy." He crossed his arms over his chest. "Make me leave."

She gaped at him.

"Throw me off your property."

"You know I can't physically remove you."

"Then I guess you'd better come up with a better way to persuade me. Maybe you'd like to kiss me until I'm too weak to remember why I'm here."

Oh, it was so tempting. "Are you laughing at me?"

He relaxed his features until there was no hint of a smile. "What if I am?"

"I'm not fooled by that pose, McCord." Her voice rose fractionally. "You think you're so smart."

He held out his hands, palms up. "I'm just trying to be agreeable."

"Like hell." She slapped his hand and assumed her best teacher voice. "You're playing a cat-and-mouse game. And I refuse to be the mouse."

"Okay. I'll be the mouse. You can be the cat." He leaned a hip against the wooden rail of the stall. "Go ahead, Ms. Parrish. Make your first move. Pounce."

When she stood perfectly still, his hand suddenly snaked out, snagging her wrist.

"Time's up. Now it's my turn. And believe me, I know how to pounce." With a growl in his throat he dragged her close.

"Jesse, don't you dare…"

His mouth covered hers, swallowing her protest.

Splinters of fire and ice collided along her spine, leaving her trembling. She'd never forgotten the feel of that hard, sculpted body pressed to hers. It was the most exquisite torture.

His lips moved over hers, seducing, sending her pulse racing. When his mouth left hers to explore her neck, her throat, she closed her eyes and gave herself up to the pure pleasure of the moment.

"Why are you wearing all these clothes?" He slid the parka from her shoulders before drawing her close and raining kisses across her cheek to her ear, where he plunged his tongue inside, driving her half mad with need.

"Jesse."

It was all she could manage before he gathered her firmly into his arms and kissed her long and slow and deep, while his hands, those clever, work-worn hands, began a lazy exploration of her body. When his thumbs found her nipples, they stroked until, her breathing ragged, she pushed away, dragging air into her starving lungs.

"Oh. That's right." His lips curved. "I'm supposed to leave. That is, if that's what you really want."

"You devil." She couldn't think. What she wanted and what she knew she ought to do were in direct conflict. She needed to send him away. It was the sensible thing. But now that he'd touched her, and kissed her, and had her fully aroused, there was nothing else she wanted but him. Just him. The thought of giving in to her desire had her mind clouding, her heart beating overtime.

"You were saying?" His grin was back, causing her poor heart to stutter.

"What I want…" Need won out over sense. She'd never had a lick of sense where Jesse McCord was concerned. "Is the same thing you want, and you know it."

Feeling bold, she lifted a hand to the buttons of her old denim work shirt.

Jesse's eyes followed every movement.

She slipped the shirt from her shoulders, revealing a nude, lace-edged bra that barely covered her breasts. "So, if you've had a change of heart, McCord, speak now, or suffer the consequences. But I warn you, if you try to leave here, I'll have to kill you."

This was one of the things he'd always loved about her. The way she lifted her chin, defying any challenge. There had always been a fearlessness in Amy Parrish that spoke to a brashness in his own soul.

He managed a husky laugh, though it nearly choked him. The sight of all the cool, pale flesh had the blood draining from his head and rushing to another part of his anatomy.

"I'd be a fool to risk death. Do with me what you will, Ms. Parrish."

With a laugh she wrapped her arms around his waist and ran hot, wet kisses down his chest to the flat planes of his stomach.

She felt his muscles quiver before he clamped his hands at her hips, lifting her off her feet.

With their eyes level, he covered her lips with his and whispered inside her mouth, "Woman, you know exactly how to drive me mad."

Very slowly he lowered her to her feet, allowing her body to brush his before fisting a hand in her hair. His mouth was almost bruising as he nearly devoured her with a kiss so intense she could do nothing more than hold on as he took her on a wild roller-coaster ride.

Oh, this was what she'd wanted. This was what she'd craved with a gnawing hunger and raw desire. A touch, a kiss that melted away all the years and the fears until they were nothing more than a blur of vague memories.

He kissed her until they were both gasping for air.

As she started to pull back he kissed her again. Inside her mouth he growled, "Before we're through, I'll make you forget everyone and everything except me. And this. Just this."

"How could I ever forget? I had the best teach..." Her words were cut off with a kiss that spun on and on until, driven by half-crazed need, he turned and drove her back against the rough door of the barn, his body straining in desperation against hers.

He lifted his head and fixed her with a look so hot, so fierce, she couldn't look away.

"No more teasing, Amy. No more jokes. Tell me you want this as much as I do."

She didn't hesitate this time. "I want this, Jess. I want you…"

His mouth closed over hers, stealing her words, her breath. Stealing her very heart.

CHAPTER SEVENTEEN

J esse." It was the only word Amy could manage as his mouth continued taking her higher with each kiss.

His body was pressed to hers, pinning her firmly against the door.

"Shh." He nibbled her lower lip while his hands, those clever, work-roughened hands, moved over her.

Despite the frigid air in the barn, her flesh was so hot she wondered that she didn't set off sparks and start a major fire.

This was what she'd wanted. What she'd hungered for. His hands on her. His mouth on hers. This knife-edge of excitement that had her breath burning her lungs, her pulse throbbing in her temples.

Jesse unhooked her bra and watched the lace drift to the floor. His lips curved into a wicked grin. "You've moved up in the world. What happened to those plain white cotton underthings?"

"In case you haven't noticed, I've grown up."

"Oh, yeah. I've noticed. It's not something I could ignore." His hands dipped to the snap at her waist, and her faded jeans joined the rest of her clothes.

His smile grew. "Why, Miss Parrish, is that a thong?"

"A gift to myself when I started teaching school."

He roared with laughter as he stripped it aside. "I'll never be able to look at you dressed like a schoolmarm again without seeing this in my mind."

His laughter faded as he lowered his head and covered her mouth with his, while his hands moved over her, slowly driving her mad.

She needed to get her hands on him. Her fingers played with the hair on his chest and she thrilled at the ripple of muscle beneath her touch as her hands moved lower, across his stomach. When she reached for the metal button at his waist, he helped her, until his clothes joined hers at their feet.

At last they were free, with no more barriers. Free to feel, to taste, to savor. And they did. With murmured words and soft sighs they lost themselves in the pure pleasure of the moment.

As his mouth moved over hers, he sensed that this kiss was different from all the others. Always before she'd held back, as though unwilling to admit to the depth of her feelings. Now she poured herself into it. Heart. Mind. Soul.

That freed him to do the same. To show her, with each touch, each press of his mouth to hers, just how much she meant to him.

His hands at her shoulders were almost bruising as he gathered her close, desperate to feel her, flesh to flesh, all the while savoring her lips. He couldn't get enough of the wild, sweet taste of her. The press of her body to his had the blood roaring in his temples. The need to take her hard and fast nearly staggered him. In order to slow down he changed the angle of the kiss and felt the quick jolt of nerves race through his system.

"Do you know how long I've dreamed of this?" He drew back, his eyes steady on hers.

She saw the hint of danger in those eyes and felt a sudden flare of heat deep inside. She'd always loved this dark, dangerous side of Jesse. "How long?"

"Every day since you left." He ran hot, wet kisses down her throat, sending delicious sensations skittering along her spine. "And when I saw you again, the dreams were back, stronger than ever."

She drew his head up, needing to feel his mouth on hers. "Kiss me, Jesse."

He did as she asked, with a hunger that had their hearts thundering.

"I need you to touch me, Jesse. Take me." She hated that her voice was trembling, but there was no way to hide the need.

"Oh, I intend to. But I won't be rushed. I've waited too long. Wanted this too much."

He dipped his head and closed his lips around one erect nipple, nibbling and suckling until she felt her legs buckle.

"Jess." She clung to his waist and would have fallen if she weren't pinned between his body and the rough wood of the barn.

"Afraid?"

"No." She tried to laugh, but it sounded more like a sob.

"You ought to be." His eyes held hers. "You can't even begin to imagine all the things I've dreamed of doing with you. To you."

Her chin came up in the defiant way he'd always loved. "Show me."

His strong, clever hands began moving over her, driving her and himself slowly mad.

She wrapped her arms around his waist. He could hear her labored breathing, the pounding of her heart like a runaway herd of cattle.

With teeth and tongue and fingertips he moved over her at will, kissing her face, her throat, teasing her nipples until she moaned and writhed, desperate for release from the madness that had overtaken her.

She let her head fall back, giving him easier access.

Except for their sighs, and the sound of their labored breathing, the night had grown still. The air around them seemed charged with the same electricity that flowed between them.

He pressed soft, feathery kisses down her neck, pausing at the sensitive hollow between her neck and shoulder. When she shivered and sighed, moving catlike in his arms, he moved lower, to circle her breast with his tongue.

Her purr of pleasure had his pulse rate climbing.

Just as she began to relax in his arms he found her hot and wet. Without warning he took her up and over the first peak. At her stunned expression, he gave her no time to catch her breath as he took her higher, then higher still.

She was wonderful to watch. He saw her eyes widen in surprise, then seem to glaze over as the waves of sensation rolled over her, carrying her along in their tide.

"Jesse." Her eyes snapped open and she clutched at him as he brought her to the edge yet again.

Her arousal deepened his own, and he knew that he couldn't hold out much longer.

Heat rose up between them, pearling their flesh, clogging their throats.

His hands cupped her hips, dragging her firmly against him. He lifted her and she wrapped her legs around him as he drove himself into her. That unleashed a firestorm of passion that took them over completely. Their breathing shallow, their heartbeats thundering, their bodies slick, they began to move, to climb, as though scaling a high, sheer cliff.

The world beyond this barn no longer mattered. A night owl called to its mate. A horse nickered in a nearby stall. They were beyond hearing. The perfume of fresh-cut hay, the earthy scents of cattle and dung drifted on the air, but they took no notice.

There was only this man, this woman, and this incredible need that had them climbing toward a distant star. With shuddering breaths and urgent whispers they moved to a rhythm as old as time.

"Amy. Look at me. I need to see you."

At the sound of her name she struggled to focus on his face. All she could see were his eyes, hot and fierce, fixed on her. All she could hear was his heartbeat, thundering wildly, matching hers.

"Jesse. Dear God, Jesse."

With unbelievable strength they moved together, climbing ever higher until, in one last burst of strength, they reached the pinnacle.

Soaring through space, they shattered into millions of glittering pieces as they drifted back to earth.

"You okay?" Jesse pressed his forehead to hers, waiting for his world to settle.

"Fine." It was all she could manage over a throat clogged with tears. To hold them at bay, she lifted a hand to his cheek.

Jesse had always been able to take her to places nobody else could even imagine. She'd wondered if, after their years apart, it would be the same. Now she had her answer.

He felt so good here in her arms. She thought she could stay this way all night, just so, flesh to flesh, heartbeat to heartbeat.

Pure heaven.

He moved his head a fraction so he could see her face. "Sorry. I didn't mean to go so fast."

"Fast?" She managed a throaty laugh. "If you'd made me wait any longer, I'd have died."

"I feel like I already did." He brushed his mouth over hers. "I've died and gone to heaven. And I don't ever want to go back to earth."

She wrapped her arms around his neck and kissed him long and slow and deep.

When at last she lifted her head she muttered, "Jesse?"

"Hmm?"

"Would you mind moving a little? This barn wood is awfully rough on my bare backside."

"Oh." He chuckled. "Sorry about that." Still holding

her in his arms he turned and carried her to the stall, lowering her to his bedroll in a mound of hay.

"Umm." When he'd settled himself beside her she sighed. "Much better."

"Let me make it up to you." He drew her close in his embrace and began rubbing her back.

"Oh, that's so nice."

"I'm sure I can do better." With his hands still massaging her back, he began running nibbling kisses across her face. Against her temple he whispered, "Baby, you still rock my world."

"I'm glad." She found herself smiling dreamily. She turned to him, wrapping her arms around him. She buried her face against his chest and breathed him in. There was something so wonderfully, potently male about him. Everything about him was achingly familiar.

"Why?" His fingers combed through her hair.

"Why what?" She was still floating, still drifting among the stars, barely able to focus.

"Why are you glad?"

"Oh." Her smile grew. "Because you rock my world, too."

"I do?"

"Um-hmm."

When he lowered his mouth to her throat, she sucked in a quick breath. "That tickles."

"Good. Part of my plan to see if I can get you to let me have my way with you again."

"Oh, right. This soon?" She looked up. Though he was grinning, she could see the glint of fire in those eyes. "Who do you think you are? Superman?"

He threw back his head and laughed. "Since I've been accused of that twice lately, I think it only fair that I try to prove I can live up to that name."

"Careful. I might believe you're serious."

"Believe it. I'm about to show you all the amazing, superhuman things I can do, as long as you're not in any hurry to send me home."

"You still want to stay?"

"I do." He had that look in his eye. Not as hungry as before, but more wolfish. Hunger laced with knowledge. "I feel I ought to redeem myself."

"Redeem?" Her fingers played with the hair on his chest, and he felt his stomach muscles tighten at her mere touch.

"I was...eager. Too hungry. Starved, in fact. I moved too fast. Now that we got that out of the way, I'd like to show you that I can take my time."

"Really?" She couldn't help laughing at his serious tone. "You need to prove that you have staying power?"

"Something like that. Especially since I plan on being here all night." He rubbed his mouth over hers before bringing his lips to the sensitive column of her throat, and was rewarded with her sudden intake of breath. "I thought I'd show you..."

He began nibbling his way down her body, between her breasts, down her stomach, and felt the way her heart took a sudden quick bounce before beginning to race as his lips moved lower still. "...All the things I've been wanting to do with you since you returned to Gold Fever."

"Jess..." The protest died on her lips as he followed his words with bold action.

"Oh, Jess." That was all she could manage before being taken on a slow, glorious ride to paradise.

At the sound of a rooster crowing up in the hayloft, Amy stirred. The first thing she saw when she opened her eyes was Jesse, leaning on one elbow, staring down at her.

"Morning." She yawned, stretched, then went very still as he bent to press a kiss to her lips.

"That's just about the nicest sound in the world."

"What is?"

"Your voice. All warm and sleepy." He brushed a strand of hair off her forehead. "And seeing you like this is just about the prettiest sight in the world."

"Careful. You keep up those compliments and I won't be able to get my head through the doorway."

"Then I'll just break down some timbers to make way for my favorite girl."

That had her shaking her head. "Who are you, lavishing praise like this, and what have you done with that brash cowboy I once knew?"

"Jesse McCord is a changed man. In the space of one night some gorgeous female kissed away all his rough edges and turned him into a sweet-talking gentleman."

"Think it will last?"

"I'm betting on it."

"We'll just have to see." She sat up and spied her clothes lying in a heap near the barn door.

He snagged her wrist before she could stand. "Where're you going?"

"Time to get up and dressed and ready for the morning."

He allowed his gaze to move slowly over her. "I like you better like this."

"I just bet you do, cowboy. That's why I'd better get dressed before you get any ideas."

"Give me five more minutes."

Amy laughed. "That's what you said last night. A number of times, in fact. But you know what happened each time I gave you five more minutes."

"Yeah. And it's about to happen again." He drew her into his arms and kissed her until she could feel her bones begin to soften, and her resolve begin to slip.

"Jesse."

"You know you want to."

"Mind reader." With a sigh she wrapped her arms around his neck and gave herself up to the pleasure he was offering.

Amy and Jesse lay in a tangle of arms and legs, pleasantly sated.

"You warm enough?" Jesse lay with one arm behind his head, the other around Amy, who was snuggled against his chest.

"Any warmer and I'd set this hay on fire."

They both laughed before Amy sat up. "Jesse, I need to say something."

At the seriousness of her tone he sat up beside her and took her hand in his, linking their fingers. "Okay."

She stared down at their joined hands. "I can understand that my sudden departure right after graduation was a shock to you."

"That's an understatement..."

She touched a finger to his lips. "It was a shock to me,

too. My aunt was my mother's only family, and I couldn't let Mom drive up to Helena alone."

"Of course you couldn't. But..."

Again she stopped him. "I never thought we'd be gone the entire summer, but Aunt Morgan's illness lingered, and then..." Amy shrugged. "She was gone, and it was time for college to begin, and I found myself swamped with new classes and new friends, and grieving the loss of my aunt and the loss of you..."

It was Jesse's turn to still her words. "You wouldn't have had to lose me if you hadn't shut me out, Amy. I tried to find out where you were..."

"You couldn't have tried too hard. I told you everything in my letter."

He shook his head. "There was no letter."

She looked bewildered. "It may have happened in the middle of the night, but I'm sure I didn't dream it. I wrote you."

"And I'm telling you I never got a letter from you."

"Look, I get that there's been a lot of time between then and now. Time can blur a lot of images." She paused, thinking of all the hours she'd spent waiting by the phone, by the mailbox, waiting, hoping, dreaming. Crying her heart out.

Her tone hardened. "If you insist that you never got my letter, all I can do is insist that I wrote you. Are you implying that I'm lying?"

"I'm not calling you a liar, Amy. I'm just telling you that I never got a letter."

Though it didn't make any sense, she took one look at the exhaustion in his eyes and let out a huge sigh of exasperation, fully aware that this was going nowhere

fast. "Can we talk about this another time? I really have
to get dressed. Dad will be awake soon, and he'll need
some breakfast."

His lips curved into a dangerous smile and the hungry
glint returned to his eyes. "What about what I need? I
love it when you get all heated with temper."

At his teasing tone, her smile returned. "You're a very
greedy man."

"Can you blame me? For years I've been on a starva-
tion diet. Now I have this glorious, wonderful feast, and I
can't seem to stop myself."

"Speaking of feasts..." Coming to a sudden decision, she pushed herself free of his arms and crossed the
barn before picking up her clothes. "You're coming in to
breakfast."

Jesse got to his feet, unmindful of his nakedness. "Are
you serious?"

She turned and sucked in a breath at the beauty of his
body. He was all muscle and sinew from years of tough
ranch chores. And that fabulous body was all hers, she
thought with a sudden shock of recognition. To enjoy as
she had all night.

She stepped into her jeans and buttoned her denim
work shirt. "I guess, if you're going to spend your nights
in our barn..."

"With you."

She looked over. "If you're going to spend your nights
in our barn with me," she added for emphasis, "I won't
sneak around behind my father's back. We're not a couple
of kids now, Jesse. I intend to be honest and up front with
my dad."

"He might decide to throw me out."

"He might. Are you up for it?"

He tugged on his jeans and boots and plaid shirt before crossing to her. Tipping up her chin he brushed his lips over hers. Then he gave her one of those heart-stopping smiles. "I'd walk through fire for you, Amy. And I'm guessing it won't get much hotter than what I'm about to face in your house. If you're ready, so am I."

Together they walked hand in hand out of the barn and up the path to the house.

CHAPTER EIGHTEEN

J esse paused in the doorway while Amy moved around the kitchen, snapping on lights, cranking up the heat.

At the sound of her father's voice calling to her, she turned. "Make yourself comfortable while I help my dad through his morning routine."

Alone in the kitchen, Jesse began opening cupboards until he located Amy's stash of pots and pans. Then he rummaged through the refrigerator and hauled out eggs, cheese, bread, and assorted vegetables. Rolling up his sleeves, he set to work, humming to himself.

By the time Otis Parrish and his daughter walked into the kitchen, the table had been set and Jesse was busy turning sausage links in a heavy skillet.

"What the hell...?" Otis stopped dead in his tracks.

"Morning, Mr. Parrish." Jesse gave him a quick smile before turning his attention to the omelet he had cooking in another pan.

"You made breakfast?" Amy peered over his shoulder. "Oh, that smells fabulous."

"It'll taste even better." He winked. "If you get that toast, everything's ready."

He crossed to the table and began dividing the omelet into three portions. When he noted that Otis was still standing in the doorway he added, "Better enjoy this while it's still hot."

Giving Amy's father no chance to argue, he returned to the stove and began scooping sausages onto a platter.

"And you made coffee." Amy breathed in the wonderful fragrance before filling three cups and placing one beside each plate.

When Otis dropped weakly onto his chair, she added lamely, "Dad, I hope you don't mind, but I've invited Jesse to join us for breakfast. Of course, I invited him before I realized he'd be the one doing the cooking."

The two shared a grin, while Otis merely glared.

As Amy picked up her fork her father slammed a hand down on the table. "Stop this foolishness and tell me what this is about. You said a McCord was here. You didn't tell me he'd be in my house, making himself at home."

"I tried to tell you, Dad. Jesse's worried about the accidents..."

Jesse held up a hand to stop her. "Mr. Parrish, I talked things over with Sheriff Wycliff, and he agrees with me that these weren't accidents. Someone is deliberately targeting you and your daughter."

"What business is that of yours?"

"You're my neighbor. That ought to be enough of a reason. But there's another. I care about your daughter. What happens to her is my business."

"Are you suggesting that I can't take care of my own?"

"I never said that. But right now, your first priority has to be taking care of your health."

He saw Otis wince, and he wished there had been an easier way to say it. But there it was, laid bare. Now Otis would have to deal with it.

"So, while you're busy regaining your health, I've decided to do what the sheriff and his deputy can't, for lack of time and manpower."

"By sitting in my kitchen and eating my food?"

The older man's temper had Jesse grinning. "Not exactly what I had in mind. But since I'm here, why don't you taste my special omelet and see if you still object."

Otis glowered. "I don't need some smart-mouthed McCord telling me what to do."

"Suit yourself."

"Dad, the least you can do is eat something." Amy tasted the egg mixture and gave a sigh of pure pleasure. "Oh, this is delicious. Where'd you learn to cook like this, Jess?"

"I guess all those years of Dandy's good cooking just rubbed off. Once in a while I look over his shoulder, just to get an idea of how to stay alive if I'm up at one of the bunkhouses during a storm. I haven't mastered his corn bread yet, but I can get by with the essentials, like eggs and meat and potatoes."

Out of the corner of his eye he saw Otis take a taste of his omelet. Though the older man never said a word, he soon cleaned his plate. Then he sat back, sipping strong, excellent coffee, his eyes narrowed on Jesse.

The color had returned to the older man's skin. Skin

that just minutes earlier had been the color of chalk. The food had given him renewed energy.

"How long have you been here, McCord?"

"Since last night."

Otis set his cup down with a clatter. "You spent the night under my roof?"

"I slept in the barn, Mr. Parrish."

Just as Otis began to relax, Amy added, "That's where I found him when I went out to check on the herd."

His gaze shifted to his daughter. "Last night."

Her chin came up in that infuriating way she'd had since she was no more than a toddler. She'd spent a lifetime challenging him and his authority.

"That's right."

"And when did you come back to the house, girl?"

"This morning." She met his eyes, refusing to look away.

He hissed out a breath. "You know how I feel about the McCords."

She nodded. "You've always known how I feel about Jesse."

He shot a quick glance at Jesse's face, then returned his attention to his daughter. "You know I could order you to leave my house, girl."

"I know." She held her breath.

"And maybe I would, if I didn't need you right now."

Need. Not love. His choice of words was an arrow through her heart.

He took no notice of her pain. Now that he'd given in to his anger, he couldn't seem to stop himself.

"I never thought I'd see the day that my daughter would give up the warmth and comfort of her own bed to sleep in the barn like an animal. With a *McCord*." He spat the word like a curse.

"It's my choice."

Amy watched as her father shoved away from the table. With an effort he got to his feet, leaning heavily on the back of his chair. He fixed Jesse with a look of pure hatred.

"You may be a good enough cook. But you'll never be good enough for my daughter. And if you know what's good for you, you'll never set foot in my house again."

He turned and walked slowly, painfully from the room.

At the table, neither of them spoke until they heard the slam of the bedroom door.

Jesse reached across the table and caught Amy's hand. It was cold as ice.

"I'm sorry, baby."

She shook her head. "Don't be. This isn't just about you. You heard what he said. He needs me. That's all. Just need. Well, that's not good enough for me. When he's strong enough to get along without me, I'll be gone again. And this time for good."

"Amy..."

She pulled her hand free. "Don't, Jess." She managed a weak smile. "You were right. That was an excellent breakfast. You cooked, so I'll clean up."

He walked to her chair and pressed his hands on her shoulders, holding her when she tried to stand.

"Sit and enjoy your coffee. I'll have this mess cleaned up in no time."

She was too drained to argue.

True to his word, in short order he had the kitchen gleaming.

When he'd hung the kitchen towel on a hook by the door, he crossed to her and kissed her forehead. "Time to head home and see to my chores. I'll see you tonight."

"You heard my dad."

"He said not to set foot in his house. He didn't say anything about the barn."

She merely nodded.

When she heard the sound of his truck, she stood and walked to the back door.

What had she done? At a time when her father was most vulnerable, she'd hit him with the hardest news of all. She'd let him know that she had chosen to give her love to the grandson of his enemy.

Her love.

She put a hand to her middle and leaned heavily on the door. She did love him, desperately, though she hadn't planned to. Instead of feeling good about the knowledge, she was feeling more miserable than ever.

No matter the outcome, she could see no happy ending to this situation.

Jesse drove like a man on a mission, sending up a cloud of dust as he sped along the dirt road leading to his ranch.

Otis Parrish was a hardheaded fool. Couldn't he see what his careless words were doing to his daughter? That he was fighting a deadly illness didn't give him the right to unload his temper on Amy. She'd already given up a career she loved to come home and take care of a thankless old man who seemed to enjoy picking a fight with her. How much more should she be asked to endure?

As he tore up the driveway and headed toward the

barn, he was forced to stand on the brakes when a vehicle came lumbering up from behind the barn.

"You idiot!" Jesse slammed out of the truck, itching for a fight.

Rafe leaned a head out the stake truck's window. "You ought to know by now that ranch implements have the right-of-way around here. Where's your brain this morning?"

Zane and Wyatt ambled out of the barn, trailed by Cal and Jimmy Eagle. All of them looked up as Rafe jumped out of the truck.

"Why should I bother to ask? You probably left your brain in the same place you've been parking your body. Over at the Parrish ranch."

That had everyone laughing, until Jesse grabbed Rafe by the front of his shirt and hauled him up until their faces were mere inches apart.

"What I do and where I sleep are none of your business."

Rafe slapped his hand away. "I don't see why I should be any different. Everybody in Gold Fever knows about you and Amy shacking up."

After building up a head of steam over Otis's treatment of Amy, Jesse's blood was hot to fight. And Rafe and his smart mouth made him the perfect target.

Jesse charged him, driving him back against the barn door. While the others watched in silence, Rafe brought up his knee, catching Jesse in the groin.

"Let that be a lesson, Jess. You fight me, you're going to regret it."

"Uh-oh." Wyatt turned to Zane. "I'm betting that got Jesse's attention. I wouldn't want to be Rafe now."

Zane shrugged. "I don't know about that. Rafe's got fifty pounds on Jesse. Ten says Jesse's going down for the count."

Wyatt dug into his pocket and held up a bill. "You're on."

Jesse threw a quick, hard punch to Rafe's chin, snapping his head back.

In retaliation Rafe brought a fist into Jesse's gut, doubling him over. When Jesse straightened, he shook his head to clear it before pummeling the stocky man with a series of blows that had both men struggling for breath.

While they fought, several other wranglers stepped out of the barn and crowded around, making bets on the outcome.

Jimmy Eagle shook his head, refusing to get caught up in the gamble.

Rafe landed another solid blow before Jesse lunged forward, taking him to the ground. The two men rolled over once, then twice, each getting in their licks.

Jesse was the first to regain his footing. He stood, wheezing in shallow breaths as he fought to clear his head. Seeing Rafe sitting in the dirt, blood oozing from a cut over his eye, he reached out a hand to help him up.

Rafe stared at his outstretched hand for several long seconds before slapping it aside and easing slowly to his feet.

His anger spent, Jesse wiped an arm over the blood oozing from a cut over his eye, smearing it down the side of his face. "You pack a mean punch, Rafe."

The wrangler shot him a look of pure venom. "Some of us didn't grow up on a big, fancy ranch, having people around to watch our backs. I learned to make sure my first punch did the job, in case there wasn't a second one."

Cal stepped between them. "Fun's over, boys. Time to get to work."

As Jesse turned toward the house, Wyatt slapped him on the back. "As far as fights go, it was okay, though I'd have landed a few more blows before calling it quits."

Laughing, Zane added, "Me, too. Still, this was a great way to start the day."

When they stepped into the mudroom, the three took pains to wipe their boots and wash their hands.

As they turned away from the sink Wyatt gave a quick shake of his head. "Uh-uh. I think you'd better get rid of the blood before you set foot into the kitchen, just in case Aunt Cora happens to be there."

Jesse followed his cousin's advice and winced when he touched the cut over his eye.

Zane grinned. "I think it's your turn to have a lovely shiner."

"Won't be the first time." Jesse punched his shoulder good-naturedly.

The three were grinning as they walked into the kitchen. Seeing it empty, they relaxed and helped themselves to the last of the hot coffee.

Wyatt leaned a hip against the counter. "So, does Otis Parrish know you were there?"

Jesse frowned. "Otis knows and is beyond furious."

Just then Cora stepped into the kitchen and stopped at the sight of her nephew's dirt-stained clothes and his face bearing bloody cuts. "Jesse. Are you saying Otis Parrish did this to you?"

"No, Aunt Cora." Jesse set down his coffee mug and poured a mug for his aunt. "I think I'd better explain."

He led the way to the big table and sat, waiting until

they were settled around it before filling them in on all that had happened.

Nobody spoke until Jesse had finished.

It was Cora who said, "How long do you think you can continue working the ranch here, and then spending your nights in the Parrish barn?"

Jesse shrugged. He'd been asking himself the same question.

"We could spell him."

At Wyatt's words, they turned to stare at him.

Wyatt glanced at Zane. "We could take on more of your chores during the day. Or, we could take turns sleeping in the barn. And we can certainly ask the crew here to keep an eye on the Parrish ranch whenever they're nearby."

Jesse shook his head. "I don't like the idea of asking everyone to do double duty."

Cora laid a hand over his. "That's what family does in time of trouble." She glanced around the table. "If Coot were here, I know he'd be proud of the way you three are coming together to solve this problem." She pushed away from the table. "I'll be in my studio if you need me. But I want Amy and Otis to know that they're welcome here."

Jesse brushed a kiss over her cheek. "Thanks, Aunt Cora. I doubt that Otis will accept your offer. But it will mean a lot to Amy."

When their aunt was gone, the three remained at the table, discussing their options.

Now that his anger was spent, the depth of Jesse's worry was obvious to both Zane and Wyatt.

When he finally made his way to his room to shower

and dress for the day, Wyatt and Zane bent their heads close.

"Jesse's a hardheaded cowboy. He really thinks he can handle all this alone, but he can't. Nobody can." Zane drained his cup and set it in the sink.

"You're right." Wyatt followed Zane from the house to the barn to begin their daily chores.

As they worked they made a pact. They would do all they could to lend a hand in whatever way possible until this crisis was resolved. Even if it meant that all of them had to go without sleep.

CHAPTER NINETEEN

———◆◆◆———

Y ou don't like my pot roast?" Dandy stared at Jesse's plate, still heaped with beef and garden vegetables and potatoes swimming in rich brown gravy. "It's always been one of your favorites."

"I'm just not hungry."

Dandy narrowed his eyes. "You sick? Or in love?"

Cora looked across the table at her nephew. "Aren't you feeling well, Jesse?"

"I'm fine, Aunt Cora."

Wyatt and Zane shared a private smile.

Cora pushed away from the table. "Dandy, we'll have our dessert in the great room when Amy joins us."

She left the room, trailed by her three nephews.

By the time Amy arrived they had already laid out the dozens of slips of yellowed paper and were busy trying to match them up.

"Sorry I'm late." Amy hurried across the room and paused to kiss Cora's cheek before greeting the others.

Jesse took her hand, linking his fingers with hers, relieved that he'd managed to talk her into continuing their treasure-hunt meetings. It was the perfect way to get her mind off her troubles.

"We've found a few more matches. Nothing earth-shattering, but we're definitely seeing a pattern. See this?" He held up the slips they'd already paired.

Amy's smile widened. "I'm so glad. I know, with enough time, we'll be able to figure out exactly where Coot was heading in his search."

Cora studied their joined hands and felt a lightness around her heart. She'd known, of course, that Jesse still carried a torch for Amy. What she hadn't been certain of, until now, was that it was reciprocal. The light in Amy's eyes was all the proof she needed to know that these two shared the same strong feelings.

Love.

It was what she wanted for each of her nephews. A love strong enough to see them through life's good times and bad.

She'd had her share of lovely romances. A suave, sophisticated museum director in Italy. A wild and reckless sculptor in Paris. The very thought had her smiling. But though she'd fancied herself in love any number of times, and had her heart broken more than once through the years, Cora had never experienced the sort of deep, soul-stirring love that her brother, Coot, had enjoyed with his beloved Annie, and it was one of her biggest regrets. That kind of love was rare indeed.

Amy glanced at Wyatt. "Have you done any more with that clear overlay?"

"Yeah." He moved it over the map and they studied it in silence.

"I don't think there's any doubt now." Amy traced a finger over the path he'd drawn from the slips of paper they'd matched. "Coot was definitely closing in on Treasure Chest Mountain."

"I have to agree with you, dear." Cora had to blink away the mist that suddenly sprang to her eyes. "I believe Coot is still showing us the way."

They paused in their work when Dandy entered with a tray of fudge brownies topped with vanilla ice cream and warm caramel sauce, along with a pot of coffee. After passing around the plates of dessert and cups of coffee, he left them alone.

"Oh." Amy took a first taste of brownie and sighed with pleasure. "Finding Coot's treasure would be a wonderful bonus. But for now, I'll settle for just this."

Jesse, sitting on the hearth with the warmth of the fire to his back, smiled in agreement. It wasn't the sweet confection he was admiring, but the woman facing him.

He was more than happy to give up another night's sleep to stay in her father's barn, as long as she was there to spend the night in his arms.

Jesse arrived home to find Wyatt and Zane waiting for him in the ranch kitchen. They had been talking quietly, heads bent in earnest conversation. They both looked up when he entered the room.

Wyatt studied Jesse's red-rimmed eyes and fresh growth of stubble. "You look like hell. Do you ever sleep?"

"Not if I can help it. What about you? Do you ever work? I saw the crew heading out when I drove in."

"You'll owe me an apology for that after you hear what I've dug up."

Jesse poured himself a mug of coffee and dropped down onto a kitchen chair. "Okay. What've you dug up?"

"On my world wanderings, I've met some...interesting characters. One of them, Archie, is a private detective and bounty hunter."

"A bounty hunter." Jesse came close to snickering, but seeing the intense look in his cousin's eye, he held himself back. "And what did this bounty hunter tell you?"

"He did a little sniffing around and got a lead on our bikers."

Jesse set down his mug with a clatter. "How'd he do what the law couldn't?"

"I didn't ask. All I know is that he found them."

"Where the hell are they?"

"Just listen." Wyatt held up a hand to silence him. "They claim someone contacted them online and invited them to Gold Fever to earn some serious money. When they got to town, Buck, the beefy guy who's the leader, received a call on his cell from someone who used an electronic device that modifies the voice. Buck couldn't tell if he was talking to a man or a woman, or even a human. He said it sounded like an android from some cheap sci-fi flick. He was asked if he and his buddies would be willing to kill someone for a great deal of money. They claim they flat-out refused. Then they were offered a sum of money to break a few of some cowboy's bones."

"Mine?" Jesse's eyes went wide.

Wyatt nodded. "They figured it was easy money. But Buck claimed that when Zane and I joined the fray, all bets were off. By the time we were through with them, our bikers decided to leave town without payment, and stated they would never be back."

"You believe them?" Jesse's coffee was forgotten.

Wyatt shrugged. "What reason would they have to lie?"

"Can your pal Archie find out who contacted them? And why?"

Wyatt gave a shake of his head. "He said it's like looking for the proverbial needle in a haystack. Using an Internet connection, it could be anybody, anywhere. So the better question is, who do you think it is? Who would want you dead?"

Jesse mulled that before saying softly, "I don't know. I'm sure I've made some enemies in my life, but I can't think of anybody who hates me enough to want me dead. And if it's me they're after, why are they using Amy?"

Wyatt glanced at Zane. "We think it's because she's your weakness. Now that their plan A failed, they've decided that they don't just want you dead, they want you to suffer."

"There's something else," Zane added. "Amy and her dad are completely isolated over at their place. Nobody around for miles."

"So whoever wants to get me finds a way to lure me to Amy's, then he knows exactly where to find me."

Wyatt's tone was low. "That's the way we figure it."

Zane nodded in agreement. "If our theory is correct, you're falling right into their trap. You've got to persuade Amy and her father to move over here until we find this madman."

Jesse gave a short laugh. "I'd have a better chance of seeing hell freeze over. Otis may be feeling weak, but not where we're concerned. If anything, his hatred is stronger than ever. And Amy won't leave him alone while he's fighting a serious illness." He stood, hoping a shave and a shower would help clear the thoughts that were spinning through his brain. "Since I can't afford to leave Amy alone at the mercy of whoever is doing this, it looks like I'll just have to be more careful while I'm at the Parrish ranch. At least until I figure out who wants me dead."

As he strode away, Wyatt and Zane watched with matching looks of concern.

Wyatt turned to Zane. "You ready to give up some sleep, cuz?"

"Won't be the first time." Zane picked up the camera that was never far from his reach. "I'll take first watch tonight. I've been meaning to try my new night lens. I hear the Parrish ranch has some great views of Treasure Chest Mountain."

"Keep your cell phone charged, and have my number and Sheriff Wycliff's on speed dial. You see anything suspicious, you call first and ask questions later."

The two conspirators parted to begin their morning chores.

The night had turned frigid. The truck's headlights illuminated a whirl of snowflakes dancing across the road, whipped into a frenzy by a bitter wind.

In Jesse's truck Amy cranked up the heater and huddled inside her parka. "I watched your aunt Cora's face tonight while we were working on Coot's trail. I'm so glad we're doing this, Jess. It's giving her such pleasure to be involved in her brother's treasure hunt."

He nodded thoughtfully. "I've noticed. I guess I was so caught up in the pain of my own loss, I forgot just how much Coot's death affected her. He was her big brother. The guy she always turned to. She has to miss him every day."

"I never heard how he died. I only know what the townspeople had to say. And most of them figure it was the curse."

"The curse." He huffed out a breath. "He was doing his usual thing, climbing around the foothills of Treasure Chest, when he fell. Probably the result of a rock slide, since there were a lot of loose rocks around him when we got to him."

"How did you know he was in trouble?"

"He phoned Cal on his cell. Didn't want to worry Cora. Said where he was, and that he'd taken a bad fall. Cal phoned Marilee Trainor for a medical backup, then we all headed out to the site of the fall. We were too late."

She heard the catch in his voice and laid a hand over his on the wheel.

They drove the rest of the way in silence. When they drove into her yard, Jesse stopped at the front porch.

She glanced over. "Why are you stopping here? You always park your truck behind the barn."

"The night's too cold for you to sleep in the barn tonight. You go ahead inside."

She drew close. "I'd rather sleep with you. We can generate enough heat to keep from freezing."

He chuckled against her temple. "Yeah. We're good at

that. But you need to sleep in a warm house tonight. In your own bed."

He stepped out of the truck and walked around to open her door. When they paused at the front door he drew her close for a quick, hard kiss, while the bitter wind blew swirls of snow in their faces.

Amy shivered. "You're right. It's too cold. Why don't you stay inside with me?"

He grinned. "It's bad enough that a McCord is sleeping in your father's barn every night. I won't add insult to injury by invading his home." He lingered over her mouth, wishing he could just ignore this damnable code of honor and take her up on her invitation. "Good night, Amy. Sleep well."

"Night, Jesse. Will you come up to the house for breakfast before you leave in the morning?"

He shook his head. "You said your father has another treatment tomorrow. No point in adding to his discomfort. Now," he said, turning her around, "be sure you lock your door."

He waited until he heard her throw the lock. Then he climbed back into the truck and drove it to the barn.

With the wind whistling around the roof and rustling the hay in the loft, it promised to be a long, cold night. Not that it mattered. As long as he could be here, close to Amy, keeping her safe from harm, he'd endure whatever discomfort the universe sent his way.

CHAPTER TWENTY

Amy checked on her father, relieved to find him snoring softly. Today's treatment had left him weak and nauseous as always, but by suppertime he'd begun to feel some of his strength returning. The doctor suggested that he may have turned a corner and was now beginning to rebound. The news had given both father and daughter a great deal of hope.

She tiptoed from his bedroom and made her way to her own room. Before she could begin to undress she heard a soft tap on the back door.

Jesse. She gave a delighted laugh. He'd had a change of mind. Hadn't she told him it was too cold to sleep in the barn?

She raced to unlock the door and threw it open. "Jess..."

Rafe Spindler took a step inside, his stocky body filling the open doorway.

Startled, she simply stared at him. "Rafe. What are you...?"

His hand snaked out, catching her roughly by the shoulder. "You're coming with me."

"With you?" She was more indignant than afraid. "Does Jesse know you're here?"

"Not yet. But he will."

He tossed an envelope to the floor.

For a moment she merely watched as it skidded across the kitchen tile. Then she looked up, her tone pure ice. "Leave my house this minute, Rafe."

"Shut up." He jammed a hand in his pocket.

"Now you listen..." Her words died in her throat as she caught sight of the glint of something as he withdrew his hand from his pocket.

He was holding a small, silver handgun, aimed directly at her heart.

He saw the way she looked around wildly, searching for something, anything, with which to defend herself.

"You got two choices. Come with me now, without a fight, or"—he waved the gun in the direction of the hallway—"I blow your old man's brains out while he's sleeping."

"My father...No. Wait. Do whatever you want, but leave him out of this."

"I figured you'd see it my way."

With a moan of despair she allowed her hands to be tied with a leather cord before being dragged to Rafe's idling truck. Once inside he tied the end of the cord to his own wrist, assuring that she couldn't leap to freedom.

Agitated, staring around with the eyes of a wild man,

he stomped on the pedal hard enough to send snow-covered gravel flying.

Zane left his truck parked in the hills and started hiking toward the Parrish ranch. While he picked his way in the moonlight, he turned his camera on the moon-washed countryside, already dusted with snow.

Breathtaking.

He loved the look of it, at times stark and forbidding. At other times, with the canopy of stars hovering over the tips of Treasure Chest, it looked like a Hollywood set. Too perfect to be real.

At moments like this he had to remind himself that he was really here, back in the place his heart had never left.

California had all that golden, liquid sunshine. But Montana had everything he'd ever wanted. Space. Grandeur. And right this minute, with snow falling in his hair and coating his lashes, a winter wonderland that was like no other place on earth.

The cell phone in his pocket vibrated, and he paused to see who was calling him.

He flipped it open. "Hey, Wyatt. What's up?"

"You at the Parrish ranch?"

"Almost. Why?"

"Keep a close watch. I just heard something I didn't like."

"What's that?"

"I thought I'd join in the poker game out in the bunkhouse. Figured I might hear a little gossip."

"And?"

"The buzz is that Rafe Spindler has been smarting for

some time now over the loss of his favorite stallion to Jesse in a card game."

"Everybody knows that. You think he'd hold a grudge against Jesse over a horse?"

"Maybe. Maybe not. But there's more. There are rumors that Rafe has been gambling somewhere other than on the ranch. Some of the guys in the bunkhouse tell me he's been spending a lot of his nights away. Rarely gets in before morning. Maybe he goes to town, though I couldn't find anybody who's seen him there. I phoned Daffy. She and Vi claim he hasn't spent an evening in their place for a week or more. I even checked the Grizzly Inn, and Ben Rider hasn't seen Rafe in over a month. There's talk of some high-stakes gambling at a ranch somewhere far enough from town so nobody sees where the trucks are parked."

"You think he's been gambling to try to win enough money to buy back his stallion?"

"I don't know. It could be. Or maybe he has a gambling problem. Hell, maybe he's just looking for a little excitement. A lot of wranglers get the itch. Whatever the reason, I thought I'd pass along the fact that he's mad as hell over the loss of that stallion."

"I can see, if he's still simmering over his stallion, why he'd enjoy a good fight with Jesse. But that doesn't explain why he'd be threatening Amy and her father. I can't see a man going to this much trouble over a horse." Zane swore as he lost his footing on a rock. "I'm almost at the ranch."

He lifted his camera and stared through the night lens. At first he wasn't sure what he was seeing. Then, as it became clearer, he swore again. "There's a cloud of snow, as though a vehicle is hightailing it out of there. No tail-lights that I can see. Call Jesse and see if it's his truck."

As he tucked away his phone and started running toward the ranch, Zane prayed that the churned-up snow he'd just seen through his camera lens was caused by Jesse's truck, and not that of a stranger bent on doing harm.

"Jesse."

Zane pulled up short when he saw Jesse looming up out of the darkness, running out of the barn.

Jesse's breath was coming hard and fast, as though he'd fought his way through a nightmare. He was still pulling on his jacket. "Wyatt said you saw someone?"

"Someone in a big hurry."

The two cousins raced toward the back door of Amy's house. Seeing it standing open, they ran inside.

Jesse headed for Amy's room. Finding it empty he raced down the hallway to her father's room.

Shoving open the door he shouted, "Amy? You in here?"

Her father sat up, sleep-fogged and disheveled. When he caught sight of Jesse he heaved himself out of bed. "Have you gone crazy? What in the hell are you doing here in the middle of the night, McCord?"

"Looking for Amy."

"She isn't with you?"

Jesse tore from the room, shouting over his shoulder, "I left her here half an hour ago."

"Jesse." Zane handed his cousin the envelope he'd found lying in the middle of the floor.

As he took it from Zane's hand, Jesse's heart nearly stopped.

In Rafe's childlike scrawl was written the words *she's dead*.

He tore open the envelope and read the crude note inside.

> *Come alone. Cliffs of Treasure Chest.*
> *You bring help, she's dead.*

Crushing the note in his fist before tossing it aside, Jesse spun away and raced toward his truck in the barn, leaving Zane and Otis Parrish to stare after him with matching looks of stunned surprise.

Jesse drove like a madman. What was this about? Why would Rafe Spindler do a thing like this? Had something inside the cowboy snapped?

It didn't seem like a random or spontaneous act, but rather something he'd given a lot of thought to. Still, it was so out of character for Rafe. He had a mean temper when he was pushed, but he'd never been dangerous.

Until now.

Amy. Dear God, Amy.

The thought of her, alone and frightened, had his jaw clenching. If Rafe hurt her in any way, he'd kill him. Or by God, he'd die trying.

Though he wasn't a man who prayed often, he found himself storming heaven with but one thought: *Keep her safe. Please, keep her safe.*

By the time Zane had raced back to his truck parked in the hills and returned to the Parrish ranch, Otis Parrish was dressed and pacing the front porch.

As the older man climbed into Zane's truck, it occurred to Zane that Otis was fighting valiantly to hold himself together. The interior truck light illuminated his sickly pallor. The poor guy was being forced to fight two battles at once. A deadly illness, and the threat of real physical harm to his daughter. No wonder he was as pale as a ghost.

To offer him some hope, Zane said softly, "Wyatt has already phoned Sheriff Wycliff, who's contacting the state police to ask for their help."

The older man smoothed out the wrinkles from the note Jesse had tossed aside. "He told Jesse to come alone or he'll..." He couldn't bring himself to say the word.

"Wycliff knows that. I told Wyatt what the note said, and Wyatt relayed the information to the sheriff."

"If that madman harms my daughter..." Otis's voice was choked with a combination of fear and rage. "Amy told me that your family offered us shelter. I couldn't bring myself to accept help from them, but I should have agreed to let Amy go to your ranch until this was resolved. This is all my fault."

"I'd say the fault is Rafe's. And believe me, Mr. Parrish, if anyone can stop Rafe and save Amy, it's Jesse."

Otis stared out into the darkness. "I wish I had your faith. I wish..." His words trailed off as he fought the fear that clutched at his heart and squeezed until he could scarcely take a breath.

"Tell me what this is about, Rafe." Amy clung to the door of the truck as it bumped up a steep incline and lurched, with stomach-churning speed, headlong down the other side.

She was shivering so hard her teeth were chattering. Rafe had given her no time to grab a parka. Her thin shirt and denims offered little warmth against the frigid night air that whistled past the truck's windows.

Rafe was taking no chances on being stopped. He avoided the roads and instead kept to the wild country-side, his headlights extinguished. He navigated by the light of the moon, and at times barely avoided crashing into darkened boulders.

She had a flashback to that night when she'd fled for her life across this very stretch of landscape. "It was you!"

"You don't know what the hell you're talking about." He kept his gaze firmly fixed on the path in front of them.

"I know you tried to run me over. Why?"

He shot her a quick glance before returning his attention to his driving. "Believe me, if I wanted to run you over, you'd already be dead."

"Then why were you chasing me?"

"How do you know I wasn't just having some fun?"

"Fun?" She turned to face him. "There's more going on here. I don't believe you."

He made a choking sound that could have been a laugh or a sneer. "You think I care what you believe? I was told to scare you good."

Her head came up sharply. "Told? Who told you?"

"Shut up."

"No. I have a right..."

His hand shot out, slapping her so hard her head snapped to one side and stars danced before her eyes.

"Now maybe you'll keep your mouth shut. I got nothing more to say."

As they continued their way across the rough terrain, Amy blinked back tears as she thought about her father and Jesse, her two fierce protectors, and the helplessness they would feel when they learned that she'd been taken while they slept.

At least, she thought with a sob lodged in her throat, they were safe.

Swallowing back her fear, she stared around at the darkened landscape. This was no time for tears. She couldn't let fear paralyze her. She needed to think. To plan. To concentrate on any means possible of escaping this nightmare.

She vowed to do whatever it took to stay alive. She was smart and she was strong. There had to be a way out.

She saw the bulge of the handgun in Rafe's pocket and shivered. She couldn't afford to think about what was awaiting her. All that mattered was that, for now, she was alive. When the time came to face whatever this madman was planning, she needed to be ready to fight for her life.

CHAPTER TWENTY-ONE

J ess." Wyatt's voice on the cell phone sounded as though he'd been running a marathon. He'd already filled Jesse in on what little they knew about Rafe's gambling problems. Now he had more unpleasant news. "Cal just told me that Rafe's stallion is gone. Jimmy Eagle thinks Rafe could have stashed the horse and some essentials in one of those canyons. He might be planning on dumping the ranch truck and taking off across the hills on horseback."

Jesse's mind started racing. "Rafe grew up in these hills. He could elude the police and hide out in the wilderness for years."

"Yeah, that's what we're thinking." Wyatt paused. "We've alerted the sheriff and the state police. They're hoping to get into position without Rafe spotting them."

"You tell them to back off. Keep their distance. I can't afford to have that nutcase going off half-cocked and hurting Amy."

"They know that. But if they can get a couple of sharpshooters in a position to pick him off, the odds get a little better."

"I'll take all the advantages I can get." Jesse saw the foothills looming in the darkness and charged ahead toward the distant cliffs. "Just so they know what's at stake here."

What's at stake.

Amy. Just the thought of Rafe hurting her had the blood in Jesse's veins turning to ice. He would do whatever was necessary, pay whatever price was required of him, to see her safe.

He was going into this blindly. All these miles, and he hadn't come up with a single plan. He had a rifle in the truck. Anyone who lived on a ranch of this size had one or more. But what good was a rifle if Rafe was holding a weapon to Amy's head?

Why? There were pieces to this puzzle that just didn't fit.

What had caused Rafe to snap? What would he possibly gain by hurting them?

Jesse needed to know what was going on in Rafe's mind. Maybe, just maybe, when they stood face-to-face, he would understand. For now, he had no clue.

He knew one thing. He couldn't afford to let himself think about all the things that could go wrong. He would concentrate instead on how to get Amy free. Unless that happened, his own life wasn't worth a damn.

Amy stood shivering in the night, ankle-deep in snow at the high elevation, her wrists bound tightly to a tree limb above her head. Rafe stood a little away, intently watching the road far below through night-vision binoculars.

He'd chosen an isolated spot near the cliffs, where he could see for miles. The ranch's four-wheel-drive vehicle had brought them halfway up the hill. At that point they'd abandoned the truck and walked the rest of the distance.

So what, she mulled, did he plan to do with her? Rape? Hold her for ransom? With either choice, she would be a witness to his crime. A liability. She would be a loose end he couldn't afford to have around.

That thought had her scalp prickling.

There would be no bargaining for her freedom. Rafe had already decided her fate. But why? What was the point of all this? He wouldn't go to these lengths just to frighten her.

Jesse.

She remembered the envelope Rafe had tossed on the floor. This wasn't about her. He'd used her as the bait to get Jesse alone.

She saw twin pinpricks of light pierce the darkness. As she watched, the lights drew nearer, and her heart plummeted.

She heard a door slam and Jesse's voice shouting out her name. It bounced around the cliff walls and echoed down the canyon.

"Answer him." Rafe crossed to her and pressed the pistol to her temple. "You heard me, answer him."

"What are you going to do if I refuse? Shoot me?" She clamped her mouth shut, taking comfort in even this small act of defiance.

"Suit yourself." He turned and cupped his hands to his mouth. "She's up here."

Amy waited, straining in the silence, praying that Jesse would keep his distance. Her heart was pounding in her temples.

Suddenly she made out a shadowy figure. In the swirling snow, Jesse was walking toward certain death. She had to warn him.

At the top of her lungs she shouted, "It's a trap, Jesse. Don't come any closer. Tell the sheriff…"

Rafe's hand closed over her mouth and nose, cutting off her breath. Unable to fight him, she kicked and bit, but he continued holding her tightly until spots danced in front of her eyes. There was a strange buzzing in her ears, and she could feel herself beginning to fade. The need for air caused her to go limp in his arms.

Just when she thought she would surely suffocate, he released her and lifted the gun to her temple as Jesse stepped into the clearing.

Amy stood, sucking in deep draughts of air, watching helplessly as Jesse advanced toward his fate.

"Okay, Rafe." Jesse took in the scene and fought an overwhelming urge to run to Amy and gather her close. The sight of her, arms tied to a tree limb over her head, the cold barrel of a gun pressed to her temple, tore at his heart. "I'm here."

"Take off your parka and turn your pockets inside out." Jesse did as he was told.

"Now turn around. I need to see if you thought you'd be cute and hide a weapon in your waistband."

Jesse turned, then turned back. "Satisfied?"

When Rafe gave a barely perceptible nod of his head, Jesse added, "You can release Amy now."

from this with clean hands? Didn't it ever occur to you what this is really about?" Jesse turned to Vernon. "Tell him, counselor. Tell him why you set him up."

Vernon calmly faced Rafe. "Everybody knew how much you hated losing that stallion. It wasn't much, but I figured it was enough of a motive to satisfy the sheriff."

"And while the law is chasing Rafe, what do you get out of all this?"

"What I've wanted from the beginning." Vernon gave a chilling smile. "A chance to search for Coot's gold without interference from any other...interested parties."

"What about my aunt and cousins? Do you think killing me will end their interest in the search?"

"I figure once you're...eliminated, they'll lose their appetite for the hunt. Lord knows, Coot never did. I listened to him for years, charting the trails he'd taken, the dead ends he'd dealt with, keeping a detailed map for my own sake. I waited as long as I could, hoping he'd get too old to continue searching, or die. When that didn't happen, I just had to help him along."

"What're you saying?" Jesse's eyes narrowed in stunned surprise at the lawyer.

"I've been trailing Coot for years, until I got sick and tired of waiting for the old man to step aside. When I saw him climbing one of Treasure Chest's cliffs, I figured a little rock slide would be a convenient way to eliminate him."

Jesse's voice was filled with shock and rage. "You followed Coot and...killed him?"

"The mountain killed him. I just greased his trail with a few well-placed rocks. As for following him, I've been doing it for years, hoping he'd lead me to the gold."

"You bastard! My grandfather trusted you. Trusted you with all his business."

"So will your aunt and cousins. I figure dealing with another death in the family will curb any appetite they may have for the family treasure."

"And you'll just happen to have some legal papers drawn up for them to sign when they withdraw from the search, pretending to be from Coot, making the treasure fair game for anybody who happens upon it?"

The lawyer threw back his head and laughed. "You're smarter than I gave you credit for, Jesse."

"And Amy? Why did you involve her in this?"

"Just call it killing two birds with one stone. The Parrish ranch is a bit too close to these foothills for my taste. Since Coot's trail was edging closer and closer, I figured I'd eliminate any more witnesses while I continue my search."

Jesse looked over at Rafe. "Do you still believe he's going to let you ride out of here? Think about this, Rafe. By now the entire ranch knows what's happening. By tomorrow the whole town will know. Whether or not you're the one to pull the trigger, you've become an accessory to a murder. Montana isn't big enough to hide a killer."

"All I did was erase a gambling debt. The rest of this isn't my business. What Mr. McVicker does after I'm gone has nothing to do with me." Nervous, Rafe put a foot in the stirrup. "I know this country better'n anybody. Once I lose myself up in these hills, nobody will ever find me." He pulled himself up into the saddle and touched a hand to the brim of his hat.

Vernon lifted his hand. "I'm afraid Jesse's right again.

You've been set up, Rafe. You see, I need you here so that when the law finds Jesse and Amy, they'll also find you. Dead, of course. And the case will be closed as easily as Coot's death."

Instead of a salute, he took careful aim with his pistol and fired.

Rafe's eyes went wide with surprise. His body stiffened before he tumbled to the ground and lay perfectly still, while his lifeblood drained into the snow around him.

Stunned and reeling, Amy gave an involuntary cry of horror. Her shoulders shook as she sobbed silently at the sight of such cold, calculated murder.

Vernon crossed to Rafe's body to check for a pulse.

Using that instant of distraction, Jesse was on him before he could blink, driving him back against a tree.

Stunned, Vernon shook his head, then pistol-whipped Jesse with such force that blood spurted from his temple.

The two men fell to the ground and rolled around in the snow.

Jesse's fist connected with Vernon's nose, sending a river of blood flowing down his parka.

The lawyer brought a knee into Jesse's groin, doubling him over. Through a haze of pain, Jesse saw Vernon getting to his feet. Jesse kicked out a foot, sending him sprawling.

When the gun slipped from Vernon's hand and dropped into the snow, Jesse gave a vicious kick, sending it flying.

As it skidded across the clearing, both men made a mad dash and fell on it.

Vernon's hand closed over the icy metal and he fired.

The sound of the explosion echoed and reechoed through the hills.

Jesse's body jerked, and his hand reached automatically to his chest.

Vernon staggered to his feet, still holding the gun, as blood spilled from beneath Jesse's parka. "Last chance to say good-bye to your girlfriend, Jesse."

He took careful aim at Jesse's heart.

"No!" Amy's cry had Vernon turning slightly, sending his second shot wide of its mark as she used the tree limb to pull herself up and kick out with both feet.

The thrust caught the lawyer by surprise and sent him sprawling.

Amy looked over at Jesse, lying as still as death. "Oh, Jesse. Please don't die. Get up. Please, Jesse, get up."

Jesse could feel himself fading. He knew he had to finish this before he passed out. He had to get to Vernon and take possession of the gun for Amy's sake. But though he moaned and struggled to move, his body refused to respond.

Amy watched helplessly. There was so much blood mingled with the snow.

As Amy mentally willed Jesse to move, she saw Vernon get slowly to his feet, wearing a look of smug victory. In his hand was the glint of the pistol as he aimed it at her. "I didn't realize you were such a fighter. Too bad it was a wasted effort. Time to finish this. Starting with you."

Amy watched, mesmerized, as his finger curled around the trigger. Inside her brain she heard the click. Though her first impulse was to squeeze her eyes tightly shut, she forced herself to face down her killer.

"You'll have to look me in the eye…"

An explosion of sound echoed through the cliffs and canyons.

Amy waited for the pain she knew would follow. Feeling no pain, she numbly waited for death to claim her.

Instead, as she watched in disbelief, Vernon's eyes went wide with the shock of recognition. His gun slipped from his hands as he seemed to fall forward in slow motion. With a cry she watched as the lawyer's body sank into the snow beside Jesse, an ever-widening pool of blood spilling from the bullet wound in his back.

When she looked up, the area was swarming with uniformed deputies and state police officers, all of them moving carefully around the crime scene, looking like actors in a dark movie.

Sheriff Wycliff led the charge, shouting out orders.

At this moment, none of them mattered. All that mattered to Amy was the fact that Jesse lay crumpled in the snow, as still as death, blood flowing from an ugly, gaping wound and staining the ground around him.

CHAPTER TWENTY-TWO

"Cut her down." Sheriff Wycliff's voice had one of the uniformed officers following orders.

Amy let out a cry as the blood began flowing once more through her numb limbs.

She couldn't feel her feet as she raced to Jesse's side and dropped down in the snow. "Is he...?" She couldn't speak the word. All she could do was stare in horrified fascination as several officers knelt beside Jesse's body, checking for vital signs.

His limp body was lifted onto a portable gurney and the straps secured.

Finally one of them spoke. "He's not dead, ma'am, but I'm betting he feels more dead than alive right now. That gunshot has to be causing him some big-time pain."

"Alive?" Amy's heart began beating again as she grabbed hold of his hand, needing desperately to feel the connection. "Jesse, can you hear me? Oh, Jesse, you're alive. Stay with me, Jess. Please, stay with me."

"I'm...here." His lids flickered but remained closed. "McVicker?"

"He's dead. Killed by a police sharpshooter."

"You—" Jesse's teeth were chattering so hard he could barely get the words out. "You okay?"

His eyes opened, and he stared up pleadingly at Amy.

"I'm fine, Jess. Save your strength now."

One of the uniforms helped her into a heavy parka. But when she saw Jesse's gurney being moved, she raced to keep up.

As they bumped along the rutted path, he clenched his jaw at the pain that jolted through him. So much pain. As though he'd descended into hell and his entire body was on fire.

Amy continued holding his hand as she kept pace with the officers carrying the gurney. "There's a plane waiting to take you to town as soon as we get you down the mountain."

Pain had him drifting in and out of consciousness. The sight of his suffering nearly broke Amy's heart.

As they neared the plane, Amy recognized Marilee Trainor and felt a wave of relief.

Marilee was an emergency medical worker who partnered with the local and state law enforcement agencies, flying ranchers in need of medical services to the town's clinic. More serious accidents were taken by medevac to the hospital in Helena.

"Amy. You look like you've been through a war." Marilee caught her in a bear hug.

"That's what I feel like." For a moment Amy leaned

against her, soothed by this young woman's quiet competence.

Marilee turned to her patient. "Hey, Jesse. Got yourself shot, I hear."

"Mmmm." It was all he could manage.

"He's freezing." Amy caught his hand, which was cold as ice, despite the mound of blankets that enveloped him.

"Shock. This will help." Marilee withdrew a syringe from her black bag and shoved aside the blankets, injecting it into his vein.

By the time he was secured in the rear of the small plane, with Amy and Sheriff Wycliff on either side of him, Marilee had the engines revving and they were soon airborne.

In no time they arrived at the rodeo grounds on the far side of town, where an ambulance was waiting to transport them to the clinic.

Inside, Dr. Wheeler and his staff whisked Jesse away to an examining room to assess the damage.

"How about you, Amy?" One of the nurses studied the blood that stained Amy's clothes.

"I wasn't shot. This is Jesse's blood. Please see to him. He's in so much pain."

"Then take this." The nurse removed Amy's police-issue parka and draped her in a heated blanket before walking away.

Amy turned to face the chaos that had already reached fever pitch and saw Jesse's aunt Cora hurrying toward her. She wasn't surprised that Jesse's family was here waiting when the ambulance arrived.

"Oh, my dear." Cora wrapped Amy in a warm embrace and began to weep softly.

Instead of being soothed, Amy found, to her dismay, that she was the one doing the soothing. This sweet old woman had already been through so much with the recent loss of her brother. How she must have suffered over the threat to her beloved nephew.

Framing the old woman's face in her hands, Amy whispered, "Jesse's going to be fine, Aunt Cora."

"I know he's young and strong. But a bullet..."

"You can't think about that. You just have to trust that he's in the best possible hands." Amy wiped Cora's tears with her thumbs and looked toward Cal, who, sensing her discomfort, turned Cora into his arms, where she continued to weep silently against his shoulder.

Wyatt enveloped Amy in a bear hug. "The police are hailing you as a hero."

"Hero?" She gave a long, deep sigh. "All I did was survive. That doesn't make me a hero, Wyatt."

Zane stepped close to wrap her in his arms. "All I know is you and Jesse made it back from hell. That makes you both heroes in my book."

"Oh, Zane. Wyatt." She stepped back and took in a long, deep breath. "I was so scared. And the truth is, I'm still afraid."

"Hey." Zane patted her hand. "Vernon's gone. Rafe, too. There's nothing to be afraid of now."

She shook her head, then lowered her voice so that Cora wouldn't overhear. "It's Jesse. I'm afraid for him. There was so much blood. So much." She dragged in a ragged breath. "He has to be all right. He just has to."

Hearing the thread of panic in her tone, Wyatt and Zane led her away from the others.

"Jesse's going to be just fine, Amy." Wyatt tipped

up her face. "He's always been the toughest McCord of all. Now you just have to believe in him a little longer."

She nodded and swallowed the lump in her throat that felt like a boulder.

"Amy..." At the sound of her father's choked voice she turned.

He was standing alone, apart from the others, staring at her with a look that tugged at her heart.

"Dad." She stepped toward him. "I didn't know you were here."

"Zane brought me. He took me to the McCord ranch first, where we could stay in contact with the state police. As soon as we heard about the shooting, we drove to the clinic. We wanted to go out to Treasure Chest, but they told us you would be brought here. For a minute I thought..." He swallowed and tried again. "I was so afraid you might have been the one shot."

"You must be relieved to know it was Jesse."

"That's not what I meant." He frowned. "But I deserve that. I haven't been fair to him, or to you. I just want you to know..." His voice nearly broke. "I want you to know how much I love you, Amy."

"Oh, Dad." Touched by his admission, she stepped into his arms and he held her to him, his face pressed to her hair, his shoulders shaking slightly as he gave in to the emotion that rolled over him in waves. "I love you, too, Dad. I've always loved you."

It occurred to Amy that she and her father hadn't been this close in years. Even his serious illness hadn't been able to bring them together the way this crisis had.

When he could trust his voice Otis said, "I'm proud of you, girl. So damned proud."

"Thank you." She stayed in his arms for long minutes, reveling in this newly discovered bond.

At last she pushed slightly away, dreading the fact that her next words just might sever their bond. "I need to tell you something, Dad, even though it will hurt you. When I thought I'd lost Jesse, I realized just how much he means to me. What I'm feeling for him is real. I know you'll never approve, but I have to be honest, not only with you, but with myself. I love him, Dad. I'm not going to give him up, even to please you."

"I understand, girl. And I'm grateful for your honesty." He looked away, mulling over what he was about to say. "Maybe it's time I was more honest, too."

Though she wondered at his words, there was no chance to question his meaning. The door opened and Dr. Wheeler strode into their midst.

Everyone flocked around him.

"How is Jesse?" Cora's tone was pleading.

"Jesse's fine. The bullet didn't hit any vital organs. It was fired at such close range, it passed directly through the flesh of his arm. That's why there was so much loss of blood. An entry wound and an exit wound. But he's strong and healthy. He'll be up and moving in no time. In fact, we'll probably send him home tomorrow, if he promises to remain quiet and take the drugs we prescribe."

His gaze skimmed the crowd before he spotted Amy standing with her father. "Amy, Jesse isn't going to give us any peace until he sees you."

While the others hugged and exchanged high fives,

Amy made her way through the crowd and stepped into the examining room.

After the level of noise in the outer room, the quiet seemed a little unnerving.

Amy moved silently toward the examining table.

Jesse lay as still as death. At the sight of him her heart contracted.

As though in church her voice became a whisper. "Jesse?"

His eyes opened. "Oh, Amy. You look so good right now."

He lifted a hand and winced at the sudden, shocking pain.

She caught his hand, holding on for dear life. "How bad is it?"

His words were slow and thick. "Just a twinge now and then. Doc Wheeler has me all shot up with something."

"Then I guess getting shot up is good."

He grinned. "I never thought about that. But yeah, it's nice to have the pain gone. Doc said it'll be back tomorrow with a vengeance. But each day it'll get a little easier. He'll be sending me home tomorrow." He closed his eyes a moment before adding, "You know how good that sounds? Home. For a little while, I doubted I'd ever see home again."

"Shh." She placed a finger on his lips. "Don't talk about it."

When she started to lift her hand away he caught it and pressed it to his lips. His eyes opened and he gave her one of those heart-stopping grins. "My brave, fierce Amy. You were amazing."

She shook her head. "I didn't do a thing. I was so scared, I couldn't even think."

"Baby, you saved my life."

"And you saved mine."

"We're quite the pair." He was still grinning when she suddenly flung herself across his chest and began to weep.

"Hey, now. What's this about? It's all over, Amy."

"Oh, Jesse. I thought you were going to die."

Now that the floodgate had been opened, she couldn't seem to stop the flow. "I didn't even mind so much about my life. But when I thought he'd killed you, something inside me just snapped."

While her tears dampened the front of his hospital gown, Jesse wrapped his good arm around her and held on, content to just lie here holding her close, feeling her heartbeat inside his own chest.

Outside, the din faded as the crowd dispersed and the clinic staff returned to their routine. In Jesse's room, Amy crawled up beside Jesse, needing to feel him warm and safe and alive beside her. The two figures remained locked in each other's arms.

When the door to the examining room opened, Amy looked up, expecting to see Dr. Wheeler. After Jesse had finally fallen asleep, she had pulled a chair alongside his bed, where she could sit and hold his hand without disturbing his rest. She'd had this desperate need to remain connected with him, afraid to let go for even a moment.

As her father advanced toward the bed, Jesse's eyes snapped open.

"Sorry to wake you." Otis cleared his throat. "Doc says you're going to be fine."

Jesse nodded.

Amy looked over. "You should go home, Dad, and get some sleep. You'll need to be back here later today for another treatment."

"I know. Zane's waiting out there to drive me home whenever I'm ready. And he said for you not to worry about bringing me into town for my treatment. He'll pick me up."

Amy felt a wave of relief, mingled with surprise. When had her father begun to accept help from a McCord?

"Then why...?"

He stopped her with a lift of his palm. "I need to talk to Jesse. Alone."

Amy was already shaking her head. "He's been through too much..."

Jesse squeezed her hand. "It's okay. I'll bet you could use some coffee."

"I don't want..."

She saw the quick shake of his head and gave a sigh. "I guess I could use some caffeine."

Otis watched until she stepped out of the room before turning to Jesse with a long, deep sigh. "All her life, Amy has always been scrupulously honest, even when she was telling me things she knew I didn't want to hear. It was her most infuriating quality. But I've always secretly admired her for it. Now I owe her the same honesty." He walked closer. "I'm the one who sabotaged your romance years ago."

Jesse shrugged, though it cost him. "You had a right

to want to protect your daughter from someone you considered an enemy."

"That's what I told myself. But no matter how I try to justify what I did, it was still wrong."

"As I recall, it was Amy who left me right after graduation without a word, sir. Not you."

"Amy never left you, Jesse."

Jesse blinked.

"As you know, my wife's youngest sister, who lived in Helena, called to say she'd been diagnosed with a... terminal illness. Much like mine." He clenched and unclenched his fists, the only sign of his agitation. "So Amy agreed to go to Helena with her mother. They left in such a hurry, there was no time for her to let you know, so she left a letter for you in the mailbox."

Jesse frowned. "A letter? That's what she was trying to tell me in the barn. I never got a..."

"I took it out of the mailbox. It was a long, passionate letter, which I read. And then destroyed. When you came to my ranch looking for Amy, I shamelessly lied and told you she'd gone for good, that she wanted to sever all ties with you before starting a new life at college. And when she complained about having never heard from you, I told her that you'd been seen all over town with other girls." He heaved another sigh. "I told a string of lies, and they had the desired effect. You ended up hating Amy for leaving without a word, and Amy was hurt and angry with you for never answering her letter, and never making an effort to contact her, all the while seeing other girls."

Jesse was silent for so long, Otis hung his head. "I realize there's no way for you and Amy to get those years back. I'm truly sorry. And I know there's no way to make amends. I'm just relieved to learn that my daughter still loves you, as she said, whether I like it or not."

"She told you that?"

Otis nodded. "She did."

"It had to be hard for you to tell me all this."

Otis shrugged. "I thought it would be, but the funny thing is, I feel better now. I know it's too much to ask you to forgive me, but I'm still glad I finally did the right thing. I'm only sorry it took me so long."

"So am I." Jesse extended his hand. "I accept your apology, Otis. And I hope that someday you can accept my friendship and that of my family."

Otis stared for long moments at Jesse's hand before shaking it. "After what happened tonight, I'd be a fool to hang on to all those old hostilities. You and your family treated me like a neighbor, and not as the enemy. If you're willing, I'd like...I'd like to be your friend."

Jesse studied the older man's bowed head. "If you're willing, Otis, I'd like to be something more."

As Otis shot him a questioning look, Jesse added, "It would please me to be your son-in-law. In case you haven't noticed, I've never stopped loving your daughter. And I intend to ask her to marry me, if that meets with your approval."

The door fell inward with such force, Amy nearly stumbled. "Did he give his approval?"

The two men looked over at her and she felt her cheeks redden. "Okay, I admit it. I was listening at the door." She advanced on her father, hands on her hips. "You read my letter to Jesse and then burned it? And let me believe all these years that he didn't care about me?"

"Now, girl..."

"Don't you 'now, girl' me. I want you to know how many tears I shed, how much pain your lies..."

Taking pity on the old man, Jesse moaned. "Amy. Help me."

At once both Amy and her father gathered around the bed.

"Where does it hurt?" Amy demanded.

"Here." Jesse touched a hand to his chest.

She moved his hand away. "Maybe you've opened up your stitches."

"It isn't that."

"Maybe you need another shot for pain."

"Not that either." He caught her hand and placed it over his heart. "This is where I hurt."

"Your heart?" She looked terrified.

"Yeah. I think there's only one cure."

"What?"

"You have to agree to marry me."

She stepped back. "Jesse, this isn't funny."

"I agree. It's deadly serious. Now, you need to stop fighting with your father long enough to give me an answer. I've already accepted his apology, and he's given his approval. All we need now to make it final is your answer."

She glanced at her father, who was smiling. "You... actually approve?"

He nodded.

She turned to Jesse, who winked.

"Oh, Jesse." She leaned down to brush a kiss over his mouth. "I never could resist that charm."

"I was counting on it." As she started to straighten, he cupped a hand around her head and drew her back for another kiss. "Wait. You didn't answer me. Will you marry me, Amy?"

"Yes. Oh, yes. Yes, a million times yes."

"I think that was a yes." He winked at her father. "It will mean that you won't be able to return to Helena to teach."

She gave him a wide smile. "Then it looks like I'll have to find some students around here. Or maybe we could have a few of our own to teach."

Jesse couldn't think of anything he'd like better. "You know we were destined to be together, don't you?"

"There were times when I wasn't at all certain of it. But now, I know for a fact that this is our destiny."

Then they were laughing together, and kissing, and whispering words that only they could hear.

As Otis walked from the room he saw Wyatt and Zane standing in the open doorway, watching the scene and straining to hear every word.

Wyatt slapped Otis on the back, while Zane pumped his hand.

"Welcome to the family," they called in unison.

"Let's get you home," Zane said.

Wyatt held the door. "Looks like we've got a wedding to prepare for, neighbor."

EPILOGUE

———◆◆◆———

Otis Parrish turned at the sound of Amy's bedroom door opening. His eyes widened. "Are you wearing that to the wedding?"

She glanced down at her faded jeans and denim shirt. "You think, just because you're wearing that fancy suit, these aren't good enough?"

He caught sight of the long plastic bag hanging over her door and felt a wave of relief. "Okay, I get it. You're going to dress at the McCord ranch."

"I don't want to arrive all wrinkled. I'll dress in Jesse's suite just before the ceremony." She tossed him the keys. "Now that you've finished your treatments, you can drive." She took up the heavy bag. "And I'll just sit back and try to remember to breathe."

He paused and touched a hand to her cheek. "Things will probably get too crazy later, so I'd like to say this now. I'm proud of you, girl. For the way you took care of me through this...thing." Though the doctor had told him he was in remission, he still couldn't talk about his illness. "And for the way you handled Rafe Spindler and that cowardly lawyer's attack."

She closed a hand over his. "Thanks, Dad. And I'm proud of you for admitting the truth to Jesse."

"Took me long enough."

"Better late than never. You won't mind that I'll be living on the McCord ranch?"

He shrugged. "Whither thou goest, and all that. Besides, I've already been enjoying the benefits of being on the good side of that family. They really know how to treat their friends. Orley Peterson delivered our grain free of charge."

Amy arched a brow. "Did he say why?"

"He said since he was delivering to the McCord ranch, our place wasn't out of his way. I guess he sees us as part of their family now, and he doesn't want to offend his biggest clients."

"Don't let it go to your head."

"I'll do my best to remain humble."

As Amy opened the passenger door, her father put a hand on her arm. "I keep thinking how much your mother would have loved this day. You do her proud, Amy girl."

Her eyes brimmed. "Thanks, Dad."

Her heart felt lighter than air as they headed toward the Lost Nugget.

Wyatt, Zane, and Jesse stood in the middle of the great room, staring around as the florist delivered a dozen different vases and urns filled with roses, lilies, and trailing ivy.

"The place looks and smells like a damned green-house."

At Wyatt's remark, the three of them shared a laugh.

Dandy was shouting orders to the cowboys he'd coaxed to be his assistants as they set up steam tables for the buffet to be served in the dining room.

A hairdresser had his assistants running up and down the stairs as he sent them out to his van at least half a dozen different times to fetch gels, lotions, sprays.

A seamstress from town was making last-minute repairs on dresses and searching frantically for an iron and ironing board.

Wyatt watched it all with a look of astonishment. "Is there some kind of crazy rule that says all women have to go overboard for weddings?"

"Looks that way." Zane slapped Jesse on the back. "Just think, cuz. The whole town, in fact, half the state of Montana, is thriving this weekend, getting rich quick, and all because of you."

Jesse merely grinned. "I'm happy to make them all rich, as long as they make my bride happy." He lowered his voice. "I've got to see Amy. Just for a minute. Then I'll meet you outside. You know where."

Wyatt exchanged a look with Zane. "We'll be there."

Cora heard a chorus of laughter in the hallway and peered out her bedroom door. Daffy and Vi were just walking toward her, with the seamstress following behind.

"Well?" Daffy paused to pose, her hand on her hip. "What do you think of the gowns Amy picked out for us?"

"They're lovely." Cora looked from Daffy, in bright crimson, with a scooped neck and slit in the ankle-length skirt that displayed a great deal of leg, to Vi, in palest pink, with a scalloped neckline and flirty, ruffled hem. "And they suit each of you perfectly."

"Our Amy is one sly girl. When she asked us both to be her maids of honor, we nearly fainted."

"I'm so glad she asked you. You've been good friends of hers through good times and bad. And when her mother died, you two made a difference in her life."

"It's easy to be a friend to someone like Amy. I surely do love that girl." Nerves caused Violet's voice to be even softer and breathier than usual. "I just hope I don't faint halfway through the ceremony."

"Maybe you ought to," Daffy said in her rusty voice. "With those gorgeous cowboys Wyatt and Zane standing with us, I just might pretend to faint myself, just so I can be scooped up in those strong, muscled arms."

While they shared a throaty laugh, Daffy glanced at her watch. "We'd better hurry. The bride's waiting for us to help her into her gown." She paused. "Miss Cora, Amy will want you to see her as soon as she's dressed."

"Just call me when she's ready." Cora watched them dance away and returned to her room to finish slipping into her shoes.

A short time later she heard the knock on her door.

"Miss Cora?" Amy stepped into the room, wearing a strapless wedding gown of white silk that fell in a fluid line to her ankles. Her hair was worn long and loose. At her ears were the diamond earrings that Jesse had insisted on buying her for an engagement gift.

"Oh, my." Cora put a hand to her throat. "Amy, honey, you're just about the most beautiful bride I've ever seen."

"Thank you." Amy held out a white satin box. "This is for you."

"For me? Why?"

"Since my mother isn't here to share this day with me, I'd like you to be my honorary mother."

"Oh, Amy." Cora's eyes swam with sudden tears. "You and Jesse will always be like my own children." She opened the box and stared at the double strand of perfect pearls with a small, jeweled clasp.

She turned to hide her tears. "Will you fasten this for me?"

Amy drew the pearls around her throat and closed the clasp.

Cora studied her reflection in the mirror. It was the perfect accessory for the pale pearl silk gown she'd chosen. "I love them. You know I'll cherish them always, just as I'll always cherish you as my own."

"Thank you. I guess I should call you Aunt Cora now." Amy softly kissed the old woman's cheek, while Daffy and Vi looked on.

At a knock on the door Daffy hurried over to find Jesse just about to enter.

She stepped up to block his way. "You can't see the bride before the ceremony."

"Daffy, do you want to live to see another day?" Jesse's eyes looked as hot and fierce as if he were facing another gunman.

Violet giggled like a schoolgirl. "I think, sister, you'd better let the man in."

Daffy turned. "Amy?"

Amy nodded.

Daffy stepped aside and Jesse started in, then halted in midstride when he caught sight of the vision in white.

Seeing the look that passed between Amy and Jesse, Cora walked to the door and motioned for the other two to follow. When she pulled the door closed, neither Jesse nor Amy noticed. They had eyes for only each other.

Amy walked to him and lifted a hand to his cheek. "What's wrong?"

"Nothing. Not a single thing is wrong now." He let out a long, deep sigh. "It's all so right." He caught her hand between both of his and lifted it to his lips. "Do you know how much I love you?"

"Not as much as I love you."

"How did we get so lucky?"

"The fates were kind."

"Remind me to thank them later. For now..." He leaned close and brushed a soft, butterfly kiss on her lips.

There was a knock on the door and Violet called, "Amy, honey, we need time to finish in there."

Amy laid a hand on Jesse's cheek. "You need to get downstairs."

"I'll be there waiting." He started to walk away, then turned back. "I almost forgot. Carry this with your bouquet."

She looked at the keychain he handed her. "A rainbow?"

"It was Coot's. I always carry it for good luck. I figure today, getting you as my wife, I've already had more than my share."

Amy felt a mist of tears and tucked the rainbow into her pretty nosegay of white roses and trailing ivy. "For luck. Maybe it will bring us closer to the treasure."

He paused. "You realize that the search will earn you a lot of nasty jokes in town. Folks will say we're both crazy."

"I know that. Isn't that what they always said about Coot? But I intend to continue helping you search for the treasure. Folks can say anything they want, as long as I know you love me."

"I always have. I always will." He tucked a strand of hair behind her ear. "I'll leave you alone with the women for now. I'll see you in front of the preacher. I can't wait to start our life together."

Together. It was, Jesse thought as he started down the stairs and past the smiling guests, just about the happiest word in the world. And no threat, no mythical curse, could have any power over the two of them, as long as they were together.

Outside, the snow fell like a thick, white curtain. In the distance, hovering just above the peaks of Treasure Chest, hung a shimmering rainbow.

Jesse paused to look at it, then, grinning, started toward the small plot of land that his grandfather had considered sacred ground.

"Hey, cuz." Wyatt's long hair flowed over the collar of the leather duster he wore over his tuxedo, giving him the look of a cowboy straight out of the Old West.

As Jesse stepped into the small, fenced gravesite of their grandfather, Zane held up a bottle of fine Irish whiskey. "I figure you might want some of this for courage."

Jesse shook his head. He'd pulled on a sheepskin parka against the snowfall. "It doesn't take any courage to marry the girl of your dreams. Frankly, I can't wait."

"What I can't wait for"—Zane, wearing a denim jacket over his tux, grinned—"is for the formal part of the ceremony to be over so we can enjoy all that great food Dandy's been cooking for days. Have you smelled that kitchen?"

The three men were laughing as Cal Randall walked up, a small wooden box tucked under his arm. He opened it and began passing around cigars, cupping his hands around a flame while each of them puffed, until the air was redolent with the rich fragrance of tobacco.

While Zane brought out one of his video cameras and began filming, Wyatt filled four tumblers with whiskey and handed them around.

"Zane and I thought this was the right time to tell you that our grace period is up. We've decided to stick around for good and continue the search for the treasure."

Jesse looked from Zane to Wyatt. "You're both crazy. You know that?"

They chuckled, low and deep in their throats.

"It's a family trait," Wyatt said with a laugh.

"Yeah." Jesse offered a handshake to each of them. "Thanks. I know I behaved like a real jerk when you first came here."

"Now that you mention it…" Wyatt and Zane shared a laugh.

Jesse joined them. "I couldn't have said this a short time ago, but I'm really glad you're staying. I feel as though I got my best friends back."

They stood, cigars in hand, and lifted their glasses while Cal said, "Your grandfather would be a happy man today. And not just because it's your wedding day, Jesse." He cleared his throat and stared around at the three cousins. "Coot spent a lifetime searching for his family's treasure. But he made no secret of the fact that he considered his family the greatest treasure of all. When your daddies left and took part of his family away, they took part of his heart, too. I think now, finally seeing his family reunited, and willing to take up his search, he'd be the happiest man around."

Jesse's voice became solemn. "Here's to Coot."

"To Coot." The others lifted their glasses before drinking.

Jesse fought the lump in his throat as he intoned Coot's favorite words. "Life's all about the road ahead. What's past is past. Here's to what's around the bend, boys."

For long moments the only sound was the sighing of the wind as snow fell around them.

"Here's to you and Amy, Jesse." Wyatt lifted his glass. "You've been through tough times together. Here's hoping the road will be a little smoother around the next bend."

They drained their glasses and headed toward the ranch house.

Cal remained at the grave, watching the three cousins, tall, rugged, handsome, hearing their voices, their laughter, carried on the breeze.

He lifted his glass. "You did it, you old son of a bitch. You did the impossible. You brought them together by the sheer force of your will. Now you'd better see to it that they succeed in finding that treasure."

He downed his drink in one long swallow. "Here's to what's around the bend, my friend."

Then, shaking the snow from his wide-brimmed hat, he pulled it low on his head and made his way to the house to celebrate this memorable day with this remarkable family.

Marilee Trainor
likes her freedom
and lives for trouble.
But she's met her match
in sexy cowboy
Wyatt McCord . . .

———— ◆◆◆ ————

Please turn this page
for a preview of

Montana Destiny

CHAPTER ONE

———◆◆◆———

Whike Wyatt watched the action in the bull-riding ring he noticed the ambulance parked just outside. In case any fool wasn't already aware of the danger, that vehicle was meant to bring home the point. But it wasn't the emergency vehicle that caught his attention; it was the woman standing beside it. There was no way he could mistake those long legs encased in lean denims, or that mass of fiery hair spilling over her shoulders and framing the prettiest face he'd ever seen. Marilee Trainor had been the first woman to catch Wyatt's eye when he'd returned to Gold Fever for his grandfather's funeral. He'd seen her dozens of times since, but she'd always managed to slip away before he'd had time to engage her in conversation.

Not this time, he thought with a wicked grin.

"McCord." A voice behind him had him turning.

"You're up. You drew number nine."

A chorus of nervous laughter greeted that announcement, followed by a round of relieved voices.

"Rather you than me, cowboy."

"Man, I'm sure glad I dodged that bullet."

"I hope your life insurance is paid up."

Wyatt studied the bull snorting and kicking its hind legs against the confining pen, sending a shudder through the entire ring of spectators. If he didn't know better, Wyatt would have sworn he'd seen fire coming out of the bull's eyes.

"What's his name?" He climbed the wooden slats and prepared to drop into the saddle atop the enraged animal's back.

"Devil. And believe me, sonny, he lives up to it." The grizzled old cowboy handed Wyatt the lead rope and watched while he twisted it around and around his hand before dropping into the saddle.

In the same instant the gate was opened and bull and rider stormed into the center ring to a chorus of shouts and cries and whistles from the crowd.

Devil jerked, twisted, kicked, and even crashed headlong into the boards in an attempt to dislodge his hated rider. For his part, Wyatt had no control over his body as it left the saddle, suspended in midair, before snapping forward and back like a rag doll, all the while remaining connected by the tenuous rope coiled around his hand.

Though it lasted only sixty seconds, it was the longest ride of his life.

When the bullhorn signaled that he'd met the qualifying time, he struggled to gather his wits, waiting until Devil was right alongside the gate before he freed his hand, cutting himself loose. He flew through the air, over the corral fence, and landed in the dirt at Marilee Trainor's feet.

"My God! Don't move." She was beside him in the blink of an eye, kneeling in the dirt, probing for broken bones.

Wyatt lay perfectly still, enjoying the feel of those clever, practiced hands moving over him. When she moved from his legs to his torso and arms, he opened his eyes to narrow slits and watched her from beneath lowered lids.

Up close, she was even better than he'd hoped for.

She was the perfect combination of beauty and brains. He could see the wheels turning as she did a thorough exam. Even her brow, furrowed in concentration, couldn't mar that flawless complexion. Her eyes, like the palest milk chocolate, were narrowed in thought. Strands of red hair dipped over one cheek, giving her a sultry look.

Oh, man. He was a goner.

Satisfied that nothing was broken, Marilee sat back on her heels, feeling a moment of giddy relief. That was when she realized that he was staring.

She waved a hand before his eyes. "How many fingers do you see?"

"Four fingers and a thumb. Or should I say, four beautiful, long, slender fingers and one perfect thumb, connected to one perfect arm of one perfectly gorgeous female? And, I'm happy to add, there's no ring on the third finger of that hand."

She caught the smug little grin on his lips. Her tone hardened. "I get it. A showboat. I don't have time to waste on some silver-tongued actor."

"Why, thank you. I had no idea you'd examined my tongue. Mind if I examine yours?"

She started to stand, but his hand shot out, catching her by the wrist. "Sorry. I couldn't resist teasing you. Are you always this serious?"

"In case you haven't noticed, rodeos are serious business. Careless cowboys tend to break bones, or even their skulls, as hard as that may be to believe."

She stared down at the hand holding her wrist. Despite his smile, she could feel the strength in his grip. If he wanted to, he could no doubt break her bones with a single snap. But she wasn't concerned with his strength, only with the heat his touch was generating. She felt the tingle of warmth all the way up her arm. It alarmed her more than she cared to admit.

"My job is to care for anyone who is actually hurt."

"I'm grateful." He sat up so that his laughing blue eyes were even with hers. If possible, his were even bluer than the perfect Montana sky above them. "What do you think? Any damage from that fall?"

Her instinct was to move back, but his fingers were still around her wrist, holding her close. "I'm beginning to wonder if you were actually tossed from that bull or deliberately fell."

"I'd have to be a little bit crazy to deliberately jump from the back of a raging bull just to get your attention, wouldn't I?"

"Yeah." She felt the pull of that magnetic smile that had so many of the local females lusting after Wyatt McCord. Now she knew why he'd gained such a reputation in such a short time. "I'm beginning to think maybe you are. In fact, more than a little. A whole lot crazy."

"I figured it was the best possible way to get you to

actually talk to me. You couldn't ignore me as long as there was even the slightest chance that I might be hurt."

"Oh, brother." Clearly annoyed, she scrambled to her feet and dusted off her backside.

"Want me to do that for you?"

She paused and shot him a look guaranteed to freeze most men.

He merely kept that charming smile in place. "Mind if we start over?" He held out his hand. "Wyatt McCord."

"I know who you are."

"Okay. I'll handle both introductions. Nice to meet you, Marilee Trainor. Now that we have that out of the way, when do you get off work?"

"Not until the last bull rider has finished."

"Want to grab a bite to eat? When the last rider is done, of course."

"Sorry. I'll be heading home."

"Why, thanks for the invitation. I'd be happy to join you. We could take along some pizza from one of the vendors."

She looked him up and down. "I go home alone."

"Sorry to hear it." There was that grin again, doing strange things to her heart. "You're missing out on a really fun evening."

"You have a high opinion of yourself, McCord."

He chuckled. Without warning he touched a finger to her lips. "Trust me. I'd do my best to turn that pretty little frown into an even prettier smile."

Marilee couldn't believe the feelings that collided along her spine. Splinters of fire and ice had her fighting to keep from shivering despite the broiling sun.

Because she didn't trust her voice she merely turned on her heel and stalked away from him.

It was harder to do than she'd expected. And though she kept her back rigid, her head high, she swore she could feel the heat of that gaze burning right through her flesh.

It sent one more furnace blast rushing through her system. A system already overheated by her encounter with the bold, brash, irritatingly charming Wyatt McCord.

THE DISH

Where authors give you the inside scoop!

♥ ♥ ♥ ♥ ♥ ♥ ♥ ♥ ♥ ♥ ♥ ♥ ♥ ♥

From the desk of Cara Elliott

Dear Readers,

Pssst. Have you seen the morning newspaper yet? Oh, it's too delicious for words. The infamous Lord H—yes, Mad, Bad Had-ley in the flesh—has made yet another wicked splash in the gossip column. You remember last week, when his cavorting with a very luscious—and very naked—ladybird ended with a midnight swim in the Grosvenor Square fountain? Well, that was just a drop in the bucket compared to this latest *ondit.* Word has it that Hadley, the rakishly sexy hero of TO SIN WITH A SCOUNDREL (available now), has really fallen off the deep end this time. He's been spotted around Town with . . . the Wicked Widow of Pont Street.

Don't bother cleaning your spectacles—you read that right. Hadley and Lady Sheffield! The same Lady Sheffield who stirred such a scandal last year when it was whispered that she may have poisoned her husband. Yes, yes, at first blush it seems impossible. After all, they are complete opposites. The fun-loving Lord Hadley is a devil-may-care rogue, and the reclusive Lady Sheffield is a scholarly bluestocking. Why, the only thing they appear to have in common is the fact that their names show up so frequently in all the gossip columns. But appearances can be deceiving, and a friend tells me that a fundamental law of physics states that opposites attract.

Not that *I* would dare to wager on it. However, the betting books at all the London clubs are filled with speculation on why Hadley is paying court to the lovely widow. Some say that it's merely one of Hadley's madcap pranks. Others think that he's been bewitched by one of the potent potions that the lady brews up in her laboratory. But I'll let you in on a little secret: Whatever the reason, the combination of a scoundrel and a scientist has passion and intrigue coming to a boil!

How do I know? I'll let you in on another little secret—as the author of the book, I'm familiar with *all* the intimate details of their private lives.

So why did I choose to make my hero and heroine of TO SIN WITH A SCOUNDREL the subject of rumors and innuendos? In doing my research, I discovered that our current fascination with gossip and scandal is nothing new. Regency England reveled in "tittle-tattle," and had its own colorful scandal sheets and "paparazzi." Newspapers and pamphlets reported in lurid detail on the celebrity bad boys—and bad girls—of high society. And like today, sex, money, and politics were hot topics. As for pictures, there were, of course, no cameras, but the satirical artists of the Regency could be even more ruthless than modern-day photographers.

Hmmm, come to think of it, the hero and heroine of TO SURRENDER TO A ROGUE, the second book in the series (available June '10), are likely to generate quite a bit of gossip too. Lady Sheffield's fellow scholar, the lovely and enigmatic Lady Giamatti, finds that someone is intent on digging up dirt on her past life in Italy while she is excavating Roman antiquities in the town of Bath. That Black Jack Pierson is a member of the learned group stirs up trouble . . . Oh, but don't let me spoil the fun. You really ought to read all about it for yourself.

Now don't worry if your butler has tossed out the morning newspaper. If you hurry on over to www.caraelliott .com, you can sneak a tantalizing peek at all three books in my new Circle of Sin series.

Enjoy!

Cara Elliott

♥ ♥ ♥ ♥ ♥ ♥ ♥ ♥ ♥ ♥ ♥ ♥ ♥

From the desk of Susan Kearney

Dear Readers,

I came up with my idea for JORDAN, the third book in the Pendragon Legacy trilogy, while sipping a wine cooler in my hammock. I was rocking between two rustling queen palms when a time machine landed on my dock. And the hottest dude ever strode up the wooden stairs and pulled up a chair beside me. His eyes matched the blue of the sea and his muscles rippled in the Florida sunshine.

Jordan.

He'd arrived just as the sun was dipping into the Gulf of Mexico. And did you know that Jordan's history is as interesting as his looks?

Did I mention this guy may have looked in the prime of his life, but he's more than fifteen hundred years old? Did I mention that centuries ago he fought at King Arthur's side? And that not only is he a powerful dragon shaper but he knows secrets to save us all?

Jordan raked a hand through his hair. "Rion told me that you write love stories about the future."

"I do." Somehow, I knew this was going to be one hell of a story.

"In the future, Earth will be threatened by your greatest enemy."

My fingers shook. "Did you save my world?"

"I had help from a smart, beautiful woman."

"And you fell in love?" I guessed, always a romantic at heart.

"She was my boss." His voice lowered to a sexy murmur. "And we fought a lot in the beginning. You see, Vivianne Blackstone didn't trust me."

"So you had to win her over?"

"She's one stubborn woman." His voice rang with pride, a grin softening his tone.

Oh, this story sounded exciting. Lucan had told me how Vivianne Blackstone had funded the first spaceship mission to Pendragon. Just imagining such a strong woman with Jordan sent a delicious shiver of anticipation down my spine. "But surely Vivianne must have liked you just a little bit at first?"

"She thought I was an enemy spy." Jordan's grin widened. "And she wasn't too pleased when I stole her new spaceship . . . with her on board."

Oh, my. "I'd imagine it took her awhile to forgive you."

While Jordan was quite the man . . . still . . . he'd stolen her ship and taken her with him into space. Vivianne must have been furious. And scared. Although, the writer in me told me Jordan had been good for Vivianne. "So how long did it take her to believe you were both on the same side?"

Jordan chuckled. "It must have been after the second, no, the third time we made love."

I swallowed hard. Oh . . . my. "You made love while she believed you were enemies?"

He raised an eyebrow. "We didn't really have a choice."

I gave him a hard look. "Um, look. I'm afraid I'm going to need the details. Lots of details."

If you'd like to read the details Jordan told me, the book is in stores now. Reach me at www.susankearney.com.

♥ ♥ ♥ ♥ ♥ ♥ ♥ ♥ ♥ ♥ ♥ ♥ ♥

From the desk of R. C. Ryan

Dear Reader,

Blame it on Willy Nelson. My heroes have always been cowboys.

Whether they're riding the trail in the Old West or dealing with today's problems on a modern, up-to-date ranch tricked out with all the latest high-tech gadgets, I simply can't resist loving a cowboy.

In my mind, the tall, silent hero of a Western is the equivalent of the savage, untamed Highlander. Noble, loyal, fiercely independent. Impossible for this woman to resist.

Now add to that a treasure hunt for a priceless fortune in gold nuggets, and you have a recipe for adventure, intrigue, and romance.

MONTANA LEGACY is the first book in my Fool's Gold trilogy. Three cousins, long separated, are brought together by the death of their grandfather, who has spent a lifetime searching for a lost family treasure.

Of course they can't resist taking up his search. But that's only half the story. Equally important is the love they discover on the journey. And more than love—trust. Trust in one another, and in the women who win their hearts and enrich their lives.

If you're like me and love tough, strong, fun-loving cowboys in search of a legendary treasure, come along for the adventure of a lifetime.

I enjoy hearing from my readers. Drop by my Web site and leave me a message: www.ryanlangan.com.

Happy reading!

R. C. Ryan